Knot on Your Life

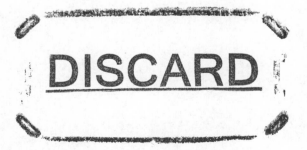

KNOT ON YOUR LIFE

BETTY HECHTMAN

WHEELER PUBLISHING

A part of Gale, a Cengage Company

LIBRARY OF CONGRESS CIP DATA ON FILE.
CATALOGUING IN PUBLICATION FOR THIS BOOK
IS AVAILABLE FROM THE LIBRARY OF CONGRESS.

ISBN-13: 978-1-4328-9082-7 (softcover alk. paper)

Published in 2021 by arrangement with Beyond the Page, LLC.

Printed in Mexico
Print Number: 01   Print Year: 2022

KNOT ON YOUR LIFE

CHAPTER 1

"That was intense," I said, coming in the door to my kitchen. Julius looked up at me with a questioning meow, or at least that's how it sounded to me. "Okay, so I'm talking to myself now," I said to the black cat. "You would too if you'd just been through what I have. How about I had to be the middle man between the Delacorte sisters, the so-called royalty of Cadbury by the Sea, and the love child of their long-deceased brother they didn't know about."

Julius did a few swirls around my ankles that seemed more about affection than plying me for some of his favorite food. Who said cats couldn't be supportive like dogs?

"We're a pair, aren't we?" I said to him. "Two wanderers who found each other." I reached down to give his sleek black fur a pet and heard him let out a loud purr.

I saw him looking toward the refrigerator and realized our emotional moment was

7

over and he'd moved on to his midmorning snack. I dearly loved him, but certainly wished he'd picked something a little less fragrant for his favorite food. I called it stink fish, and believe me, it lived up to that name. Despite multiple layers of plastic bags and wrapping, I could still detect the strong odor. I swear I could smell the fish even before the can was opened.

I assumed my closed-nose position and began the unwrapping. Finally I dropped a dainty spot of it in his bowl. He was lapping it up before I'd finished tapping the last of it off the spoon. "I hope you appreciate that I'm trying to make up for your tough life," I said as I began the rewrapping process. Or at least that was what I assumed he'd had. I'd first met the cat when he was an unwelcome guest at Vista Del Mar, the hotel and conference center across the street, and the manager had tried to shoo him away with his golf cart. I got the feeling the cat had been showing up a lot and I guessed that he'd been abandoned by someone. He must have recognized me as a kind spirit because he showed up at my door shortly after that. I let him in without question and he's been here ever since. Later I heard that cats do the choosing when it comes to their humans and it seemed that he'd chosen me.

The phone was ringing as I shut the refrigerator door. Julius was already giving his paws a little after-lunch cleaning. I grabbed the cordless without bothering to check the screen.

"So, Feldstein, how'd it go?"

"Not even a hello first, Frank?" I said.

"Okay, hello. So then how'd it go? I thought you were going to call me." Frank Shaw was a private investigator and my former boss during my stint as a temp worker in Chicago. Working for him had been my favorite of the short-term jobs. It was far more interesting than trying to get department store customers to let me spritz perfume on them, or standing on Michigan Avenue handing out samples of a new flavor of gum called Tickle Your Taste Buds. It was more like scorch your tongue. The chief ingredient was chili pepper.

Now there was almost two thousand miles between me and Frank, but we'd stayed in touch. Well, I'd stayed in touch with him when I needed help solving a murder.

Before doing the temp jobs, I'd tried law school, but after a semester knew it wasn't for me. I worked as a teacher in a private school and baked desserts for a friend's bistro until it closed. I was at loose ends when I started the temp work and was faced with having to move back in with my parents.

I was in the middle of my thirties and that simply wasn't option number one for me. So, when my Aunt Joan offered me her guesthouse in Cadbury by the Sea, California, I pretty much jumped at it. She was the one who helped me get the job as dessert chef at the Blue Door restaurant and to set up my freelance muffin making for the coffee spots in town.

I still felt a tug when I thought about her. She'd died shortly after I'd moved to Cadbury. My only consolation was that I had determined it wasn't an accident and brought the killer to justice — with Frank's help.

"What's going on, Feldstein? You're not talking. I haven't got all day. Are you going to fill me in or not?"

"Sorry, Frank," I said quickly. I let out a sigh as I saw the get-together in my mind's eye. Cora Delacorte was wearing one of her Chanel suits and too much green eye shadow. Her older sister, Madeleine, was sporting a pair of boyfriend jeans rolled up at the ankles. Neither of them knew why I'd invited them to coffee at Maggie's coffee shop. Then Gwen Selwyn had hesitated at the door. It was hard to imagine her as a

10

love child. The title conjured up peasant tops and faded-out jeans. Instead, she wore sensible slacks and a thick brown sweater I was sure she'd knitted with some yarn from her shop. Her daughter, Crystal, accompanied her. She looked more like my vision of a love child in her rainbow of colored shirts piled on top of each other and earrings that deliberately didn't match.

I'd waved them over to the table and for a moment the four women stared at each other with only two of them knowing why they were there. "I should have done more of a 'cat's on the roof' first," I said to Frank. "You know, made some comment about how there were rumors that the Delacortes had some mystery family members they'd never met."

"What did you say?" he asked.

"I just blurted it out. I said Gwen is your niece — your brother's child. Then I pushed the envelope with the paternity test across the table. Then I added that Crystal was their grandniece and reminded Madeleine how fond she was of Crystal's son Cory.

"Cora started shaking her head and pushing the envelope away. Madeleine was stunned but then she at least smiled. Gwen wasted no time in speaking up, assuring them she wasn't interested in their family fortune. It was really all about Cory and how much he loved Vista Del Mar, which their brother had owned and the sisters had inherited. She mentioned that Edmund's will had stated the hotel and conference center was to go to his offspring. She'd said she just wanted Cory to have a share of the place."

"And then war broke out?" Frank said.

"Not exactly. Cora and Madeleine were too stunned by the news to say too much. Gwen seemed at a loss for what to say after that and Crystal kept looking at the two women. I stepped in and suggested they all let everything settle in and then they could get together again. Hopefully without me," I added.

"I told you not to get involved," he said. True, he had told me to mind my own business when I'd uncovered the truth about the identity of Edmund's secret child.

"And I probably should have listened to you, but I didn't. So here we are."

"Well, if they decide to run you out of that town, I could probably find some work for you here. Even with the Internet, there is still a need for PIs, and lately business has been picking up."

"Thanks for the offer," I said, "but I'm good for now. I have a retreat coming up

this weekend." My aunt had left me everything, including her house and the yarn
retreat business. She actually left me her
house and a guesthouse, though that
sounded grander than it was. The house was
small and the guesthouse was a converted
garage. I'd already versed Frank on the
retreats, but the usual question was *What is
a yarn retreat?* Basically, a group of people
gathered for a long weekend away from it
all and spent their time doing yarn craft.

Vista Del Mar was the perfect spot for it.
The hotel and conference center was located
on the tip of the Monterey Peninsula, giving it an away-from-it-all feeling. There was
lots of fog, and the moody weathered buildings that housed the guest rooms were
sprinkled around the one hundred or so
acres of the grounds. Each of the buildings
had a cozy living-room-like space with
comfortable chairs and a fire going in the
fireplace. A boardwalk ran through the sand
dunes that bordered the property and then
there was the beach. It was beautiful with
waves that were actually sea foam green,
and the sand was so soft that no one minded
getting it in their shoes. But there were also
Danger signs, particularly near the rocky
area that went out into the water. The signs
warned that the coastline was dynamic with

crashing waves and crumbling cliffs. Rocks were slippery and large, unexpected waves could sweep you off your feet. They suggested playing it safe and not climbing on the rocks or going into the water and risk getting carried out to sea.

The fact that Vista Del Mar was unplugged made it seem even more of a getaway from the world. There was no cell service, Wi-Fi or even a television in the main building. It was unplugged, but not cut off. There was a row of vintage phone booths with pay landlines and a message board for communicating in the building called the Lodge.

I'd come a long way since I'd first inherited the business. I hadn't known much about yarn craft other than to admire the many pieces my aunt had left me. It was part of my ritual to add something to my outfit that she'd made when I dressed for a retreat.

I had learned to knit and crochet, but my skills were basic and I relied on real expert helpers for the yarn craft workshops. I looked at my job as being the arranger, the host, and the fixer if there was a disaster. I shook my head, realizing that problems seemed to be more the norm than the exception.

"It's a group coming from San Jose. They all know each other and even told me what activities they wanted, so it ought to be an easy weekend."

"And you're having it at Vista Del Mar, right?" he said.

"Sure. That's where they always are."

"And isn't one of the rich sisters' new relative one of your helpers?" he said.

"You mean Crystal?" I said. "She's my only helper for this retreat." The meaning of his comments suddenly sunk in. The meeting between the Delacorte sisters and their new family was likely to have some fallout, with me possibly in the middle. "I'm sure it will be fine," I said, trying to sound confident.

"You know where to reach me if things go south. And remember there's a job for you here." And then he hung up.

I let out a sigh, wishing I had postponed the meeting until after the retreat. There was nothing I could do about that now. All I could do was go forward and hope for the best.

Every retreat I put on was unique, but this one was completely different from the others. A woman from a knitting group in San Jose had contacted me and asked me to put together a retreat to celebrate one of their

15

members' birthday. Aileen Bursten had told me what kind of yarn workshop and other activities they wanted, and then it was up to me to make the arrangements. It was a lot easier than my usual method of planning a retreat, getting the word out so people signed up, and then hoping they'd be happy with what I'd put together.

This group was driving in and I thought they probably wouldn't arrive until the afternoon, which was lucky because I still had a little setting up to do. Aileen had been to Vista Del Mar before and she knew the accommodations were spare, to say the least, and she'd requested that I leave goodie bags in their rooms with some extras. I had tote bags to drop off with the supplies for their workshop project. I always brought over some baked goods to keep in their meeting room as well.

I always made butter cookies, but I'd topped this batch with chocolate wafers. The white tin was sitting on the table ready to go. I'd packed them in layers, using doilies as the dividers. It looked so much nicer than plain old wax paper. I grabbed my jacket and the tote bag I used for a purse and picked up the tin off the kitchen table. Julius was already sleeping on one of the kitchen chairs and didn't look up as I left.

I walked across the driveway to the guest-house, which had been where I lived while my aunt was alive. I'd stayed there even after she was gone, feeling as if the house was still hers. Finally, I'd moved into the house, but for the same reason I'd left everything as is for a while. I'd just started making some changes. I wouldn't really call it a remodel, more like redecorating. I was painting the walls and recovering the furniture since her taste was fussier than mine.

The guesthouse was now the repository for all the supplies for the retreats. It was really one big room with a kitchen area separated from the rest by a counter. At present, the counter had baskets of the different items I'd gotten for the goodie bags. I liked the idea so much that I'd decided to do it for all future retreats and had bought extra of everything. I put the tin in the plastic bin on wheels I used to ferry things for the retreats and set to making up the bags for the five people I expected. I'd gotten small white shopping bags and lined them with sheets of green and blue tissue paper, leaving the ends showing above the top. As I began to drop the supplies into each bag I thought of how much nicer the shampoo was compared to the utilitarian stuff Vista Del Mar provided. I added bags of snacks, a generous amount of chocolate, some scented soap and a lavender sachet. I'd created the sachets myself and had attached a note explaining that they could be tucked under the pillow for a fragrant sleep. My aunt would surely be smiling at that since I'd hardly been the crafty sort when I'd first come there. Live and learn.

Pleased with how the bags had turned out, I put them into the bin along with some bottles of flavored sparkling water. Crystal was going to bring the yarn and tools for the group's project, but I put in five of the bright red tote bags that said *Yarn2Go* on them to leave in the meeting room. I heard the phone begin to ring in the house. I knew without looking that it was my mother. I just wasn't up for her conversation at the moment and ignored it.

I'd finally come to the conclusion that she meant well, but both my parents were doctors, and let's just say that my life choices didn't sit well with her. How many times had she reminded me that when she was my age she was a doctor, a wife and a mother, and then left it hanging — the meaning clear: *and what was I?* She was hung up on certificates and degrees and had offered me cooking school in Paris or a detective academy in Los Angeles. She couldn't understand that I was happy with where I was, though even I knew it might not last.

CHAPTER 2

Once I was outside the guesthouse, I zipped up my fleece jacket against the cold damp air then laughed at what a wimp I'd become. Cold was really a relative term. I'd lived most of my life in Chicago and knew a thing or two about real cold weather. It was January, which in Chicago meant short bleak days with wind that cut through your coat. The January temperature in Cadbury wasn't much different from the temperature the rest of the year. Jacket weather with cloudy skies. The big difference was that January was part of the rainy season here. And even then it didn't rain that much, but when it did, it poured. But it was a nonissue at the moment and I hoped it stayed that way for the weekend since I'd planned some out-door activities for my group.

I lived on the edge of Cadbury by the Sea and it was wilder here than in the main part of town. There were no sidewalks or streetlights and the ground in front of the houses along the street were filled with native plants, which was the nice way of saying weeds.

The grounds of Vista Del Mar were literally across the street from my place. But once I passed stone pillars that marked the entrance it was like stepping into another world. It felt rustic and untamed, which was part of its charm as long as no one was expecting a posh resort with fluffy towels and a velvety green lawn.

There was no lawn here, velvety or otherwise, just dry grass and scrubby growth around the lanky Monterey pines that grew along the driveway. The buildings were covered with dark weathered shingles and blended in with the surroundings.

I heard the sound of an engine behind me and turned just as a number of cars and SUVs came down the driveway too fast. I had to jump to the side of the road to avoid getting hit. Vista Del Mar had started out as a camp over one hundred years ago, before cars were a consideration. As a result there wasn't much space for parking and the roadways that wound through the sloping grounds were better suited to golf carts.

I was surprised by the traffic and noted that the small parking lot near the building called the Lodge was already filled. Normally it was dead around here at this hour. It was the between time when people had already checked out and new arrivals hadn't checked in yet.

I had a sudden concern that my group might be part of the early arrivals. I went directly to the Lodge and pulled open the heavy door to check. The Lodge was the main building and served a variety of purposes. It was sort of a mixture of a hotel lobby and a social hall. Guests went there to register and also to hang out.

A crowd was gathered around the massive registration counter at one end of what was really a giant open space. The rest of the room seemed deserted, as expected for this hour. No one was playing table tennis or pool. The board games and jigsaw puzzles were all on the shelves against the wall. The seating area around the fireplace was empty, as were the small tables scattered around the area for card games or gathering.

I left my wheeled bin by the door and moved around the back of the crowd to get a look at what was going on. There were two distinct groups hanging out by the counter. I dismissed the larger group as not being my birthday yarn people. Not only were there about twenty of them when I was expecting five, but there were men and women and my group was all female. A lot of them were wearing khaki vests and had binoculars hanging around their necks, which were giveaways that they were the group I called the bird-watchers. They had events at Vista Del Mar regularly throughout the year. They seemed relaxed and were showing each other photos on their phones, no doubt of birds they'd seen. It was the perfect spot for them to have a getaway. They came from all walks of life and for the weekend left everything behind. Their interests really went beyond birds to all of nature. They had speakers, side trips like whale watching on Monterey Bay, and even craft activities.

A small group was to the side of them and their manner was completely different. At first I thought they were all dressed in black jeans and black turtlenecks, but then I noticed that one of them stuck out from the others. He seemed older and wore gray slacks and a light blue dress shirt. They all had dark hair and his was flaxen. I don't know why I looked at their footwear, but the light-haired guy had on leather shoes and the rest of them wore sneakers. There was no way they were my retreat group since there was only one woman in the group.

Something about them kept me watching to see what was going to happen. One of them seemed to be in charge. His dark hair was cut short and his sharp features gave off an aura of impatient arrogance. He was shifting his weight and glaring at the registration desk.

The others were looking at their phones with lost expressions. I wondered if they were just finding out the place was unplugged. They seemed like the types who viewed their cell phone as an appendage and could be going through some kind of withdrawal. I was glad they weren't my group since they appeared to be trouble waiting to happen.

Kevin St. John had just come from the business office in the back to join the single clerk manning the registration counter. He was the manager, or as he saw himself, the Lord of Vista Del Mar. He had a moon-shaped face and always dressed in a dark suit that made him look out of place in the rustic surroundings.

There were always numerous events going at Vista Del Mar each weekend, but it was surprising that so many people were trying to check in this early. I guess Kevin was surprised too, because his usual bland expression was replaced by what could best be called consternation.

Just then Cora and Madeleine Delacorte came in the other door and stopped to observe from the sidelines. It looked like Kevin St. John swallowed hard and I assumed he thought they were there checking up on him since they were the owners of the hotel and conference center. Cora, with her overly formal attire and too much green eye shadow, looked in my direction and pursed her lips as she shook her head in a disparaging manner. I noticed her gaze moved beyond me and then I understood. They were there to hold their ground, expecting that after the revelations of the morning Gwen and Crystal would show up to stake a claim on the place.

"Didn't they listen?" I said to myself. Madeleine had a weak smile when our eyes met and I almost went over to reassure them that their fears weren't going to be realized. The only reason that Gwen Selwyn had agreed to confront them was to help her grandson Cory be part of the hotel and conference center. He'd been working there off and on and loved the place. Madeleine had formed an attachment to him without even knowing he was actually part of her family and told me she wanted to help him with college.

My gaze went back to Kevin St. John, and when he caught me looking at him, he shot me a sour expression. There was no hiding it: he did not like me. He was unhappy that I had taken over my aunt's retreat business and that the Delacorte sisters had continued to give me the special rate on rooms they'd offered to her. Honestly, if I didn't get the reduced price there was no way I could have continued the business. As it was I had to supplement my income by making the desserts for the Blue Door restaurant and baking muffins for the coffee spots around town. It helped that the house my aunt had left me with was free and clear. I looked toward the sisters with sudden worry. Were they going to hold the revelations of the morning against me? Maybe Kevin St. John would get his wish after all.

I considered going to them and trying to smooth things over, though I had no idea how to do it. But I decided to leave everything as is for the moment and my attention went back to the gathered throng of people.

The manager directed the clerk to deal with the larger group while he offered a solicitous smile to the smaller group and waved for the one in charge to approach.

I heard someone come in and hoped my group hadn't chosen that moment to arrive.

"Are you in line?" a man with a deep baritone voice asked. I turned and saw that a tall dark-haired man wearing a dress shirt with the tie pulled loose had joined me. His sport coat was sitting on his suitcase. He noticed me looking at it. "I know, I seem overdressed, but I'm meeting a client. I'm an accountant. I do his books every year on the same weekend."

I told him I wasn't in line and pointed toward the door that led to the driveway, explaining I lived across the street. "I put on yarn retreats," I said. "In fact, I'm really here looking for my group. Casey Feldstein," I said, holding out my hand.

"Reese Rogers," he said in his mellow voice. "So what's a yarn retreat, if I may ask? You sit around the campfire and make up stories?"

"Not that kind of yarn," I said. "More like the kind you make sweaters with."

"Oh, you mean the thing with the needles," he said with sudden understanding.

"Actually, the group I have coming requested learning how to crochet, so no needles, just a hook." I added that this retreat was different from my usual since they were all friends coming to celebrate a birthday. Then I smiled apologetically. "That's probably much more information that you wanted."

"No problem. It's always nice to know who else will be here."

I noticed that the Delacorte sisters had moved on to the café that was named after them adjacent to the registration area. The manager noticed it too and seemed relieved.

"They're sure an intense bunch," Reese said, watching the group Kevin St. John was dealing with. "I wonder what they're here for."

I shook my head and said I didn't know. "They look like they need something to de-stress and calm down." I let out a sigh. "Luckily, I don't have to worry about them."

I was watching how the manager was dealing with them and I had a thought about why he was being so solicitous. He wanted to have as much control over Vista Del Mar as possible and had been trying to get rid of the middle men like me, who put together retreats and just arranged for rooms and rented meeting space from Vista Del Mar. I bet that whatever the group was there for, Kevin St. John had put together the whole thing.

I was sure I was right when I saw him

28

handing out folders with something stamped on the front, and a moment later he came out from the back to walk them to the door. I thought he was going to escort them to the building with their rooms, but the one who'd seemed in charge brushed him off and said he knew the way.

As soon as they were gone, Kevin St. John went back behind the counter to help with the bird-watching group.

"You just have to make sure there's birthday cake and yarn," Reese said with a smile. "I love this place. Old-fashioned with real keys to open the doors instead of those plastic cards. And no cell phones ringing incessantly or people staring at their screens like zombies."

"Then you don't mind being cut off?"

"Oh, no," he said with a smile. "I relish it. It's nice not to be reachable for a change. No phone ringing in my room in the middle of the night."

It seemed like an odd comment and I had to wonder who he was worried about hearing from, but it was none of my concern. I wished him well and slipped through the throng around the registration desk and slipped a note to the clerk, asking her to give me a call when my group showed up. Her name was Cloris and she mostly worked in the kitchen, but she was always looking for extra hours and regularly filled in wherever she was needed. She seemed to take everything in stride, but I wondered how she felt about her current assignment working so close to Kevin St. John.

I was about to leave but I stopped when a man came in. He stood out from the rest so much I did a double take. He was wearing black leggings, a loose cream-colored T-shirt and bare feet. I shivered at the bare feet and no jacket, but he seemed oblivious. His black curly hair seemed like it would have been an unruly mop if it hadn't been tied into a topknot. I watched as he joined the group at the counter. Kevin St. John threw him an annoyed look and separated from the couple he was checking in. He gestured for the barefoot man to follow him as he walked to the far end of the counter. There's that saying about curiosity killing the cat and all, but it didn't seem to make an impact on me and I changed directions as if I was going to the café, but stopped near the entrance in earshot of their conversation.

"You should have been here when they arrived," Kevin St. John chided. "I'm depending on you to make this retreat a success. I hired you to be the facilitator. I want this group to be happy so they tell their friends about this retreat. If this works we could have groups like them here every weekend." He pushed a folder on the man and said the schedule of activities was in there. "I better not hear any complaints." There was just the slightest tone of a threat in the last comment and all I could think of was *Good luck, Mr. Bare Feet.*

I'd left my bin by the door and retrieved it so I could get back to the reason I'd come. When I got outside I was struck by how quiet it seemed after the commotion inside. The breeze brought in a surge of moist air that smelled of salt water mixed with the smoke from all the fireplaces in Vista Del Mar. I didn't bother zipping my jacket since my next stop was nearby.

Sand and Sea was the closest building with guest rooms and the one I always used for my groups. It dated from the days when Vista Del Mar had been a camp and had housed the counselors. Like the other structures, it was covered in wood shingles that once had been a dark brown but now had pale streaks from the salty breeze.

The balcony on the second floor room served as a covering for the small porch that led to the entrance, and I pulled the bin up the few stairs. Inside the fire was glowing in the lobby area but all the wing chairs spread around it were empty. When I got to the hallway the cleaning crew was finishing up. I showed them the goodie bags and explained wanting to drop them off. The crew knew me so there was no problem opening the doors to the rooms my group was going to occupy. I gathered several of the small shopping bags on my arm and got ready to start distributing them when a door on the other side of the hall opened. I recognized the guy who seemed like the leader of the group wearing black. He barely gave me a glance but his eyes went to the bags on my arm.

"I'll take one," he said, reaching for it. I shook my head and pulled my arm away.

"Sorry, but they're only for my group." I realized that didn't really count as an explanation. "I put on retreats here. My group hasn't arrived yet."

"Then you work for the hotel," he said, still eyeing the bags.

"No. I just book the rooms and meeting space with Vista Del Mar. I make all the other arrangements and act as host." I held up the bags. "My group is celebrating a birthday and I thought it would be nice for them to have a few extras." He wanted to know what was in the bags and I mentioned the nicer toiletries and the snacks. "And of course a generous supply of chocolate," I said. He looked down into the bin and saw the bottles of sparkling water, and I said they all got one of those too.

He grimaced with dissatisfaction. "We should be getting all that too." With that he walked away without even a "have a nice day."

I shrugged it off and went about my business. I left the bags and water in a prominent position in each of the rooms. The final touch was to tuck a sachet on each of the beds. It would leave a lovely fragrance on the sheets and was also known as a sleep aid.

The bin was a lot lighter as I headed for the meeting room I'd arranged for the yarn workshops. I passed my favorite of the Monterey cypress trees. Most of the ones on Vista Del Mar had been shaped by the constant breeze and the dull green foliage reminded me of someone running with their hair trailing behind. But this one was protected from the wind and had more of a symmetrical shape. I took a deep breath of the damp air and enjoyed the moment of solitude. It really was the calm before the storm.

The single-story building holding the

meeting room had been added later, and while every effort had been made to make it fit in with the older buildings, it still looked more modern. Like all the other Vista Del Mar structures, it had a name and was called Cypress. There were two meeting rooms in the building and I always used the same one. The door was open and I pulled my load in.

I was glad to see that everything was ready for the first workshop we'd have that afternoon. A fire had been laid in the fireplace and was ready to be lit. The counter where the coffee and tea service sat had cups, accessories and napkins ready. I dropped off the tin of chocolate-topped cookies next to a stack of snack-sized paper plates. The long table seemed a little too big for this small group, but it was either that or just the chairs with an expanded armrest, which were too limiting. I checked the plastic bin against the wall and saw that it was loaded with sparkly yarn. A second one had crochet hooks and samples of the finished project. I took out the tote bags and added them to the last bin.

My yarn skills weren't up to teaching others yet and I was glad to hand off that task to the two yarn experts I'd come to know in Cadbury. Since this group was so small, I'd hired only Crystal to do the honors, but after the showdown earlier that morning I wondered if I'd made a mistake. What if she was upset with the way the Delacorte sisters had reacted to the news she was part of their family. Would she blame it on me since I was the messenger and then take it out on my group? I could hear Frank telling me it was my own fault for stirring everything up.

I pulled out a chair and sat down. I'd learned enough about yarn craft by now to know that it was a good stress reducer. So much so that I always carried a small easy project for times like this when I needed to let go. I pulled out the tiny pink triangle hanging on the cable between the two short knitting needles. I took a couple of deep breaths and began on the next row of the washcloth. Every row would add a stitch, and it was repetitive and easy. By the third row I was feeling better. I hoped that this retreat was going to be problem-free. Then I laughed at my own naivete. When did that ever happen?

CHAPTER 3

Just as I was about to cross the street a red Ford 150 truck came barreling down the quiet thoroughfare and then pulled up to the curb. Dane stuck his head out of the window and regarded me with a grin. "Hey, what's up?"

Without waiting for an answer, he cut the engine and popped out of the truck. Instead of his cop uniform he wore a pair of faded jeans and a T-shirt, both of which accentuated the fabulous shape he was in. He seemed to be all muscle and moved with a spring in his step. He went to hug me, but backed off when he hit my resistance, and his angular face softened as a smile danced in his eyes.

"Oops, I forgot public displays of affection are still a no-no with you." His voice, as expected, had a teasing tone.

"Just in a small town. If this was New York City, no problem at all," I said.

36

He looked up and down the empty street. One side of it was all trees and brush that hid Vista Del Mar, and the other side was populated with small houses of different styles. "Right, there are so many people watching us," he said.

"You don't know. All the neighbors could be looking out their windows with their binoculars trained on us." I tried to sound serious, but it was such a ridiculous statement that I couldn't hold back a smile.

Dane Mangano lived down the street. There had been an attraction between us from day one. No matter how I tried to keep him at arm's length, he kept pushing in closer. He'd offered me his heart and everything that went with it. It was too much, too soon. The best I could do was to acknowledge that he was my boyfriend. But I still wanted to keep it on the down low from the Cadburians. Knowing looks and winks weren't my thing. And in the back of my mind I worried that even though I liked living in Cadbury by the Sea, making sweets for the town and putting on the retreats, how long would it satisfy me? I worried that one day I'd wake up and be done with it and anxious to move on. Suddenly I'd decide to take my mother's offer of cooking school in Paris or detective school in LA.

"I know you might want to leave Cadbury someday and you're convinced I'll be broken hearted," he said. "But did it ever occur to you that you wouldn't have to leave alone?"

He grinned at my surprise that he'd read my thoughts.

But no matter what he'd just said, I knew that Dane was committed to the small town, where being a cop meant keeping tourists from driving too fast down Grand Street and reminding locals to pick up after their dogs. His cop duties were low on violence and high on working things out peacefully.

He'd taken it upon himself to avoid trouble before it happened by keeping Cadbury teens busy with gratis karate lessons in his converted garage. He also fed them and gave them advice. No matter what he said, he'd be lost in a big city and deeply unhappy.

"I can't deal with this right now," I said, still emotionally worn from the morning meeting with the Delacortes and Gwen and Crystal.

Dane picked up that I wasn't playing around and his expression faded to serious. "Why, what happened?" The flirty tone of his voice was gone.

I debated what to say. I hadn't told him

38

that I'd discovered that Gwen Selwyn was the love child of the Delacorte sister's late brother, Edmund. I hadn't told anybody, well, other than Frank, while I debated what to do with the information. Finally, I'd dropped it in Gwen's lap to do with as she chose. Only recently had she decided to face the Delacorte sisters. It seemed like the cat was out of the bag, or at least sort of. Should I tell Dane? I glanced at him and considered trying to make it sound like I was worried about the upcoming retreat, but I knew he wouldn't buy it. I'd dropped too much of a hint and he would never let it go.

"You have to keep what I'm about to tell you to yourself."

His eyes brightened and he grinned at me expectantly. "Oooh, a secret. I love a secret."

I think he was expecting some gossip I'd picked up at the Blue Door and I saw his eyes widen and his grin disappear as I told him who the very down-to-earth Gwen Selwyn really was.

"How long have you known?" he asked in an interrogation tone he must have learned in cop school. He pursed his lips with annoyance when he heard how long it had been. "Why didn't you tell me right away? Don't you trust me?"

"I didn't even tell Lucinda," I protested. She was probably my best friend in town and also sort of my boss since she and her husband, Tag, owned the Blue Door. "The only person I told was Frank and he's far away and uninvolved." When Dane still looked hurt I continued. "Frank advised me to forget about what I'd found out."

"But obviously you didn't," Dane said.

"I struggled with it, but in the end I thought Gwen had a right to know." I looked at Dane hoping for a nod of understanding before he returned to his usual teasing demeanor, but it wasn't happening. To make up for what I'd done, I reached out and hugged him.

I couldn't see his face, but I could feel him leaning into the embrace. "Aha, trying to use your feminine wiles to make up for not telling me," he said. I let out my breath, noting that his tone had lightened. "Well, it worked. I forgive you. I like this side of you, making the first move."

I was already squirming out of the hug as he suggested I might want to join him for lunch at his house. I opened my mouth to speak and before I could say the words, he said them for me. "I know, I know. You have retreaters coming and you have to gear up."

It turned out to be truer than I expected.

40

I'd just gone into my house when the landline began to ring. I barely got out a hello before Cloris spoke. "Casey, you better get over here, like right now. Your people arrived and there's a problem. A big problem."

I was on the way to the door as she was talking and dropped the cordless just before I went out. What could possibly have gone wrong already?

CHAPTER 4

I made it across the street in record time and pulled open the door to the Lodge out of breath both from running and in anticipation. Kevin St. John was standing in front of the registration counter glaring at the five women I assumed were my retreat people. I couldn't understand why he looked so perturbed until I noticed one of the women was holding a tiny white poodle wearing a pink T-shirt.

"Ms. Feldstein, do something. You know that pets are not allowed."

"But Fifi isn't a pet," the woman said. "She's my emotional support dog. The airlines let her on planes when I fly, so I can't see why this place wouldn't allow her." The woman looked around at the rustic surroundings.

"No pets for any reason," Kevin St. John repeated. The dog looked at him and let out a squeaky bark.

This was a first and I had no idea what to do. There was no doubt that the manager wouldn't bend. He didn't like pets and couldn't understand why people had them. He'd almost run over Julius when he'd strayed onto the Vista Del Mar grounds. I was surprised he hadn't tried to run off the wild deer that wandered through the property.

I introduced myself while I tried to think of a solution. They'd driven together, and if one of them was turned away they would all leave and insist on a justifiable refund. I assured the manager that I would take care of it and wished he would go away. He lingered for a moment, but then luckily was tagged by a pair of the bird-watchers holding a map.

"Aileen Bursten," one of the women said, putting out her hand.

"Oh, sure," I said, shaking her hand. I recognized the name as the person I'd dealt with about planning the event. She had a squarish face with long dark wavy hair pulled into a low ponytail. Her clothes made no impression on me other than they seemed plain. I already knew she was the organized type from our emails and phone calls setting up the weekend. She took my arm and led me away from the group. "You

43

have to do something. I'm, I mean, we're all looking forward to this weekend." She pointed to a large pink tote at the dog owner's foot. "She carries the dog around in that bag all the time. What if she kept her in the bag?"

Before I could nix it, the dog's owner joined the two of us. She had a slight build and a pixieish face. Her brown hair was pulled into something at the back of her head. It was too tiny to be called a ponytail and was more like a puff. "We could just go somewhere else in the area," the woman said. "I heard that hotels in Carmel are very pet-friendly." She turned to me. "Whatever you planned could just be moved there."

"No," Aileen said firmly. "It has to be here. This place is perfect for what we want." She looked to me for help.

"I suppose Fifi could stay at my place," I said, pointing out how close I lived. I generally liked to keep my place off-limits from retreaters, but this was an emergency. I mentioned having a cat who I wasn't sure would welcome a dog visitor and offered my guesthouse for the dog. Fifi's owner stepped in as I was talking.

"And then I could sneak her into my room at night," she said. I glanced around and Kevin St. John was out of earshot and now busy on a phone call.

"I didn't hear you say that," I said in a forced tone. "I can give you a key and you'll be free to come and go as you wish. I certainly won't be keeping tabs on you and Fifi. Just please be discreet," I said, dropping my voice. What was I doing? If Kevin St. John found out the dog was on the grounds, let alone in her room, he'd demand she leave and take the information to the Delacorte sisters. I couldn't afford any black marks against me right now. But by the same token, I wanted Fifi's dog mom to be happy.

Talk about being caught between a rock and a hard place.

Aileen grabbed my hand. "Thank you for saving the weekend." She went off to tell the other three women what was going on.

The manager was back behind the registration counter, and even when I assured him that I'd made arrangements for the dog, he insisted the woman put the dog into her tote bag.

He watched until the two of us went out the door.

"I didn't get your name," I said as we went up the Vista Del Mar driveway. Of course I knew all their names, just not which name went with which woman.

"Sorry," she said, looking down at the dog head showing over the top of the pink tote bag. "I was just so worked up about Fifi I wasn't thinking about anything else." She held out her free hand. "Deani McCarthy."

When we got across the street I opened the door to the guesthouse and brought them in. Deani gave the place the once-over. "So this is what counts as a guesthouse here?"

I wasn't sure what she meant by her comment and quickly said that I knew *guesthouse* sounded grander than it was.

Deani chuckled. "I'm afraid you took my comment wrong. I was just thinking what a place like this would rent for where our group comes from. You could get a boatload of money for a place like this." Fifi was still in the bag and making no move to get out. "This might sound a little strange, but this is too big a space to leave her in. We need something smaller."

I glanced around the converted garage. I was about to suggest the bathroom — it was barely big enough to turn around in — but then I remembered my aunt had an old dog crate from when she'd had a pet. A small part of the former garage had been kept as a storage space and I went and found the metal crate. Deani unfolded it and set it in the middle of the floor. I got a bowl for water and an old blanket to put in the bottom of it. Fifi watched it all from the confines of the bag. As soon as it was done with barely any coaxing, she jumped out onto the floor and went right into the crate. She began to root around, rearranging the blanket.

"Just give me a minute," Deani said. "I want to make sure she's okay." She did a sweep of the interior again. "You said you have a cat. It won't be coming in here, will it?" she asked nervously. "Fifi is afraid of cats."

I didn't say anything but I could see why. Julius was bigger than the tiny poodle.

I assured her I would make sure Julius didn't get a chance to meet the dog face-to-face. She seemed reluctant to leave the dog and I offered to let her stay while I went back across the street, but she seemed torn.

"I'll just stay until she get used to the place. Then I'll come back in an hour or so to make sure she isn't too lonely." Deani looked around the main area and settled into a wing chair I'd always liked to use for reading. She looked in the tote bag and took out a skein of moss green yarn and a set of circular needles. I still didn't know why they were referred to as a set since a cable ran between the shorter version of knitting needles, making it one long piece.

I watched in amazement as she began to cast on stitches without even looking. Not something I was able to do. I judged by the size of her cast on she was making a scarf. Her fingers flew as she went back and forth making row after row, all without looking.

"You're sure good at that," I said. She sighed and smiled.

"I don't sleep well and I feel better if I can do something positive with the time." She held up the work she'd completed. "I make scarves and hats and donate them." She made a face. "It used to bother Don, but it doesn't matter anymore."

Was Don her husband, her boyfriend or even another dog? And why didn't it bother him anymore? I wasn't sure how to ask, but then she answered it all for me, explaining that she and Don had been together for seven years and recently had broken up. You didn't break up with husbands, you divorced them, making it clear he'd been a boyfriend.

"Don kept telling me I ought to grow my business into something bigger. He couldn't understand why I didn't take one of my customers up on his offer." She rolled her eyes. "All his talks of apps and going national. But that's what happens when you deal with all these start-up types. I really thought I'd be getting away from it all this weekend, but then I saw one of them was here." She seemed to be having an internal discussion. "After what he did, I could kill him."

She'd lost me by now and I put my hand up to stop her. "What exactly is it that you do?"

She gave me a blank look for a moment and then it seemed like a lightbulb went off in her head. "I guess I didn't mention that. You can see I really need this weekend to catch up with myself. I've been up since five getting everything ready so I could go." She stopped herself. "There I go again rambling on and you have no idea what I'm talking about." She took a breath and let it out. "I bring lunch and snacks to offices." She stopped herself and mumbled that she wasn't explaining it well. "It's more than just bringing random sandwiches and sal- ads. I customize it. First I find out if the cli- ent has any food allergies, is vegan or vegetarian, paleo, keto, gluten-free, or has any religious or ethical dietary issues. I find out foods they hate and foods they like. And then I create lunch and snacks and deliver them."

"So you text them a menu or something

and then they order?" I said, trying to follow what she was saying.

She shook her head and rolled her eyes. "You have to know these start-up types to understand. They just want the food to appear, so I choose what I'm going to bring based on all the stuff I asked them and they accept it. They are so into what they're doing that they don't even realize they're hungry until I show up. I charge them a lot and most of them are thrilled to pay it so they don't have to stop what they're doing, look at a menu and click on their phone. They call me the lunch genie."

She looked at Fifi, who seemed very happy in the crate. "I better tell Madison who I saw. She's not going to be happy."

"Madison's the birthday girl, right?" I asked.

"Yes, and she's freaking out about turning forty, but I don't think you need to freak out until you turn fifty. Half a century? How can you still say you're young? Madison brought some pink hair dye with her. Thank heavens she's not making us all get crazy-colored hair."

"Which one exactly is she?" I asked.

"That's right, you didn't get to meet the rest of the group. She's the one with light blond hair to her shoulders. She's kind of intense and gestures a lot with her hands. She put our knitting group together." She rolled her eyes at herself. "Here I go again leaving half the story out." She took a moment to collect her thoughts.

"I met her because of my work. Madison manages one of those shared work space places that have a lot of start-ups. To say they're demanding is an understatement. Think man-sized boys who are way too smart with no common sense. She's always complaining that they think she's their concierge. She says *concierge* but she really means mother. She just doesn't want to admit that they think she's that old. But I digress. While Madison is the manager of the place, she doesn't have an office. Instead she has to man the reception desk along with everything else. To keep her sanity, she knits. I happened to see what she was doing once when I was delivering meals. A lot of my customers have space in her place. We always talked a little and I mentioned that I'd been knitting since I was a kid. She told me she'd been talking to some other people she knew about starting a knitting group. We could make things and, well, complain to each other. It sounded good to me, so I joined."

Fifi had slept through it all, but then she

began to let out little yelps and barks in her sleep.

"Oh, no, she's having a nightmare. She's probably upset about what the awful man said about dogs, as if she could even do any damage. She only barked at him because it was so obvious he didn't like her. Fifi is very sensitive and I think she can smell it when someone doesn't like her. It's just ridiculous that the manager won't allow her on the grounds."

"But he makes the rules. And as far as I know you're going to follow them. Just please be discreet whatever you do."

"Of course," she said. "But it's not like he does room checks or anything, right?"

"I hope not," I said, imagining the manager patroling the hallway listening for barks.

I was anxious to get back across the street, but Deani kept stalling by talking about the others. I heard all about Aileen and how they'd listen to her complain about her husband — how dull he was and how he didn't want to go anywhere or do anything. The group had been relieved when she finally got a divorce.

She gave me the lowdown on PJ. I should definitely not ask her what the PJ stood for. Once I heard it was Pauline-Josephine, I understood. Who would name a kid that? And because she had a vlog that focused on lifestyle hints that were now called "hacks," she was constantly looking to record stuff for it. "She's always ready for her close-up," Deani said with a laugh. "But seriously, she wants to brand herself and have a line of products, but she's a little clueless on how to go about it and maybe a little desperate. She was a housewife for years and now is trying to make something for herself out of what she did for all that time." Deani's needles kept going and she was turning out row after row as she talked. "Apparently, her husband was one of those in-charge kind of guys who wanted her to walk one step behind, if you know what I mean. And when he moved on, she was left trying to figure out how to reinvent herself. She has a grown daughter who's working on getting a master's in some obscure field."

Deani mentioned Iola last. "She's the quiet one in the group, but I figure she's hiding something under all the silence. Like maybe she's afraid to say anything because of what she'd say if she did. Like maybe the husband she mentioned doesn't really exist, or he does and she murdered him."

When I was surprised at the comment, Dean added, "Don't mind me. I'm a mystery addict so I see plots even when there aren't any. But I still think there is something going on with Iola."

"Have you ever just asked her right out?" I asked.

"No. I mean, I couldn't just say something like is your husband's decaying body sitting in a rocking chair at your place."

I nodded, thinking that Deani hadn't shown any interest in getting to know anything more about me, but then the retreats were all about the retreat people.

At least she'd given me a who's who of the group.

54

CHAPTER 5

"There you are," Aileen said when Deani and I rejoined the others in the Lodge. The four women were in the seating area arranged around the huge stone fireplace. Their suitcases were lined up under the window that looked out on the driveway. "He wouldn't let us check in until you got back." She shot an annoyed glance toward Kevin St. John, who was behind the registration counter. He seemed to be deliberately avoiding looking our way.

"No problem. We're using the time to knit and have a snack," one of the other women said. Trying not to be too obvious, I checked her out, seeing if I could figure out who she was. Deani had mentioned that one of the women was ready to video at any moment. I was sure this woman was PJ since she looked camera-ready. Her makeup was subtle but flawless. Her toast-brown hair was cut very short in a style that never got out of place. The black leggings with a long black tunic were made of a knit fabric that refused to wrinkle.

"PJ, isn't it?" I said, and she smiled and held out a cellophane bag with small crunchy-looking squares. I got a whiff of a buttery smell and she urged me to take one and then offered the same to Deani.

"You don't have to ask me twice," Deani said, reaching into the bag after I took one. She turned to me and said, "You are in for a treat. PJ makes these, and let me tell you, when I brought some samples with the food I delivered, everyone was like, these are great."

I took the opportunity to pop the one in my hand into my mouth. At first it tasted of buttery toast, but when I began to chew I tasted cheese. It tasted as delicious as it smelled. "It's like a mini toasted cheese sandwich," I said.

"They're even better in soup. The cheese reconstitutes and gets almost gooey," Deani said.

"How do you make them?" I asked, and was about to mention my other job baking, but PJ rocked her head and smiled.

"Trade secret. It took a lot of time and experiments before I figured it out. Hopefully they'll be for sale soon." She looked as

56

if she wanted to say more, but she did the move of pretending to lock her mouth with a key.

"Don't feel bad, she won't even tell us anything," another woman said. I had the choice between her being Madison or Iola. It was almost too easy to figure that she was Madison. There was the blond hair and the hand gestures, but mostly it was that she seemed so animated.

"Thank you, Madison. I won't take offense," I said. Her smile broadened, making it clear I was right about who she was.

"Iola, I'm glad you could come," I said to the last woman. She acted a little startled when I spoke to her, but then her mouth curved into what I could best describe as an apologetic smile. I understood now what Deani had said about barely noticing her. She had bland looks and nondescript clothes and seemed to blend in with the chair. I made a mental note to make sure to talk to her during the weekend. "I'll take care of getting you all checked in," I said. Deani joined the others and I went back to the front.

"Ahem," I said loudly when I reached the massive wooden counter. I know he knew I was there, but he still took his time before he looked up.

"Ms. Feldstein," he said, seeming surprised. "What can I do for you?"

"How about checking in my group now," I said in a pleasant tone. I was definitely annoyed, but I wasn't going to show it. "You can just give me their keys."

"What kind of service is that?" he said, looking across the room at the gathering of women. "You can go join them and I'll bring the keys over."

I knew that he was up to something. He never tried to make things easier with my retreats. I'd barely rejoined the women when he came into the seating area. He had put the keys in little folders with the room numbers on them, along with the name of the guest, and insisted on handing out the keys himself. When he got to Deani, he looked down at her tote bag and commented on how roomy it was.

I caught him at his game and pulled the bag open, assuring him that Fifi was safely in my guesthouse.

"Good to know," he said before focusing on me. "And of course, you'll make sure the dog stays there all weekend, right? It would be terrible if anything ruined your group's weekend."

I nodded but had my fingers crossed behind my back, hoping that it would cover up my lie.

I pulled five folders out of my tote bag and handed them out, explaining they held schedules of the retreat activities and information about Vista Del Mar and activities they offered. I added that they'd get tote bags at the first workshop. Then, even though Aileen said she knew the way to the Sand and Sea building because she'd been to Vista Del Mar before, I escorted them to the moody-looking building.

The sky was still a flat white and the light had barely changed since the morning, making it hard to decipher that it was afternoon.

I started to do my usual spiel, pointing out the living-room-like lobby area with the comfortable chairs and glowing fire and mentioning it was a nice spot to hang out and work on their projects.

Deani seemed most interested. "It's available all the time, right? Like even late at night?" I nodded and she seemed relieved. "Great, there's someplace to go if I can't sleep."

Madison was checking over the schedule I'd handed out. "We could arrange our own little gathering here during free time. I know we're going to be working on crochet things in the workshops, but I brought a couple of knitting projects with me. I saw that there's

59

wine in the café."

Aileen looked troubled. "We don't have to spend all our time together. We could make it loose. Just come if you want to."

"That sounds good to me," PJ said. "I want to get some video for my vlog." I started to explain she wouldn't be able to upload it, but she stopped me and pointed to the schedule. "I see we'll be going off location for at least one activity each of the days. I'll be able to get a signal at least and hopefully Wi-Fi then and I can upload it then."

I was glad that she seemed so easy about it. After what Deani had said about her and what I'd experienced with other groups, I was expecting her to make more of a fuss. I looked to see if Iola was going to add anything, but she just shrugged and said something in a low voice that I couldn't hear.

Now it was time to let them see the rooms. I hoped that Aileen had explained the accommodations so it wouldn't be a total shock when they saw how basic they were. Hoping to soften the blow a little, I told them about the goodie bags I'd left.

"I even left lavender sachets in your beds." They had gone on ahead of me to the hallway and were already finding their rooms when I caught up with them. Madison had her door open first. She walked in and looked around and I waited for her to say something. "I love it," she said when she came back to the doorway. "It reminds me of camp. This is going to be such a fun weekend."

By then the rest of them had their doors open and were going in. No one seemed bothered by the lack of TVs or phones. The clock radios got a lot of kudos for being so old-fashioned and easy to set.

I got ready to leave and stuck my head into Madison's open doorway. "By the way, Happy Birthday."

She looked a little sheepish. "You're a little early. My actual birthday isn't for another couple of weeks. I'm not sure why we're here now. Aileen insisted we come this weekend, she said there was a special deal."

Really? That was news to me.

That had gone much better than I expected. I'd left the five women to get settled and have a look around before our first workshop. The only problem was Fifi, but the dog was so tiny and Kevin would be busy with the other guests and probably forget all about her.

I liked having a group who were already

61

friends. I was thinking ahead of ways to promote retreats to celebrate special moments. What fun a wedding shower weekend would be. I could do baby showers and birthdays.

I followed the path and went directly to the meeting room I'd arranged. This weekend was going to be a breeze. All I really had to do was be there for the workshops and the special activities I had planned. But there wouldn't be all the hand-holding I'd done in the past.

Somewhere above all the white clouds the sun was moving across the sky, but it was invisible down here. No sun meant no shadows. I was getting used to the flat light and having no idea of the time unless I checked my watch. It was just about two o'clock, which was perfect since the first workshop started at two thirty.

The doors to both of the meeting rooms in the Cypress building were open. The workshops for all the different groups tended to start around the same time, so it figured that the room next to ours would be occupied at the same time ours was. The other one was larger and seemed like a cave somehow. I guess it was the dark green paint on the walls. The only window looked out on an enclosed courtyard with a few plants surrounded by rocks.

I walked in our room and smiled at how inviting it was by comparison. We had a window that looked out on the path. The walls were white and there was a fireplace.

I'd barely walked into the smaller room when Cloris joined me pushing a metal cart. When I'd seen her earlier she'd been wearing a blazer that the staff working the desk wore. Now she had on a white smock she wore when she was on kitchen detail.

"They have you working everywhere today," I said.

"I was just filling in this morning," she said as she unloaded a metal urn on the counter and hung a sign on it that said *Coffee*. "Back to my regular duties, catering and kitchen." She moved the other urn onto the counter and hung a sign that said *Hot Water*. "It was a mess this morning. All of those people wanted to check in early and the regular clerk didn't show up. Mr. St. John was caught off guard. He didn't seem to expect the two groups to arrive when they did."

"I get the group with the vests and binoculars are birders. But what's the story of the group in black?"

She smiled. "They're from Silicon Valley and want to clear their heads or something.

They're here for a mindfulness retreat."

"Did they realize they were going into an unplugged zone?" I asked. "Those techie types must freak out without all their electronics."

"I didn't hear anyone complaining. I think part of the mindfulness thing is going unplugged."

"What about the guy in the leggings. How does he fit in?" I asked, thinking back to seeing him in the Lodge.

"That's Sky Brooks," she said with a smile. "And don't call those leggings. He was very specific that they were yoga pants." She continued with her work. "He's the one who opened that yoga and Pilates studio on Grand Street in beautiful downtown Cadbury. Mr. St. John hired him to be the facilitator." She laughed at the word. "From what I heard, Mr. St. John put together the activities and schedule and all. Sky is just supposed to pull it off."

"His name isn't really Sky, is it?" I asked.

"I saw the form he filled out to get paid and it said Robert," she said with a chuckle. "I don't really know him, but I hope he isn't as pretentious as his name. I do know that he really wants this gig to work out. But Sky has his work cut out for him. Mr. St. John wants all the retreats or events he arranges to be optimally profitable, which means spending as little as possible putting them together." She straightened a chair that had gotten moved as she brought in the cart. "I hope your group appreciates all the extras you give them."

"I guess my focus is on making a successful retreat more than a bigger profit." I laughed. "Maybe I should be more like him, then I wouldn't have to do a bunch of jobs to make ends meet. Lucky for me that my aunt left me her house or I'd really be in trouble."

"I think your way is better," she said as she finished up. When she wasn't working at Vista Del Mar, Cloris was studying hospitality. It was one of the reasons why she actually wanted to try working different jobs at the hotel and conference center. Lately, she'd changed her playful look to something more serious. Her warm brown hair was now chin length in a sleek style. She tended to wear slacks and a sweater, which she covered with whatever uniform went along with her current duties. She always seemed upbeat and as if she really liked whatever task she was currently performing at Vista Del Mar. She was also my conduit for inside information.

She rolled her eyes. "Mr. St. John has a

lot riding on this mindfulness retreat he organized. He thinks it will lead to others, which will give him even more free rein to run Vista Del Mar as he sees fit. I heard him say that he knows how to handle the Delacorte sisters." She shrugged. "He told the bird people that next time they should let him do it turnkey for them. You should have seen the look on the face of the woman who organized it. You know that phrase *if looks could kill*? I don't think he even cared, though. He just wants to control everything and make the biggest profit possible."

They were not comforting words. If Kevin St. John started running a bunch of retreats, it was only a matter of time before he figured out a way to push me out.

She noticed the tin on the counter and opened it. "Yum, the butter cookies look delicious." I offered her one and she gratefully accepted. "Wow, up to your usual standards," she said, taking a crumb off her finger. She produced a long lighter and lit the fire. The kindling caught and it gave off an inviting glow. "Anything else?" she said as she pushed the cart toward the door.

"Who has the room next to us?" I asked.

"The mindfulness crew," she said. "I hope they aren't trouble."

CHAPTER 6

I checked my watch. Crystal wasn't late —
yet. But then her habit was to cut it pretty
close to the start time. I pulled out one of
the chairs and took out the pink triangle
hanging on the small circular needles. It
really was the perfect project to carry
around. I did the first two knit stitches and
then the yarn over, which would increase
the number of stitches in the row by one. I
still had a long way to go before I'd begin
decreasing the number of stitches in each
row. In the end I'd have a lovely square with
a pattern of open spaces along the sides. I'd
already completed a number of these wash-
cloths and every time I used one it made
me feel good to know that I'd made it
myself. I was getting up my nerve to make
one for my mother. I'd find some fancy soap
to include with it and mail it off to Chicago.

I sighed wondering if she'd be impressed.
My mother was a cardiologist who literally

fixed broken hearts. Making a washcloth didn't really put me in the same league. She was having a hard time facing that the apple had fallen so far from the tree. As much as I argued with her, I kind of understood.

I heard the sound of someone coming in and glanced at the doorway just as a man walked in. I recognized the short dark hair and sharp features of the man I'd encountered in the hall. I supposed he technically was a man since he appeared to be in his mid-twenties, but something about his look made "guy" seem like a better description.

"You're next door," I said, gesturing toward the next-door room. He ignored what I said and came further into the room. He gave me a cursory glance before going back to checking out the room.

"The bag lady," he said, and I winced at the title.

"I'd rather be known by my name. Casey Feldstein," I said. I expected him to introduce himself, but he seemed most interested in his surroundings.

"This is much nicer than ours," he said. "The fireplace, the drinks." He walked over to the counter with the coffee and tea service. Without asking for permission, he opened the tin. "Cookies with chocolate, hmm, looks good."

"I always bake some treats for my group." I did a little side pitch on the other baking I did, mentioning the desserts I made for the Blue Door and the muffins for all the coffee spots in town. I was wasting my breath because he seemed to have no interest in what I was saying.

"Can I take one?" he said. By now I'd dealt with all kinds of people so I wasn't totally surprised by his brashness. I'd made extra so I told him to help himself. Without hesitation, he picked up one of the small fluted paper cups holding one of the cookies and popped the treat into his mouth.

I watched his eyebrows go up in surprise. "This is really good. We should have something like this."

"You'll have to talk to Mr. St. John," I said. "I understand he put together your retreat." I gestured around the room. "I arranged all this for my group," I said, still holding the knitting needles. I wasn't accomplished enough to be able to stop knitting when I was in the middle of a row and quickly continued on with the stitches.

"Oh," he said as his brow furrowed. He stepped closer and watched as I finished the row. When I set it down on the table, he picked it up and looked it over. "Is there a theme to your retreat?" I thought the guys from Silicon Valley were supposed to be shy and nerdy. He seemed to be neither. He'd come in and made himself at home. I wasn't sure if it was confidence or a sense of entitlement.

"Ours is all about yarn craft and it's a birthday celebration. I'm hosting a group of knitters who requested learning how to crochet. They'll also be going whale watching and wine tasting." I pointed to my work in his hand. "That's knitting and this is crochet." I grabbed one of the crochet hooks and a ball of cotton yarn. Crystal had taught me the basics of crochet and I made some chain stitches and a short row of single crochet. I opened the bin that had the supplies for my group and took out a finished sample of the shawl the group would be making. "By the end of the weekend they'll either be finished making one of these or close to it." He kept looking around and seemed unsettled.

"I heard your retreat is about mindfulness," I said. He was making me uncomfortable and I tried to fill the dead air with conversation. "Some people consider knitting and crocheting to be mindfulness activities. You're focusing on the stitches — which puts you in the moment," I said.

At that he looked at the washcloth in

progress again. "Can I try?" he asked.

"I guess so," I said and rummaged around in Crystal's bin and found a pair of knitting needles and grabbed the ball of cotton yarn. I wasn't a super knitter, but certainly good enough that I could show him how so he could do a few rows.

"To expedite things, I'll do the cast on." I was already laying a base row on the needle as I spoke and then I handed it to him. From there I gave him step-by-step instructions like "poke the empty needle into the first stitch." I moved the yarn around the needle for the first stitch to demonstrate and helped him manipulate them so that the stitch moved onto the empty needle.

I was going to help with the next stitch but he wanted to do it on his own. He needed a little coaching to complete it and then seemed proud of himself as he moved it onto the other needle. He stared down at the two stitches. "I get it. It's all about loops. That was definitely a mindful experience. I was centered and focused."

I let him go through one row, but then enough was enough and now I was ready for him to leave. He didn't seem to be making a move, but thankfully I heard the sound of people coming up the path and going into the next room. I pointed it out to him. "It sounds like your workshop is about to begin." He glanced toward the door and apparently got the message because he went toward the doorway without so much as a thank-you.

Crystal breezed in just then, passing him. With all her colorful clothes, it was like she brought in the sunshine on the cloud-filled day. He looked at her, then did a slight double take. She had that effect on people. She had on a bright orange top covered with a purple jacket. She'd wrapped a fuchsia-colored lacy scarf around her neck. I saw his gaze stop on her ears and he seemed perplexed.

"They're not supposed to match," I said, figuring his thought.

"Crystal, this is our neighbor from the retreat next door," I said. I looked at him with a shrug, realizing I didn't know his name.

"Elex Keaton, CEO of Reborn," he said before going out.

"Okay," Crystal said with a chuckle at the way he'd added his title to his name. "He seems a little full of himself. What is he, maybe twenty-five?" She made her way to the table and took off the purple jacket and loosened the scarf.

"They're having a mindfulness retreat," I

explained and Crystal perked up.

"And I bet they're from Silicon Valley," she said and I nodded.

"Kevin planned their retreat," I explained. Crystal winced.

"Oh, good luck on that then," she said. She pulled out a ball of pale pink yarn and some knitting needles with some work hanging off of them. It was too small to tell what she was making. She read my thoughts and picked it up to give me a better view. "It's going to be a sweater for my daughter." She made a face. "Can you believe it that she's into pastels?" Her tone made it sound like her daughter was guilty of something terrible, not just liking light shades of color.

I showed her my pink washcloth in progress, and noting that for once she was actually early said I was going to join her in knitting while I gave her a heads-up on my group.

There was a commotion at the doorway and when I looked up Elex had returned with an entourage that included the guy with the flaxen hair I'd noticed earlier and Sky. Elex was in the lead and the other two seemed to be trying to keep up with him.

"Look at what they have. A fireplace, drinks and snacks. Real activities. And what do we have? A dismal empty room and —"

Elex waved a sheet of blue paper and rolled his eyes as he read from it. "A mindful walk, air tasting, finding your mantra." He moved right up to where Crystal and I were sitting with the other two close behind him. "I want what they have for us," he said.

Sky looked panicked. "All the arrangements have been made. I'm sure when you've completed the first workshop —" The mop-headed guy glanced at the blue sheet in his hand. "*Discovering What Mindfulness Means* — you'll feel differently. We do have a snack as part of the workshop. You'll each be getting three raisins. The point is to savor the taste and texture." He fumbled with the sheet and was about to say more when Elex cut him off.

"Three raisins," he said with a snort. "I'll have to talk to the manager."

"No, don't do that," Sky said, sounding a little panicky. I knew why since I'd heard Kevin St. John's threat about not wanting to hear any complaints. "We can't change anything now." He looked at the blue paper. "There's a Sound Bath Saturday night for your group and all the other guests. You'll see, it'll be a life-changing experience."

Elex seemed undaunted and looked at me. "What about you? Can you take care of what I want?" Before it could even register

74

what he'd said, the flaxen-haired man moved in next to Elex.

"We should talk first," he said in a low tone. "You need to understand things have changed."

Elex gave him an exasperated look. "I'd expect you to understand even more than me." Elex turned to Crystal and me. "Tim's used to fancy vacations at posh resorts. My vacations are picking peaches on my family's farm in Kern."

"I can make do," Tim said.

Elex seemed to shrug off Tim's comment and spoke directly to me. "Well, can you do it? Arrange for drinks and snacks, get us some of those bags I saw you giving out?" He stopped and looked at the table where his knitting attempt still sat. "Can you arrange some mindful yarn thing where we actually have something to show for our time?"

Crystal and I looked at each other, trying to absorb what he was asking. Surely we could do it without much trouble. And making some extra profit on the weekend was definitely appealing. "There'd be a charge for our services on top of any actual expenses," I said.

"No problem." Elex turned to the light-haired man. "Tim, arrange it."

Letting out a sigh of capitulation, Tim nodded at us. "If you could set up a tab, we'll settle up at the end of the weekend."

"I can't do anything about your meeting room," I said. "But I can get the drinks and snacks and leave goodie bags in your rooms. As for the yarn activity —" I looked at Crystal and she nodded in agreement.

"We could put together something for your group and arrange a workshop where everyone would learn how to knit and make a simple project, all done in a mindful manner." I had a sudden thought. "We could even have it in this room when my group isn't using it," I said. Elex seemed to like the idea.

"What about this evening?" Elex glanced at the blue sheet in his hand. "It sounds better than *mindful table tennis on your own.*"

I thought it through quickly. The birthday group only had the upcoming afternoon workshop and then the room would be free for the rest of the day. I leaned over and asked Crystal what she thought. She was available that evening and was sure we could put together the supplies and a project. I knew I could depend on Cloris for help with the drinks and I had a tin of cookies at home I could bring over. "We can do it. Shall we say seven in here?"

"Agreed," Elex said.

Sky let out his breath in relief as he did a little bow to us. "Namaste. I mean thank you." He leaned in close and dropped his voice. "I'd appreciate it if you wouldn't mention anything about any of this to Mr. St. John."

"No problem," I said with an inner chuckle. It wasn't in any of our interests for Kevin to know what I was doing. He'd be angry that I meddled in his retreat. Sky seemed to remember then that he was supposed to be the leader and urged them to go back to their meeting room.

As soon as they were gone, Crystal and I started talking about the arrangements. We discussed what sort of a project would work for them. We'd talk to her mother and have her put together kits and Cory could bring them over. The rest was up to me.

"Hmm," Crystal said when we were done. "This should be interesting. We've never worked on two retreats at the same time."

"Be interesting or cause trouble?" I said, wondering what I'd just gotten myself into.

CHAPTER 7

In the few moments between the time Elex and his crew left and my group showed up, Crystal and I talked over the events of the morning.

"I'm sorry," I began. "I thought, well, hoped, that the Delacorte sisters would be happy to find out that they had more family." I looked at Crystal. "I'm afraid everyone is mad at me now for discovering that your mother was their brother's child." I left out *love* or *illegitimate* since they seemed kind of judgy.

Crystal had picked up her knitting and was adding rows to her daughter's sweater. Without stopping she turned to me and smiled warmly. "Nobody wants to kill the messenger. At least, not me. I like Madeleine and I think she likes me. I know she likes Cory. The problem is with Cora and my mother." She let out her breath and I could only imagine what her mother had

78

said to her about the earlier meeting. "I think we have to give it some time and then hopefully we'll all be one big happy family." It was obvious by her tone that the last part bordered on sarcasm.

I was glad to let go of the subject as the birthday group, as I'd come to call them, arrived. Madison walked in first and looked around the room. Deani was right behind her carrying her pink tote bag. I couldn't tell if Fifi was hiding somewhere in it and I wasn't about to look. Iola slipped in behind Deani and took a seat on the other end of the table from Crystal and me. I tried to focus on her appearance and note her clothing, but it was like she had on an invisible cloak. Nothing about her registered. PJ came in last. I thought she was talking to herself, but then I noted that she was holding her phone up in front of her and talking to it. Deani had warned me that PJ would be collecting stuff for her vlog. She took a panoramic view of the room with the phone and I heard her say something about "roughing it."

"Where's Aileen?" I asked when they were all in the room. They shrugged in unison and looked around the room as if she might be hiding under a chair.

"She'll be here," Madison said. "She's

been talking nonstop about looking forward to this weekend."

"In the meantime," I said, gesturing toward the coffee and tea setup. The four of them went to help themselves and brought their drinks and cookies back to the table.

I introduced Crystal and said she was going to unlock the secret of crochet for them. I was glad that I knew who was who now and introduced each one of them to the workshop leader. They seemed entranced by her attire and mismatched earrings.

"What a super hack. What to do when you lose an earring," PJ said, pulling out her phone and asking if she could get a close-up of Crystal's ears for her vlog.

Crystal was uncomfortable at the attention, and to deflect it asked how the group had formed.

"You know how at the end of the day you need to let off steam. Some people go to a bar. They all come to me," Madison said. "We use the lounge of the shared office space I manage. Everyone has something they need to get off their chest. Almost everyone." She stole a look at Iola, who was looking out the window.

"So, it's as much about the stitching as the bitching," Crystal said with a chuckle.

"You know it," Madison said. "For me it's

about my mother-in-law. She's at my house now probably making a list of all my housekeeping gaffes. And my daughters. I think I'm an enlightened mother but even so they roll their eyes at every suggestion I make." She let out a snort. "And then there's the tenants, or work partners as we call them now. It's bad enough dealing with them during the week, but I just saw some of them here." She let out a big breath. "I didn't mean to start with the bitching before we even started stitching."

Crystal went to get something from her bag. "You're the birthday girl, right?"

Madison nodded. "For the purposes of this retreat, yes, but in actuality it's not for a couple of weeks." Crystal took out a lei made out of crocheted flowers and put it around her neck.

"So, you can wear it now, and then when it's your actual birthday."

Just then Aileen came in. She looked around at everybody. "Sorry I'm late," she said.

"Are you wearing mascara?" Deani demanded, staring at Aileen.

"And lipstick, too," PJ said. I took another look at Aileen and it registered how different she looked. It wasn't just the makeup — her clothes were different too. I didn't remember exactly what she'd been wearing other than it was bland-looking. Now she had on jeans that seemed molded to her body with a very fitted scoop-neck white top and a long, colorful silk scarf that hung loose.

"What's the big deal?" Aileen said. "I don't have time to think about things like makeup when I'm home. It's nice to get a little dressed up for a change." She put her things down next to one of the chairs and I pointed her to the refreshments.

They waited while she got herself a drink and a cookie.

"You probably figured that Aileen was the late arrival," I said to Crystal. "And Aileen, this is Crystal, who is going to unlock the secrets of crochet for all of you."

Aileen gave Crystal a second look and smiled. "I love the look. I bet you're a fun person."

"I'd like to think so," Crystal said. "But you better not talk to my daughter. She thinks I'm embarrassing, like I'm trying too hard."

"Oh, do I ever hear you," Madison said. It seemed the group was more interested in socializing than getting down to yarn craft. While Madison and Crystal traded stories about their daughters, PJ grabbed some more video for her vlog. She'd separated from the others and was holding her phone out and talking to it.

Curious, I edged a little closer. She'd set the camera so it was facing her and was talking about traveling.

"The best hack to traveling light is wear something like this." She stood up and moved the phone so it got her whole outfit. She noticed me listening and stopped recording long enough to ask me to hold the phone. She hit Record and then did a twirl as she went on about the merit of the black leggings and black tunic top. It took up little space in her suitcase, was comfortable, hid any spills, could be dressed up or left casual. She leaned over and pushed the Stop button.

"You sold me," I said and she smiled. I noticed there was a tiny embroidered red heart on one shoulder.

"If you think of any other hacks for coming to a place like this, please let me know. The pressure to come up with content never ends. I need to keep my followers following to get advertiser money." She let out a sigh. "I'll upload this as soon as I can get a signal."

I hadn't planned on mentioning it since this group seemed to be okay with being

83

unplugged, but it was different for PJ. It was her livelihood. "My house is across the street. If you walk into my driveway, you'll get a signal."

She instantly brightened. "Thank you. You're a life saver."

When I looked back at the group I noticed that Crystal's brows were furrowed and she was looking at her watch. The allotted time for the workshop was going by and nobody had picked up a hook yet.

I stood up and got the group's attention. "We ought to start the program." I did a flourish with my arm toward Crystal, and she joined me in standing.

"Okay, ladies, time to find out about hooking." They all chuckled before she continued. "We're getting a late start so I'll be teaching you the basics of crochet and we'll start the project next time."

I handed out the red Yarn2Go tote bags, a set of crochet hooks and a ball of cotton yarn to each of them. Since they were all accomplished knitters I had no doubt they'd pick up crochet easily. I hung around while Crystal explained that in crochet instead of casting stitches onto a needle, you made a length of chain stitches. She demonstrated how to make them, and before she'd finished they'd already picked up their hooks and were making their own.

There was no reason for me to stay and I needed to put together and distribute the goodie bags for the Silicon Valley group and get things together for their workshop.

The door was shut to their meeting room, meaning their workshop was still in progress. It seemed pretty quiet and I wondered if they were doing the mindful exercise with the raisins. I passed a few people pulling suitcases as I went through the grounds before I crossed the street and walked up my driveway.

Julius was watching me from the kitchen window. His gaze was unusually intense and I was sure he knew we had a dog visitor. I'd have to make it up to him later. For now, I went directly to the guesthouse. I was almost afraid to look in the crate, sure that Deani had come back and gotten the dog. But then the tiny white poodle let out a yip as I came in.

She was my responsibility too, so I let her out of the crate and held her in my lap while I made a quick call to Gwen Selwyn to tell her what we needed from the yarn shop for the evening workshop. Thankfully, there was no mention of the morning meeting with the Delacorte sisters and she went directly to the business at hand. She promised to get the kits together and have them dropped off at the front desk.

"I have to warn you, I'm a cat person," I said to the dog when I'd hung up the phone. "But you're awfully cute." I gave her a snuggle and she licked my arm in what I took to be a dog kiss. "Okay, now I have to get to work," I said, putting the dog on the floor. She did a little shake and went back into the crate and stayed in there even with the gate open.

I put together the five bags in record time, giving myself a pat for having thought to buy lots of extras of everything. Though I altered their bags a little. I left off the sachets and doubled up on the snacks and chocolate. I added bottles of sparkling water and I was ready to go. I checked Fifi's water and gave her a few pets before I shut the door to the crate, grabbed the packed bin and went to the door.

I went looking for Cloris and found her on my first stop. She was sitting at one of the tables in the Cora and Madeleine Delacorte Café. I pulled the bin up to the table and must have seemed a little breathless.

"Is something wrong?" she asked.

"Sorry to interrupt your break," I said, and then told her about what I was doing for the Silicon Valley bunch.

"No problem interrupting. I find breaks boring. I'd rather be doing something. Just tell me what you need." She smiled at me. "And take a breath. Whatever it is, we'll get it done."

I hated to admit it but I was a little overwrought. I did as she suggested and took a deep breath before continuing. "I promised them drinks and snacks for the workshop this evening. I'll bring a tin of cookies."

"But you need drinks."

I nodded. "I suppose you could do a setup like my group has. And I need to get these bags into their rooms." I gestured toward the bin.

"So you need access to their rooms," she said with a shrug. "No problem. Like I said, I'd rather be doing something." She followed me out and picked up the master key from the clerk at the registration desk.

"I knew that Mr. St. John's way wasn't going to fly with that group," she said when we were outside where no one could hear. "His mantra is no extras. I like the way you do your retreats so much better. That's why when that woman called inquiring about the birthday weekend, I turned it over to you."

I turned to her with surprise. It hadn't occurred to me until that moment to wonder how Aileen had found me. "Well, thank you," I said. "Kevin St. John certainly wouldn't like that."

"I won't tell," she said with a conspiratorial smile. "It's too bad one of them brought a dog." She shook her head and let out a sigh. "Mr. St. John is adamant about pets, even on the grounds."

I assured her that I'd just seen Fifi and she was in my guesthouse.

"Good, because I heard him say that if he found the dog on the premises, the guest would have to leave even if it was the middle of the night." She leaned a little closer. "It's almost like he wants to find the dog in the room."

That wasn't anything I wanted to hear, particularly since I couldn't control what Deani was going to do. "I can't worry about that now," I said, checking my watch. "I want to get these bags in their rooms before their workshop lets out."

"No problem," she said in an efficient voice as we walked up the small hill to the Sand and Sea building. She had the list of names and room numbers and it turned out the five of them were in rooms across the hall from the birthday group. She opened each door and told me who was staying

88

where. I tried to be quick about it, but I couldn't help taking a quick look at the rooms. The first room belonged to Elex. His black duffle bag matched his clothes. It was open on the bed but appeared still packed. A couple of books were next to it and I glanced at the titles. Both were on mindfulness. One said something about it being an antidote for anxiety and the other promised to clear the way to better business decisions. A computer bag with some papers sticking out sat on the bed. I put the paper shopping bag and bottle of sparkling water next to the clock radio.

When I got back in the hall I looked at my watch and realized there was no time for being nosy. Cloris announced the next room belonged to Tim Moffat and I remembered he was the one with Elex when he'd made the arrangements. He stood out from the others thanks to his light hair and preppy attire. I rushed in, barely noting that his incidentals were lined up along the sink in the room. As I moved toward the table with the clock radio, my jacket caught on his open laptop sitting on the bed. I grabbed it just in time to keep it from falling and must have hit a button because the screen came on. I got a quick glance and saw a picture of a bag of something. My heart was still thudding when I got back in the hall. I didn't want to think of the consequences if the laptop had hit the floor and broken.

A floral scent greeted me as Cloris opened the next door. A pile of clothes sat on the bed and several pairs of women's shoes were on the floor below. No surprise the room belonged to the sole woman in the group, Julie Stanton.

"These guys are sharing," Cloris said, opening the last door. "Their names are Jackson Gordon and Josh Williams." They had so much stuff in the small room I felt claustrophobic. I had to step over their suitcases and computer cases to get to the table. I dropped off the bags of treats and bottles of water and left the room quickly. I assumed that since they were sharing a room they must be underlings.

Cloris said she'd drop the key off and then she had to get to the kitchen and start work on dinner. She assured me the drinks would be in the meeting room in time for the evening workshop.

When I went back to the Cypress building both meeting rooms were empty. I knew my group had free time until dinner and I remembered the other group had some sort of walk. I did a quick cleanup of our room and moved the tote bags with their work off to the side. I was glad that I'd marked them with their names before I'd given them out so there wouldn't be any mix-ups.

The next stop was the Lodge. I told the desk clerk to expect something to be dropped off. I looked out the window at the fading afternoon and let out a sigh. I felt like I'd been rushing forever and I needed some time to reenergize. My favorite go-to was taking my knitting to the beach. The fresh salty air mixed with the rhythm of the waves and the movement of my needles always left me feeling restored. I felt in my pocket for the circular needles and ball of pink yarn. I left my tote bag at the front desk, wanting my hands to be free. More people had checked in and were hanging out in the gathering spot. I deliberately didn't check to see if any of my group was there and went out the door on the deck side.

I took the boardwalk that went across the dunes. The area on either side was covered in tall bushes and squat plants. I was sure there were probably some deer wandering through the plantings.

The boardwalk ended at an archway that marked the end of the Vista Del Mar grounds. The street that ran between the grounds and the beach was quiet, but even so I made sure to look before I crossed. With all the curves a car could appear out of nowhere. Particularly now that fog had started to roll in.

When I got to the beach side of the street I saw that shimmering mist was coming in on long fingers that shrouded some areas in mystery and left others completely clear. I considered changing my plan, but then I knew the area so well I could find my way in the fog.

In an effort to protect the native plants growing in the sand from being trampled, the whole area along the street was fenced off and an entrance had been created that led to the expanse of beach. My feet sank into the silky white sand and I stopped when I got to the end of the entranceway. The tide was coming in and the waves were loud as they rolled in, reclaiming the beach they'd backed off of earlier. It was a little scary and thrilling to realize I was on the edge of the continent.

The fog kept shifting with clear spots and invisible areas. Even without being able to see it, I knew there was a big *Danger* sign on the rocky area to my right. The rocks they warned about went all the way out into the water almost like a pier, but as the tide came in more and more of it would disappear under the crashing waves.

I was surrounded by the good kind of ions and took a deep breath. I forgot about the workshop and the baking I still had to do after that. I chuckled to myself, realizing I was having my own mindful moment.

I heard some noise I couldn't place and caught sight of something black in my peripheral vision, but before I could identify it, it had disappeared. I walked back to the street to check but it was deserted.

The fog cleared over the rocky area as I returned to the beach. I was looking it over thinking of the tide pools that must be hidden in the crevices when I noticed something light-colored against the dark rocks. I ignored the *Danger* sign and climbed onto the uneven surface to get a better look.

It was still impossible to tell what it was. I knew I should let it go, but I also knew it would bug me if I didn't check it out. I was glad that nobody could see me because I was hardly graceful as I made my way over the jagged surface. I looked again and this time got a better view. Now I could see there was another color. Red, bright red and lots of it. I upped my speed as I reached a smooth mound of rock.

As I got closer I recognized that it was a man wearing a blue shirt and he was sprawled on his back. The red was blood on his face, and shirt. I fell to my knees and leaned over him. Instinctively I reached for his neck to check for a pulse. I thought I felt something.

Just then I heard sirens in the distance. "Thank heaven help is on the way," I said out loud, hoping the figure on the ground could hear me. The siren got louder and then abruptly stopped. A moment later people in uniforms were climbing over the rocks coming toward me.

There was a lot of shouting, though I couldn't make out the words. When the paramedics reached us, they pushed me away and scooped him onto a stretcher and rushed back over the rocks — as much as you could rush on such a bumpy uneven slippery surface. It was only then that it registered that it was Tim Moffat. The pale blond hair and preppy outfit were the give-away.

Two cops had come with them and they were yelling something at me. Whatever it was got carried off with the breeze. The next thing I knew one of them had grabbed my arm and was pulling me away.

I'd started to protest, but he pointed toward the water and for the first time I saw that the tide had brought the waves almost to the spot where I'd been kneeling. A few more minutes and Tim and I would have been pulled out to sea.

CHAPTER 8

"Do you want to explain what you were doing on the rocks hovering over the victim?" Lieutenant Borgnine said to me. He was wearing the rumpled herringbone jacket that seemed to be his uniform. The scowl seemed to be his default expression. He had a build like a bulldog and had bristly, mostly gray hair with an open spot on top.

I would have liked to say no, but clearly it wasn't an option. At least he wasn't rubbing his temple this time. Or at least not yet. Dealing with me seemed to bring on a headache. He was a seasoned cop and I'd had just a few weeks' experience of working for a private investigator, and yet I'd solved a number of murders that he'd been wrong about. It really bugged him that he'd used my help on occasion. On a positive note, he was a fan of my baking. Whatever I said was going to cause trouble.

As soon as the ambulance had driven

away, the cop who'd pulled me off the rocks had taken me across the street to a bench on the boardwalk. Instead of taking a statement from me, he'd made me wait for the lieutenant's arrival.

I'd offered the officer a thank-you for getting me away from the incoming tide. I knew that he knew who I was because it was a small town and because of my relationship with Dane, but he stayed in official police mode, calling me ma'am and saying he was just doing his duty.

"It's not how it looked," I said to Lieutenant Borgnine. "I went to the beach for a little solo knitting time and I saw something on the rocks and went to investigate." His scowl deepened at the last word and I wished I had chosen a different one. Why poke the bear?

"Investigate?" he bellowed. "I thought we were in agreement about that." If there was an agreement it was on his side only. He wanted me to stay out of his business because, well, I had solved a number of crimes. I think it bugged him that I'd worked for a PI, too. Frank was always telling me that cops didn't like private investigators.

"Poor choice of a word," I said, hoping I could diffuse things. "When I realized it was a person I went to see if I could help."

"Then you know the victim?" he asked.

"It depends on your definition of *know*," I said.

"Don't be cute," he said with a groan.

"I know his name is Tim and he's from Silicon Valley."

Before I could say more, Kevin St. John and Sky had joined us. The manager seemed beside himself and Sky froze when he saw me. I tried to send him a signal that I hadn't said anything about my arrangement with the group. I wasn't good at this signal thing and it came across as me making a bad attempt at flirting.

"I just heard there was an accident," the manager said. He looked at me and the blood on my hands. "What did you do, Ms. Feldstein?" he demanded.

"Nothing. I got there after he fell. But that's just conjecture. I'm assuming he fell. It's not like I saw him fall. When I got there he was lying on his back."

"Who was lying on his back?" Kevin St. John demanded.

"She said his name is Tim and he's from Silicon Valley," Lieutenant Borgnine said, referring to me.

The manager turned to Sky. "He must have been on the mindful walk. What did

98

you tell them?"

Sky put up his hands defensively. "I didn't tell them anything. I read them what you wrote about how to make the walk a mindful experience. They were supposed to go by themselves and experience the moment."

"You should have told them not to walk on the rocks," Kevin St. John said angrily. "Somebody has to go to the hospital." He gave Sky a dubious look. "I better go. You stay here and take care of the rest of them." The manager rushed off with Sky following behind him.

"What's going on with them? Isn't the barefoot guy the one who opened that yoga store?" Lieutenant Borgnine asked.

"I think it's called a yoga studio," I said.

"I knew that," Lieutenant Borgnine said. I gave him the rundown on the retreat that Kevin St. John had set up.

"Mindful?" he said, glancing in the direction that Kevin St. John had gone. "I get it, and he has the yoga guy working it."

He looked at my hands and clothes with a disparaging shake of his head. "How did you end up like that again?"

I explained leaning over him while I checked for a pulse.

"So there wasn't an altercation between the two of you?" He looked me in the eye.

"No. I told you I saw him lying there and went to —" This time I stopped myself.

"So did you find a pulse?" he asked.

"I think so. But it was weak. And that's all I know," I said, trying to end it. I was absolutely not going to tell the lieutenant anything about enhancing the retreat.

Just then two uniforms arrived to take the place of the earlier cops. One of them was Dane. I saw him swallow hard when he saw the blood on my hands.

"Are you sure that's all you know? I could certainly arrest you. You were hanging over the victim and you say you were looking for a pulse, but someone else might think you'd been fighting with him." I think he enjoyed the look of panic that came across my face.

"Really? You're not serious."

"I said I could, not that I was going to. It was just an encouragement for you to tell me everything." He shrugged, and I tried to hide a guilty look knowing that I'd left out my relationship with the group. "As much as I'd like you out of the way, I don't think you are responsible for what happened. Most likely it was an accident. Another fool ignoring the signs so he could prove how daring he was." He gestured to Dane. "Will you help her out of here." He leaned closer to Dane and said something I didn't hear.

"I can manage myself," I said, standing up. The lieutenant looked me in the eye as Dane moved in closer.

"I'm sure you can. I know you want us all to think you're supergir— uh, woman, but with all this, this . . ." He gestured toward me and I realized there was blood spattered on my clothes too. "Well, you might be more shook up than you realize." Dane took my arm as I took a step. Much as I hated to admit it, Lieutenant B. was right, sort of anyway. I did feel a little like I'd gotten a punch in the gut. As we started to walk away, he called out after me, "I'll be wanting to talk to you again, so don't leave town or anything." It was impossible for me not to roll my eyes at his comment. Was that his idea of a joke?

Despite experiencing a slightly wobbly feeling as soon as we were out of Lieutenant B.'s line of sight, I tried to pull away. "I can take it from here," I said, trying to get my arm loose of his, but Dane held on fast. It was not my style to be leaning on someone.

"My orders are to take you home," Dane said in his cop tone. Then he leaned in. "It's no shame to accept some help from time to time."

"I would if I needed it," I countered. "But

I'm fine. Just fine." I couldn't see his face, but I sensed he was shaking his head with consternation. Dane certainly knew a thing or two about taking care of needy people. His mother was an alcoholic and as kid he'd had to take care of her and his sister, Chloe. Actually, he still did. Every time his mother relapsed he had to step in. His sister was on her own for the moment but who knew how long that would last.

Before I could suggest another way, Dane led me up the steps to the Lodge and said we'd cut through it. We got a lot of strange looks. I could see why. The way Dane was holding my arm and steering me, it wasn't clear if he was marching me through as a suspect or helping me.

"This was Lieutenant Borgnine's idea, wasn't it," I said, twisting my head back to face him. His lips curved into an impish grin.

"Yes," he said with an air of resignation. "Sorry, but it was this or I'd have to work the graveyard shift on Christmas."

Just then we approached the man I'd met that morning when Kevin St. John'd had the flurry of early check-ins. His name reminded me of peanut butter and then it came to me — it was Reese, like the peanut butter cups. He eyed me with concern and

I remembered the mess on my hands and clothes and rushed to explain.

"I'm fine. There was an accident on the beach."

"Glad to hear you're okay," he said as his eyes rested on the bloody shirt. He glanced up at Dane as if he was trying to figure out why I had a police escort.

"One of the perks of living in a town like Cadbury," I offered with a smile. "The cops assist more than they arrest."

I felt Dane move a little faster and now he was pulling me toward the door on the other side of the Lodge instead of holding me in front of him.

"Who's he?" he demanded as soon as we got outside.

"Don't go all alpha male on me. He's not even my type," I said. "He's just a guest I met this morning. He comes here every year on this weekend to meet with a client. I think he's an accountant. Probably a geeky accountant," I added.

He lightened up. "Sorry for overreacting," Dane said. I waited to see if he was going to say anything else. This was one of the reasons I held back on our relationship. I had to be free to deal with men without worrying about Dane getting all possessive.

We got to my place without encountering

anyone else. I was particularly relieved we didn't pass any of the birthday group. It would have been awkward to say the least.

"Okay, no one can hear now. Are you going to tell me what you left out telling the lieutenant?" Dane said as we walked in my kitchen door.

"What makes you think there's anything else?" I asked, trying to bat my eyes in a bad attempt at looking innocent.

He rolled his eyes. "You don't really think I'm going to fall for that?"

"I was hoping for comic relief." I batted my eyes a few more times with a smile.

"And to change the subject. Now I'm sure you didn't tell him everything."

We had stopped inside my kitchen. The noise had awakened Julius from an early evening nap and he sauntered in. He looked at me and then focused on Dane before letting out a plaintive meow. I didn't know cat language but I bet there was something in that meow about a dog staying in the vicinity.

"I've got this," Dane said to me before turning to the cat. "I know what you want." He went to the refrigerator and took out the stink fish. He held the can out toward me as he unwrapped it from all its layers of coverings. "Tell me or I might just accidentally wave the can in front of your nose."

I put up my hands in capitulation, gagging at the thought of confronting the smell. "Fine, but I was just thinking of you. I wouldn't want you to be in an awkward situation with Lieutenant B. because you knew something he didn't."

I explained that I did know the victim a little more than I'd let on and told him about the deal I'd made with Elex. "Tim didn't seem in favor of it," I said. I also explained why I didn't want the lieutenant to know.

Dane seemed disappointed. "That's all? It's hardly what I'd call a relationship. Though I get why you wouldn't want the lieutenant to know. There's no way he wouldn't say something to Kevin St. John about it." He took another look at me and shook his head. "You might want to do something about that." He waved toward my clothes and I looked down.

I hadn't realized how bad it was. My beige fleece jacket had come out unscathed, but the cream-colored turtleneck I had on underneath was splotched with blood. My hands were a mess too.

"You could probably use a shot of something," he said. I was pretty much a non-

105

drinker and Dane was for sure since he'd spent too much time dealing with his alcoholic mother, so he suggested a cup of coffee.

"I am feeling a little weak in the knees," I said. His head shot up in surprise.

"Did you really just say that? Did you really just admit that you're not an iron woman who can deal with anything and not be affected?"

"You got me," I said. "But you know I'm already better. I don't need the coffee. Just a shower and a change of clothes."

I could smell the coffee beginning to brew as I went into the bathroom. I'd left the jacket in the kitchen. I stripped off the turtleneck and threw it in the trash. The only way to get the blood out completely was by using bleach and it would ruin the shirt, plus it would be a reminder of finding Tim.

When I returned to the kitchen showered and dressed in fresh clothes, the coffee was brewed and there was a note on the table saying he'd gotten a call and had to go and that he'd see me later. He'd signed it with a heart. "Why can't I do stuff like that?" I said out loud.

CHAPTER 9

The dinner bell was ringing as I went back across the street. Meals came with the rooms at Vista Del Mar and were served in the Sea Foam dining hall. Using a bell to call people to meals was a leftover from when it had been a camp. Since Aileen had been to Vista Del Mar before and she'd been the one to make the arrangements, I assumed she'd told the rest of them about how the meals were served and what they were like. The menu was heavy on comfort foods like meat loaf and macaroni and cheese, *heavy* being the important word there. It was delicious but not exactly gourmet.

I was less concerned about the menu for dinner than what I should tell my group about what had happened to Tim. And the big question was would there be any news about his condition. I was pretty sure I'd felt a pulse, but beyond that I had no idea.

I breezed through the grounds with ease since I knew them by heart after all this time, but Vista del Mar was very dark at night. The outdoor lighting was limited to small low-watt lamps along the paths. The lack of bright outdoor lighting added to the rustic feeling of the grounds and made the buildings seem like cozy outposts.

The Sea Foam dining hall was located a short distance from the Lodge. The name of that building was simply Lodge, but it just seemed odd not to put a *the* before it. The dining hall was built in the same Arts and Crafts style as the other buildings, which meant lots of wood and stone. The building itself blended in with the darkness and only the tall windows showed, spilling light onto the ground outside.

A staff member was stationed at the host stand just inside the door checking meal tickets and giving them a punch. He smiled at me and waved me on without asking me for a meal ticket.

A fire glowed in the huge stone fireplace, which made the high-ceilinged room seem more inviting. Round wood tables were scattered around the interior. Seating was not assigned, but the groups seemed to always sit together, and once they'd chosen a table they stuck with it for the weekend.

Food was served cafeteria-style with an entrance to the line at the back of the room.

Everything seemed very ordinary, which led me to believe that no one knew about Tim's accident. But then the ambulance and police cars had been on the street and not on Vista Del Mar property.

While I was checking for my group I saw Elex and the other three in black clothes come in with Sky hovering around them. Sky turned in my direction and then they were all looking at me. What should I say to them? Before I could make a decision, Elex crossed the room and came up to me.

"Sky said that you were the one who found Tim," he said. "What happened? How bad was he hurt?"

All I could do was tell him the truth and repeat my story of how I'd found him. "Have you heard how he is?" I asked.

Elex shrugged. "Sky told us that the manager is at the hospital with him. How bad could it be? You said you think he fell."

"I didn't see him fall, but I assume that's what happened," I said.

"I don't know what he was thinking — walking on the rocks. He's not that well-coordinated to begin with and he insists on wearing those ankle boots with the leather soles."

"He must have lost his balance and fallen backward," I said. "He wasn't conscious when I saw him." I let it sink in for a beat. "I'm sure you're all upset by what happened. Do you still want the workshop this evening?"

Elex nodded. "Yes, this accident just made us all the more tense. I'm sure Tim would want things to go on normally."

I said I'd be in the meeting room at our appointed time and suggested he get some dinner. I watched him take a deep breath and then close his eyes momentarily, as if he was trying to calm himself before he went back to his associates. I did a quick survey of the area, looking for anyone from my retreat group.

I recognized Madison-the-birthday-girl at a table by the window. It was hard to miss the crocheted flower lei that Crystal had given her. Deani was next to her. Her hairstyle with the tiny ponytail gave her a stark look. My eye went to the floor and her tote bag wondering if Fifi was hidden in there. My gaze moved away quickly. I didn't want to know. The last person at the table was a complete surprise. Lucinda Thornkill was holding a pitcher of iced tea and hanging by the table. She owned the Blue Door restaurant, which made her my boss since I made their desserts, but she was also my best friend. She'd come to all the retreats that I'd put on except this one since it was really a private party.

"What are you doing here?" I said when I joined her at the table. She hugged me with her free hand.

"Someone ordered some food from the Blue Door." She glanced at the noisy dining hall. "I guess they wanted something a little more romantic. They even requested some candles." She looked toward the two women at the table. "After I dropped off the package at the registration desk, I thought I'd say hi and see how things were going. Cloris pointed me to this table, and when I saw you weren't here I thought I'd step in and act as host in the meantime. I was just about to make the rounds with the pitcher."

She took a sideways glance at the table. "You only have two people for the retreat?"

"No, there are five of them. The rest of them are either late or in the back getting their food. Thanks for stepping in for me," I said. "I wonder where the people who ordered the dinner are planning to eat it."

"They had me bring paper plates and utensils, so I'm guessing either the beach or in their room."

"Was there a name with the order?" I

asked, curious who it was.

"Rogers," she said. "I think it was Reese Rogers."

"Oh," I said, surprised. "I met him. He said he comes here every year on this same weekend to see a client. I guess he doesn't like the food."

"It was dinner for two," she said.

"He's alone, but I suppose he might have invited his client."

"I wonder what kind of client. He wanted to know if we had oysters," she said with a smile. "By the way, he's a fan of your desserts. Well, he didn't mention you exactly, but said he knew we had fabulous desserts and ordered two pieces of the apple pie."

"Maybe he's not such a geeky accountant after all," I muttered.

"What?" Lucinda said. I sighed and told her about my encounter with Reese and Dane's reaction.

"You make it so hard for him. You can't blame him for trying to stake out his territory."

"I'm not his territory," I said. "I'm not his anything, except sort of his girlfriend."

"Sort of?" she said, making a tsk sound. "I know, you're just thinking of him and you don't want to break his heart if and when you abruptly pull up stakes. But you know when you find the right guy . . . ." Her voice trailed off, but then she added, "Even if he comes with a few issues."

I knew she was talking about herself. But she had to realize her story was more the exception than the rule. I mean, how many people reconnect with their high school sweetheart years and years later when both of them just happen to be single? And end up getting married? The issues she mentioned were all her husband's, Tag. Apparently, it hadn't been evident in their high school years, but he bordered on obsessive-compulsive. It drove him crazy if one of the Blue Door's servers set up a table with the silverware even slightly askew. And it drove her crazy that it drove him crazy. But somehow they managed and she seemed to have no regrets.

I glanced around the room and was surprised to see Iola was hanging by one of the tables the birders had taken over. With only five of them in my group it was pretty easy to keep track of who was who. I remembered Iola as being the quiet nondescript one. But she was talking to a man now and he offered her a seat next to him. Hmm.

Aileen was coming across the room with a tray. After a moment she joined the other two as Lucinda and I watched.

113

Lucinda turned to me. "Why exactly was Dane leading you through the Lodge? You said he was in uniform."

I pulled her a little further from the table. "I haven't told them yet and I'm going to downplay it, but I can tell you the whole story." I used my elbow to surreptitiously point out the group in the black clothes. I explained the situation with Tim.

"Oh, dear, and you found him," she said, shaking her head at the thought. "At least it wasn't somebody in your group." She glanced toward the table just as PJ arrived with her plate of food. "I better do the honors." She held up the pitcher of iced tea.

I took the opportunity to introduce her to all of them. "It seems Iola decided to sit with some other people," I said, nodding in the direction of the birder group.

"Maybe she'll have more to say to them," Aileen said. "She never dumps like the rest of us. Sometimes I think she's some kind of spy."

"Spy?" Madison said with a laugh. "Who would she be spying for?"

"Isn't that the thing about spies? They're supposed to be stealthy so you don't know who they're working for," Deani said. She was looking at her plate of food. Tonight's offering was meat loaf, mashed potatoes and

114

green beans. I wanted to look away, afraid she might be dropping tidbits to Fifi in her tote bag, but all her attention seemed to be on her eating the food. I chuckled to myself, calling that thing Deani carried a tote bag. It was more like a pale pink mini suitcase. "This is delicious, and the best thing about it is that I didn't have to do anything with the preparation or delivery." She explained her food service to Lucinda.

"Maybe she just has nothing to say," PJ said. She had rearranged the food on her plate and was taking photos of it. She noticed Lucinda watching her. "I have a vlog about lifestyle hacks. I'm doing travel hints this weekend." She looked at the plate of food again. "I thought I'd say something about how to watch your diet when you're on the road." She moved the plate again and in the process knocked over the glass of iced tea that Lucinda had just filled. Lucinda grabbed a napkin and mopped up a lot of it, but some of the amber liquid had flowed off the table onto PJ. She looked down at her black tunic and leggings.

"It's a good thing you aren't wearing a light color," Madison said, glancing at her own pale pink linen top.

"I already used this outfit in a vlog post, but Madison's comment made me see the outfit in another way. Anything to get some more content." She stood up and photographed herself in her entirety. "Don't let a spill ruin your travel day," she began.

Aileen rolled her eyes and leaned in close to Lucinda and me as PJ continued taping her narration. "She's obsessed with that vlog. I bet she sleeps camera-ready. On the ride here, she did a whole post about bathrooms on the road." PJ heard her and stopped taping.

"I don't sleep camera-ready. As for the rest of the time, yes, I'm always in makeup and dressed to look good on a video. And there's a reason I did the post about restrooms when you travel," the vlogger said. "The company that makes packets with toilet seat covers and wipes paid me to feature it."

"I can't keep up with you," Madison said. "Wasn't there something else you were working on that was going to solve everything?"

PJ's expression faded. "There's been an obstacle." Then she brightened and turned to Lucinda. "If you have any hacks about anything, I'd be glad to interview you for the vlog."

"I thought the point of this weekend was to celebrate Madison's birthday and get

116

away from it all," Deani said, giving PJ a pointed look.

"I can't get away from it all," PJ said. "There's a lot of pressure with the vlog. I have to pump out content to keep my followers watching, which is bringing me advertisers like the bathroom supplies people."

I'd been waiting for an opening to bring up Tim's accident. I planned to keep the details to a minimum since they didn't even know him and just to use it as a reminder not to go walking on the rocks. But I quickly realized there was never going to be a lull in their conversation and I was going to have to just jump in. Finally, I put up my hand to stop the conversation. "There will probably be some kind of announcement, but I wanted to give you a heads-up," I began. "One of the Vista Del Mar guests had an accident. He fell while on a walk . . ."

Before I could say more, they all started shooting questions at me. *Who was he? Where did he fall? How did he fall? How bad was he hurt?*

"As for the who, he's someone from one of the other retreats here this weekend. You asked where he fell." I described the rocky section next to the beach. "There are plenty of crevices to catch your foot on and the surface of the rock is extra slippery when it's wet. What made it even more dangerous is that it was almost high tide and the waves were sloshing over the rocks," I said. "I'm guessing that he probably tripped." When it came to his injuries I didn't know what to say and tried to sound cheerful. "I'm sure he's getting the best care and he'll probably be back with his group by tomorrow." I'm afraid I didn't sound that convincing about the last part. I gestured toward the group in black and said it was one of them. I heard an intake of breath from the group at the table as it went from the abstract to a real person.

"I'm surprised they didn't already make an announcement," Madison said. "You'd think the management would want everyone to be warned."

"I'm sure there will be something like that," I said. "The manager went to the hospital with him."

"You certainly seem to know a lot about it," Aileen said. I turned to Lucinda and she shrugged and nodded as a way to encourage me to tell them the rest of it.

"I sort of came across him on the rocks," I said. "I was there when the paramedics took him away and I talked to the police about what happened."

"Police?" PJ said. "I thought you said it was an accident — that he fell. What were the police doing there?"

Lucinda put her hand on my shoulder and took over. "When anything like that happens the police investigate. But you don't have to worry about it. Casey is on the case," she said with a smile at her pun. "You probably don't know this, but she was an assistant private investigator in Chicago. Getting to the bottom of something in a place like Cadbury is nothing for her after dealing with the mean streets of the big city. Just go ahead and enjoy your weekend. I'm sure if there's anything to find out, she'll do it."

The four of them examined me with new interest. Lucinda had laid it on a little thick. It was debatable what my position at Frank's agency had been. I called myself an assistant detective, but detective's assistant was probably more accurate. "I did do some work for a PI," I said, trying to downplay it.

"A private investigator," Aileen said with a smile. "It sounds romantic. Was he one of those renegade bad-boy types? You know, always fussing with the cops and bettering them. Handsome in a world-weary way?"

I had to contain a laugh. Frank was none of that — well, maybe fussing with the cops.

But handsome in a world-weary way? Not exactly.

"If anyone is bettering the cops, it's Casey," Lucinda said. "She's far too modest to say it, but she's solved a number of local cases that stumped the cops."

Madison chuckled. "I guess then we can rest easy knowing that Sherlock Feldstein is on the case." She announced that it was time for Operation Pink Hair and she pushed away her plate.

"So then no knit-together this evening?" Deani asked.

"We don't have to hang together all the time," Aileen said. "I'm looking forward to putting my feet up and reading in my room."

"I'm in for a knit-together," PJ said. "I'll see if Iola wants to join us." They bid Lucinda and me a good night and all headed for the exit.

The two of us sat down at the empty table. She found the coffeepot and poured us each a cup before asking me if I was going to get food.

"I lost my appetite," I said. "Too much going on."

"At least they're more resourceful than your usual groups. You didn't even have to suggest the knit-together." Lucinda smiled.

120

"I like that term. You're still coming to the Blue Door later, right? We need your desserts for the weekend. And the Saturday-morning coffee crowd will be expecting your muffins."

I nodded and she patted my hand.

"You're like the postman, what's the saying — neither rain nor storm nor dead of night can keep you from your rounds."

"I'm not sure that's the way it goes, but I certainly do my best to make sure Cadburians have their carbs."

Just then Kevin St. John came into the dining hall. His moon-shaped face was placid as usual, but his eyes appeared frantic. He looked over the area and then walked directly to the table with his retreat group. His back was to me and all I could see was their reaction to what he said. I watched as their expressions changed from concern to shock.

"That's not good news," I said. "I wonder if they'll still want the mindful knitting workshop tonight."

"They probably need it now more than ever," Lucinda said.

CHAPTER 10

Whenever I put on a retreat the days were epic, but this one seemed even longer than usual. It seemed like eternity since I'd had the meeting with the Delacorte sisters and their new relatives. I felt bad about not telling Lucinda about the situation, especially after telling Dane. Actually I regretted spilling the beans to him, but I couldn't undo it now.

It felt a little strange to be free of my group. But I'd never had such an independent group before. Normally, I'd be hanging around to make sure their evening plans were going smoothly, but they'd made plans on their own.

I still had the Silicon Valley group to deal with. If I'd known one of them was going to die I never would have agreed to help them out with their retreat. The last thing I needed was to be involved with another death in the area. I was sure it had just been an accident. Elex had said Tim wasn't that well-coordinated and leather-soled boots were just asking for trouble. I had my doubts if they would even show up for the workshop, or maybe it was wishful thinking. Even so, I headed for the Cypress meeting room ready for whatever happened.

I met Cloris just as we reached the Cypress building. She was pushing a cart and stopped, looking at the two doors.

"We're using my room," I said. I felt a little guilty about using my group's room for the Silicon Valley bunch, but they had no workshop planned and it was much more cheerful than the room on the other side.

I opened the door, flipped on the light and went inside with Cloris right behind me. I was surprised by the rattle of bottles as she pushed the cart in and wheeled it to the counter. I'd expected her to bring the coffee and tea service like my group got, but I saw she had a bunch of dark-colored bottles. I thanked her again for helping with the arrangements and keeping it on the down low.

"It's my pleasure," she said, going to light the fire. I looked over the cart of drinks and checked the labels. "I wasn't sure which they'd want so I brought enough so they could have a bottle of each." I made a face when I saw there were two kinds of kombucha. The drink was made from fermented yeast, bacteria, black tea, sugar and other ingredients and was supposed to have health properties, but the smell had been enough to keep me from wanting to try it. She was closer to them in age and I guessed that she'd used her own judgment when picking the drinks.

The fireplace came to life with a warm glow and Cloris began to set up the drinks. "I suppose you heard what happened," I said. I made a last sweep of the table to make sure all of my group's supplies and swatches were in the bin with their tote bags.

She nodded. "But orders are to keep it quiet. Mr. St. John doesn't want anything that will reflect badly on Vista Del Mar." She dropped her voice. "What he really means is he wants to keep it quiet that someone died on the retreat he organized. I suppose if it had been like a heart attack or something he wouldn't have been so freaked. But someone dying from an accident related to an activity he set up . . ." She put up her hands in capitulation. "Of course, he's blaming it on Sky."

Crystal rushed in and seemed a little breathless. She and Cloris exchanged nods of greeting as Cloris pushed the empty cart toward the door. "Well, I think you're all set. Good luck."

Crystal put the wheeled bin against the wall and took the lid off. She looked at the counter with the refreshment setup. "Good choice about the kombucha."

I chuckled. "It was all Cloris. She's the best."

Crystal nodded in agreement and began to lay out supplies on the long table. "Cory brought everything over earlier." Her smile had faded and I was surprised how distressed she seemed. "I'm beginning to regret that we had that face-to-face with the Delacorte sisters. My mother is too. They're never going to agree to give up anything. Corey loves Vista Del Mar and now they're treating him like he's the enemy. Poor kid didn't know why, but he said the sisters gave him odd looks when he dropped off the bin, like they thought he was up to something."

"Ugh, sorry," I said, feeling like it was all my fault. "I know that Madeleine is very fond of Cory. They're probably just in shock. Once they get used to the idea maybe they'll come around."

"I hope so. He wondered if he'd done something wrong. How could I tell him the only thing wrong was who his great-grandfather was." Crystal, with all her colorful clothes and mismatched earrings and

125

socks, seemed so young and fun, and I had to remind myself that she was also the mother of two teenage kids. And seemingly a very good mother at that.

She looked at the tote bags she'd set out and checked her watch. The door to the outside was open and it was obvious no one was coming up the path. "I hope they didn't change their mind," she said.

"About that," I began. "There's been an accident. And now there's only four." I grabbed the fifth tote bag and put it on a chair. I gave her the details of what happened and my involvement.

"How awful. Kevin St. John must be frantic. The first retreat he organizes all by himself and someone dies." She shook her head. "It was just an accident, right?"

"As far as I could tell," I said.

"All I can say is that they're sure dressed for the occasion. What's with all the black clothes, anyway?" I shrugged as an answer.

Just then there was the sound of voices coming up the path. "It looks like it's show-time," I said and we both put on friendly smiles.

"There are five of them after all," Crystal whispered as Sky came in with the group.

Sky noticed me staring at him. "I thought I should stick with the group and, er, look after them," he said. He seemed nervous and kept glancing back to the open door. "Maybe we should close this. Who knows who might walk by." He pulled the door shut.

We both knew he meant Kevin St. John.

The four others had stopped inside the doorway. "Come in, come in," I said. "Help yourself to drinks. There're some snacks in the tin." They went over to the counter and followed my suggestion and came back to the table with bottles and cookies and took a seat.

"I'm Casey Feldstein. I put on yarn retreats here," I said, trying to sound upbeat. "And this is Crystal Smith, yarn teacher extraordinaire. She's going to lead you through a mindful knitting experience." I looked to the four of them expecting them to introduce themselves, but I actually had to push them to do it.

Elex took the lead as expected. "We've already met, but I'm Elex," he said and gestured to the woman sitting next to him. "You're up next."

This was the first time I was getting a good look at the woman in their group. She had long wavy hair that seemed left to its own devices. If she wore any makeup it was so subtle as to appear non-existent. Her clothes had a baggy fit, hiding her shape. "Julie," she said in a nasal tone. She gave Elex a sharp look. "And no matter what some people think I don't know how to knit just because I'm a female."

Crystal rushed in to make sure they all knew that sailors had knit nets and it was a unisex hobby. "And you are?" she said to the other two men when she'd finished. Maybe it was because they were both dressed in the black outfits, but they appeared almost like twins. Both had close-cropped dark hair and bland features. They gave their names as Josh and Jackson, but to be honest I wasn't sure which name went with which guy.

I knew I had to say something to them about Tim. I wanted to say something brief and move on. While I was thinking of what to say, Crystal turned to Sky, who was standing in front of the door while he gazed out the window that was across the room.

"You can join us if you'd like," she said. He was so focused on staring out the window that it took a moment for what she'd said to sink in and then he shook his head, making his topknot wobble.

"I'm a facilitator, not a participant," he said. He threw in a *Namaste* and made a bow before going back to his Kevin St. John watch.

I knew Crystal was about to begin, so it was now or never that I said something about Tim. I went for the basic and said, "I just wanted to let you know how sorry I am about your friend."

Elex gave me a strange look. "Tim wasn't exactly a friend. More like a business associate."

"Well, whatever he was to all of you, I'm sorry for your loss," I said. I hoped that would be it and Crystal could get on with the program, but one of two other men spoke up.

"What's going to happen now?" Josh or Jackson asked.

"The manager contacted his next of kin. His wife will be here tomorrow."

"That's strange," Julie said with a furrowed brow.

"Not really," Elex said. "She's the one who'll have to make the arrangements." It sounded like either Jackson or Josh said something about that being a lucky break for her, which seemed like an odd comment.

"Maybe we should get started," Crystal said. But it went unheard.

"That's not what I meant," the same dark-haired man said who'd made the earlier comment. "I meant what happens to us now."

"We keep going as planned, Josh," Elex said. I now realized I could tell them apart. Josh, who'd just spoken, had a big zit on his forehead.

"But what about —"

"Everything is under control," Elex said, cutting him off before he could finish. The nosy part of me wondered what Josh was about to say and of course why Elex wouldn't let him say it. But I also wanted to stay out of it.

"You guys are from Silicon Valley, so I'm guessing you're involved in some kind of start-up," Crystal said, obviously trying to change the subject. "And I bet you're going to change the world." She had a small grin. "But isn't that the mantra of all the start-ups?"

"I don't know about the others," Elex said with a little edge. "But we actually are going to change the world. Our company is called Reborn because the big plan is to bring back old things in a new way. Our first project is all about delivering produce. What's the one thing people complain about when they get groceries delivered — they're not happy with the produce. Things like the lettuce is wilted and the apples are mealy.

But what if it was like the old days and a truck came to them loaded up with the best fresh produce?" He looked at Crystal and me for our reactions. "All they'd have to do is step outside and pick out what they want." Elex let out a sigh. "When I went to Stanford this isn't what I expected to do. I grew up on a peach and almond farm and thought that was all behind me. But then I heard that in the old days trucks used to drive around city neighborhoods with produce. I thought about what I knew and it seemed like the perfect idea to pursue."

Julie appeared a little doubtful. "All of us didn't grow up on a farm, but that doesn't mean our ideas aren't valid," she said.

Elex ignored her comment. "We have proof of concept, now we just have to roll it out bigger." He glanced at his group. "And we can do it without Tim."

"I can't believe that Tim went walking on the beach. He was so fastidious about everything," Julie said. "And I thought I heard him say he was going to walk up the driveway and do his mindful walk on the street outside the grounds."

"Well, obviously whatever he said, he did walk on the rocks," Elex said. "It was a dumb idea to tell us to walk solo." He turned to Sky.

The man in the yoga pants threw up his hands in exasperation. "I was just following orders. Mr. St. John is the one who said you should walk alone." He hesitated for a moment. "Sorry to be the bearer of bad news, but Mr. St. John said I should let you know that the police want to talk to all of you."

"What?" Jackson said. "Why? It was an accident, right?"

Crystal looked at me. "Maybe you should tell them."

"It's up to the medical examiner to determine the manner of death and there's always an investigation when someone dies like that."

"Casey knows her stuff," Crystal said. "She's like a local hotter Miss Marple. I'm sure she'll be keeping up with the investigation, particularly since she's the one who found your associate."

Elex already knew, but the other three looked at me with surprise and insisted on knowing the details. Once again I went over the whole thing of finding him sprawled on his back.

"Did he say anything?" Elex asked.

I shrugged. "He was unconscious." I heard Elex let out a sigh and it was impossible to tell if it was from disappointment or relief.

"Can we get going on the workshop?"

Elex said.

"Absolutely." Crystal looked at her watch. "I was just going to suggest the same thing."

She gave them a moment to settle and then began. "The plan is I teach you the basic of knitting. Just making a swatch is boring, so I came up with a simple project." She pulled out a long strip of knitting that went from shades of orange to shades of blue. They all had blank looks. "It's a tie. I thought it would jazz up those outfits a little." She put it around Elex's neck and he looked down at it and began to fiddle with it.

"I'm not good at tying ties, but you can tie it the traditional way or actually any way you want," Crystal said. I couldn't see Elex's expression because he was still checking out the long thin length of knitting around his neck. He finally looked up and gave her a thumbs-up.

"I like it. We'll have a souvenir of the weekend."

She had them look in their tote bags and take out the yarn and needles. "There are six stitches already cast on, so all you have to do is keep knitting across the rows as you lose yourselves in making the stitches."

She gave them a quick lesson on how to do the knit stitch and they began to awkwardly work their way across the short row, looking at each other's work as they did.

Just as they were settling in the door opened. Sky acted on impulse and blocked it from opening all the way. He appeared panicked as I saw someone poke their head inside. It was not the moon-shaped face of Kevin St. John. Actually, I didn't even catch the face of the intruder at first. All I saw was a bunch of hair the color of cotton candy. Obviously Operation Pink Hair had been a success.

"It's okay," I said to Sky and pushed him away from the door to let Madison in. She looked at the table and the group around it. I muttered something about them being from next door and I was helping them out.

"I wanted to get something from my bag," she said. I showed her where I'd stowed them. She found hers and extracted the crochet hook. She held it up and waved it at Crystal. "I thought I'd play around with what we learned." Then she was out the door and Sky took up his position at blocking it. Surprisingly, her entrance and exit had been barely noticed by the Silicon Valley bunch. They had truly become lost in working with all the loops of yarn.

I let them continue on as long as I could, but Crystal pointed to her watch and began to pack up her things. "Time to call it a night," she said. She had to repeat it several times to get their attention. "There are knitting instructions in your bag, along with the pattern for the tie."

"It can't be time already," Elex said. He held up the few inches of rows he'd completed. "This is the first thing we've done that seems actually mindful," he went on. "I knew adding this was the right thing to do." I waited, expecting him to say thank you to me and Crystal, but he didn't. Instead, he looked at his group and repeated the brilliance of his decision.

Sky took his attention off the door for a moment and addressed the group. "Just you wait until you experience the Sound Bath on Saturday night. I put it together and it's going to be a mind-blowing mindful experience." Sky turned to me. "It's open to all the guests so be sure your group comes." So, Kevin St. John had actually let Sky plan something. I asked for details and he insisted it had to be experienced to be understood.

"You can't leave us like this," Elex said. "We need at least one more session." Crystal looked to me.

"I'll see what I can work out," I said, promising to let them know. They packed up their things and finally got up to go.

Crystal watched them go to the door and then broke into a smile. "Now I get the clothes. You are trying to be like Steve Jobs."

The four of them gave her a blank look. "You're all wearing the Steve Jobs look, the black turtlenecks and the jeans," she said.

"If we happen to make people think of Steve Jobs, so be it," Elex said. There was just a touch of annoyance in his voice. "He wore blue jeans with his black turtleneck, and if you notice, we wear black jeans. It was my idea we dress this way. We all just have so much bandwidth for decision making and why waste it on clothing choices." He pointed to Julie. "She can get dressed in a few minutes because she doesn't have to spend any mental energy deciding what to wear. I bet it takes you a lot longer," he said, looking at Crystal. "The point is why spend energy on unimportant decisions like what to wear or what to have for lunch."

"Whatever works for you," I said. "Be sure to take your tote bags with you." I was going to add that they could take the extra drinks, but they were already grabbing them.

When we were alone, Crystal turned to me. "I guess Tim didn't go along with the idea. Funny how it was the guy in preppy clothes who was the outsider."

Crystal rushed off ahead and I stayed behind to straighten up. They'd left a mess. I gathered up the empty bottles and cleaned the crumbs off the table. The drinks had certainly been a hit. I'd have to compliment Cloris on her choices. I put my group's bags back on the table and turned off the lights.

I was wishing it had been one and done, but no such luck. I'd have to figure out how to arrange another session.

"Case," a voice called out in the darkness as I headed up the pathway. There was only one person who called me that. Sammy thought of it as a nickname, but really all he did was take off one letter, even if it was a syllable.

"Sammy?" I said, turning in surprise. "What are you doing here? Don't tell me you have some emergency magic show and you expect me to be your assistant."

"No, Case," he said as he caught up with me. "But look what's in your hair." I looked up just as he magically made a glowing butterfly appear.

Sammy was my ex from Chicago and he really shouldn't have been in Cadbury. He insisted he hadn't been following me when he showed up in the small town. Sammy

137

was Dr. Samuel Glickner, M.D., who specialized in urology, but magic was his real passion. He'd gotten a temporary position in Cadbury doing his doctor stuff away from the critical eyes of his parents, who thought the magic business was monkey business and should be locked up in a trunk with all his illusions and the key thrown away.

My breakup with Sammy had been totally nondramatic. It came down to the fact that he was a nice guy who had all the attributes of husband material, except one. There was zero chemistry — at least on my side. I wanted to believe his story that he was there following his passion for magic and not for me, but I had my doubts.

He'd started out doing table magic on weekends at Vista Del Mar but had moved on to doing actual shows and I'd gotten hooked into being his assistant. It was supposed to be temporary, but he didn't seem to be looking too hard for a replacement. And there was something else. Though he'd planned to be a serious magician, there had been some screwups the first time he tried to "cut me in half," and it had turned into more of a comedy routine. The audience ate it up and he'd changed his show. He insisted that no one got him but me and I could play into the comedy stuff.

I took the butterfly and looked it over before handing it back to him. "It's a new prop," he said. "Note the colors are like a monarch butterfly." Monarch butterflies were a big deal in Cadbury since every year huge numbers of them wintered in Cadbury. The town celebrated with a whole week of activities every year in the fall.

"It's certainly more charming than pulling a quarter out of my ear," I said with a smile before asking what he was doing at Vista Del Mar.

"I got a call from Kevin St. John asking me if I could do some close-up magic over the weekend. He said something about an accident and wanting to add a distraction."

I told Sammy about the mindful retreat and that Kevin St. John had arranged it for the group. "It was one of his retreaters who had the accident," I said. "He has to be freaking out. It's bad enough when something happens to a guest at Vista Del Mar, but when it's someone from a retreat he put together —" I rolled my eyes and put up my hands.

Sammy looked at me. "And I suppose you know all about the accident."

"Know about it?" I said, shaking my head. "I ended up in the middle of it." My lip curled in distaste with the memory. I went

139

on to describe the scene I'd come upon and my attempt to find a pulse. "He must have slipped and fallen on his back. It was awful. I ended up with blood on my hands and clothes."

"You say he fell backward," Sammy said. I thought about why I'd said that and the image of Tim came into my mind's eye.

"I assume that's what happened. He was lying on his back."

"Did you cradle his head while you looked for a pulse?" Sammy asked and I shook my head.

"I knelt down next to him," I said. "I leaned over him when I went to check his neck for the pulse. I must have touched his head and his clothes."

"It's not the end I usually deal with, but if he fell backward on the rocks, you'd expect the blood would be on the back of his head. How did you end up with it on you?" I'd been purposely avoiding the mental picture of Tim on the ground and now I was recalling it a second time. I closed my eyes and let the image flow. "The blood was on his face. The worst was on his forehead." I gagged at the thought it had ended up on me.

Sammy shrugged it off. "Maybe he moved or something." He gave my shoulder a reassuring pat. "It's not your worry." He paused and took a breath. "And on another note — I was hoping you'd be my assistant for the close-up magic. We could do some of the comedy stuff."

"Okay, as long as I don't have to wear that spangly romper," I said, relieved to have the subject changed. It was more pleasant to think of Sammy's magic act than the vision of Tim on the ground. Sammy was fine with me wearing my street clothes, even if he would be wearing his performance tuxedo.

When we got to the driveway of Vista Del Mar, Sammy looked across the street. "I went to your place first and I saw someone going in the guesthouse with a key. What's going on?" He sounded upset. He'd been living at a bed-and-breakfast since he'd come to Cadbury and had asked about renting the guesthouse. I knew it was a bad idea and rather than just turn him down, I told him if I ever rented it, he'd be the one. I quickly reassured him that the person he'd seen was a woman and that the only being staying there was a tiny poodle. His mood lifted immediately.

"Well, then, see you tomorrow," Sammy said as he started to walk away. He turned back. "Thanks, Case. You always come through."

CHAPTER 11

There was always a different feeling when I crossed the street to my place. I felt away from it all when I was on the Vista Del Mar grounds and back to the real world when I went up my driveway. Julius was watching from the kitchen window. I wanted to stop in the guesthouse and check on Fifi, but at the same time I didn't. Sammy had seen Deani going into the guesthouse, but it wasn't clear what she was doing. Was she visiting the dog, dropping her off or horror of horrors, picking her up?

My nightmare scenario had Deani keeping the dog in her room and Fifi letting out a bark as Kevin St. John was in the hallway. The doors were so thin, the sound would carry and he'd barge into the room. Better to be in the dark, I thought, and I went directly to my kitchen door without a sideways glance.

Julius jumped down and began doing

figure eights around my ankles as soon as I walked into my kitchen. "I can't stay," I said, but even so I sat down on one of the kitchen chairs and he jumped into my lap. He rubbed against me and let out a rumble of purring as I stroked his back.

"Don't worry. Fifi is just a temporary guest," I said. "Maybe a little too temporary." If Kevin St. John found the dog on the grounds I was going to get the blame.

I gave Julius his nightly dab of stink fish and got ready to leave. It was time to put all thoughts of Vista Del Mar and my retreat group on the back burner. I was not going to think any more about Tim and how he'd gotten blood on his face if he'd fallen on his back. It really wasn't my concern anyway.

The deal I had with the Blue Door was that after I'd made the desserts for the next day, I could use their kitchen to bake the muffins that I took around to the coffee spots in town. I added the perishables to the bag of ingredients I'd packed earlier. I had a whole repertoire of muffins that I made, but every now and then I made something new. That was the plan for tonight.

There was always an issue of what I was going to call something new. I liked names like Plain Janes for vanilla muffins and The

Blues for blueberry ones, but the town council had a thing about what they considered cutesy names. They wanted things to be called what they were. As if the name of a muffin was that important. I had no choice but to go along with them, so instead of calling my new creation A Raisin to Be, I'd have to call them Raisin Biscuit Muffins. Where was the romance in that?

The streets were never busy in Cadbury, but by this time of night they were really dead. I didn't pass another car as I drove down the street in front of my house and only passed an occasional one on the rest of the ride. The main drag in town was called Grand Street. It certainly deserved the name. A parkway ran down between the two directions of traffic, making the thoroughfare wide and impressive.

By now all the shops but one were dark and long since closed. Light spilled onto the sidewalk in front of the twenty-four-hour pharmacy and a cluster of cars were parked in front.

It was hard to see it at night, but the downtown area was authentically charming with a mixture of architecture. There were actual Victorian buildings painted in bright colors with fish-scale siding. Some of the shops and businesses were housed in blond brick buildings that seemed to be mid-century style. And the white stucco post office with the terra-cotta tile roof was Spanish style. The Blue Door restaurant had at one time been a residence. The wood frame building was situated so that the side of it faced Grand Street and the front on the side street.

As I parked my car, I could see Lucinda through the uncurtained windows that faced the main street. I went up the stairs to the narrow porch that ran along the front. It was used as an outdoor seating area, but now the tables had the chairs on top of them.

The front door really was blue — at least the bottom half. The top was glass.

Inside things were winding down and only two of the tables were still occupied. The diners were just finishing dessert, which I noted was the pound cake I'd baked the day before served with strawberries and whipped cream.

Lucinda rushed up to me. "Tag heard about the accident at Vista Del Mar. He's going nuts worried that it could have been me," she said. I glanced across the former living room that was now the main dining area. It was hard to miss Tag Thornkill. Though well into his fifties, he had such a

145

thick head of brown hair it seemed like a wig, but it wasn't. He was hanging over a server who was setting up the tables for the next day, readjusting the silverware as she put each piece down. The poor girl kept closing her eyes with consternation.

"Have you heard anything more about it? Did the group he was from show up for the workshop?" Lucinda asked. She was wearing the same Ralph Lauren denim dress she'd had on when she came to Vista Del Mar. It still looked as fresh as she did. Lucinda always appeared put-together. I often joked to myself that she probably put on lipstick to get the mail.

"The group did show up and they seemed to blame his fall on his leather-soled shoes and bad judgment," I said, setting down the recycled shopping bag full of ingredients. "I got the feeling they were more concerned about how his death was going to affect their business than the loss of him." I explained what their business was and that from the way they talked about Tim and the way he dressed it seemed like he was an outsider.

"You don't think that someone might have wanted him out of the way," she said, dropping her voice.

"You mean like someone made it happen?" I started to say there was no reason to suppose that, but then I thought about what Sammy and I had talked about and at the same time there was something in the back of my mind trying to get my attention. I closed my eyes for a moment hoping that the hidden thought would suddenly appear front and center. It didn't, and finally I put up my hands and said, "I don't know."

"Just be glad you don't have to concern yourself with it," Lucinda said with a smile. "Even if I did tell your group that you'd be in the know about the investigation."

"I will have to let them know that Tim died." My friend gave me a reassuring pat on my shoulder just as Sammy had done.

The two couples got up and went to the front to settle their checks. Tag went to take care of them and the server cleared the two tables.

Lucinda glanced at the couples as they went out the door. The server took off her apron and left a moment later. "That's it," Lucinda said. "We're officially closed. The pound cake was a big success, as usual. We sold out of the apple pie hours ago. Those couples both ordered their dessert when they made their reservation." She pointed toward an empty pedestal stand on the front counter and all that was left were a couple of crumbs.

"I'm glad the pound cake worked out so well because I'll be making more tonight," I said. It was hard to do the baking when I was in the middle of a retreat, so I tended to make standbys that I could practically make in my sleep. I'd thought about making one for Madison's birthday, but she'd made such a point that it wasn't really her birthday that I let it go.

I picked up the bag and went toward the kitchen. The chef came out and grunted a greeting at me. I was used to this changing of the guard by now. He was territorial about the kitchen and always seemed a little perturbed that I was taking it over. I understood because I viewed him as being an intruder in my space.

My first order of business was the desserts for the restaurant, and once I put on my apron, I began to lay out the ingredients. Lucinda poked her head in to tell me they were leaving and the place was mine.

As soon as I heard them go out the door, I went into the dining room to turn on some music. I liked to bake to soft jazz. Something felt off and I stopped in the middle of the room and looked around with an uneasy feeling. I felt as if someone was watching me. I went to one of the windows and looked out. A dark SUV was parked next to my Mini Cooper. It didn't seem like anyone was in it.

I went to the front door and tried to look out on the porch, but I couldn't make out much in the darkness. I had started to think that I was being foolish. The car parked out front didn't mean anything. The side street was all residential and someone could have parked there and gone to one of the houses.

Even so, I couldn't seem to shake the feeling. Maybe if I checked the porch and saw that no one was there I'd calm down and be able to get to my work. I had my phone in my hand as I pulled the door open and stuck my head out. I gave the porch the once-over and was about to chide myself for my foolishness and go back inside when I heard a rustle. I looked over the dark area again and this time I saw something move in the shadow.

"Who are you and what do you want?" I said, trying to make my voice sound big while fighting the sudden adrenaline flow.

There was no answer and I remembered my phone. I swiped on the flashlight and pointed it at the corner.

CHAPTER 12

"Deani!" I said. The big sound had gone out of my voice and the adrenaline flow had taken over and I sounded high-pitched and squeaky. "What are you doing here?" She was slender and even though she had the tote bag the size of a small suitcase that could have had who knows what inside, I didn't really see her as a threat.

"I was hoping to get away without you seeing me," she said. She seemed to be backing toward the stairs at the end of the narrow porch.

"Not without an explanation. Why don't you come inside." It was more of a command than a suggestion. I opened the door wider and waited until she complied.

She seemed uncomfortable as she came into the restaurant. She looked around at the empty tables. Just then a fuzzy white head popped over the top of the tote bag. Fifi saw me and let out a yip.

I had my arms folded and was almost tapping my foot as I waited for her explanation. "I was expecting a little more action at night than Vista Del Mar offers. Everybody kind of disappeared and there was nothing much to do. I'd forgotten to bring toothpaste so I used Aileen's SUV to go to the drugstore. I saw you getting out of your car when I was on the way there. When I saw your Mini Cooper was still parked there on the way back, I wondered what you were up to since this place is obviously closed." She glanced around the empty dining room.

"Oh," I said, unfolding my arms.

"And after what your friend said about you being some kind of detective and that you'd be checking out the investigation of the accident, well, I thought it might be related to that."

I laughed thinking what she must have imagined. "Come with me and I'll show you what I'm doing." She'd told me that she ran a food service that provided lunch and snacks for offices and I thought she'd be able to relate.

She followed me into the kitchen and I pointed to the butter, eggs and sugar on the counter. "I make the desserts for the restaurant and bake muffins for the coffee spots in town."

151

"Really," she said, surprised, as she took a look around the kitchen. "Then we're kindred spirits. Though my customers are down on sugar. I brought samples of a cookie recipe and they weren't even interested. But they loved the samples of the snack item PJ made, well, except for the vegans and nondairy people." She asked me for details of how I worked and it turned out we both operated in similar old-fashioned ways.

"I could use an app to handle my business, but I prefer to deal in person."

"Well, now that you've seen what I'm doing —" I left it hanging, hoping she'd take the hint and leave but she didn't make a move.

"So then you didn't find out anything more about the accident?" she asked.

I checked her expression. She seemed interested, but not overly concerned. "Bad news. The victim died," I said.

Deani was pale to begin with but whatever color she had drained from her face as she took in what I said. "That's terrible." She leaned against the counter for a moment, before saying that she had to go. Her reaction caught me off guard and I followed behind her trying to think of something to say to her. She mumbled a good night before she went out. She seemed so upset and I wondered if I'd been too blunt or she was just one of those sensitive types. Either way I didn't think it was a good time to remind her that Fifi should spend the night in the guesthouse.

As soon as she was gone I resumed making the cakes, trying to move faster since I was now behind. I was almost back on schedule as I poured the batter into three tube pans and put them in the oven. It only took a few minutes for the air to smell of buttery vanilla sweetness.

I realized I'd never turned on the radio and just as I went into the other room there was a knock at the door. No mystery this time — Dane was standing with his face close to the glass. He made it a habit to stop by when he worked the night shift. He came in carrying a holder with two cups of coffee and a bag with grease marks.

A midnight blue canvas jacket covered his uniform of the same color. He leaned in and gave me an affectionate kiss before looking around to see if there were any witnesses. "No worries, it looks like no Cadburians saw that." He had a serious expression but his tone was joking. "I have to worry about my rep. Can't be caught kissing while on duty." He sniffed the air. "No cinnamon." He sniffed again. "But I smell vanilla. Pound cake?"

"Good detective work," I teased and his mouth curved into a grin.

"That's me, the cake detective." He let out a sigh. "Better than the call I had a little while ago. Tonight's big event was someone getting trapped in the bathroom at the wine bar." He put up his hands to demonstrate his solution: "All it took was a good shove to the door."

He followed me into the kitchen. "What else are you making?" he asked.

"Rustic cherry pie," I said. He chuckled and shook his head.

"I still can't believe that someone who makes such fabulous desserts relies on frozen food." He put down the coffee and took out two submarine sandwiches wrapped in paper.

My eyes lit up at the food and he feigned a grumble. "And here I thought you were excited to see me."

"Sorry. Of course I'm glad of your company. But I'm famished. With everything that happened I never got around to eating." I gave him a hug. "I'd starve if it weren't for you. You bring me sandwiches and you leave pasta for me a couple nights a week when you cook for the karate kids."

The truth was Dane was a whiz at dinner food. The tomato sauce he made from scratch was so delicious that I was tempted to lick the plate.

"You look a lot better than when I saw you earlier. Too bad they couldn't save him." As he said that the thought that had been lurking in the back of my mind finally came to the front. How had I not thought about it before?

"Someone else was there," I blurted out.

"Someone else was where?" Dane said, sounding confused.

"Someone had to have seen what happened and called for help. I can't believe that Lieutenant Borgnine didn't figure that out."

"He assumed that you called," Dane said. He was looking at the sandwiches. "Where should we eat these?"

I forgot about my ravenous hunger for the moment. "I couldn't have called. There's no cell signal there. I can't believe he doesn't know that." I was pacing in the kitchen now. "There's something more. I'm sure he was lying on his back when I found him, but there was blood all over his face. Sammy said you'd think the blood would be on the ground around him."

"Okay, what's your point?" he asked.

155

My shoulders slumped. "I don't know. Maybe somebody hit him in the head with a rock. You should tell Lieutenant Borgnine."

"I'm sure he'll figure it out," Dane said, waving the sandwich under my nose. The smell of garlic and Italian dressing made my mouth start to water, but I took one last shot.

"So, you aren't going to say anything?"

"Don't poke the bear," he said.

"But you'd think he'd be happy to get the help," I said and Dane rolled his eyes.

"Don't worry about it. From what I've heard, it sounds like a simple accident. There's a reason for all those warning signs. And it's not like you're involved with the group the victim was with," he said. He peeked out of the kitchen. "Let's take our food out on the sunporch. Though I suppose now it's a moon porch." He picked a table near the window and I moved the place settings out of the way.

"As long as we put everything back just the way it was. We don't want Tag to throw a fit." The smell of the meat and cheese and condiments was swirling around my senses, overriding all other thoughts, and I felt drunk with hunger.

He watched as I practically inhaled the

sandwich and downed the coffee.

"What would you have done if I hadn't come by?" he asked.

I shrugged. "Who knows? Passed out — eaten one of the pound cakes? I'm just glad you did."

"I'd like to take that to mean you were glad to see me, but I get it. It really is all about the food, isn't it?" He faked a hurt expression.

"I'm glad to see you, too," I said, looking in the bag to see if there was anything else. He rolled his eyes and handed me the rest of his sandwich. "You need this more than I do." A moment later there was nothing left but crumbs. Now that I wasn't consumed by hunger I remembered to tell him I'd offered to let Fifi stay in my guesthouse. "So if you see someone going in or coming out, don't call out the cavalry," I said. I was about to tell him about Deani's strange visit when his radio began to crackle and I heard something about trouble on Lover's Beach.

"Got to go," he said. He went to pick up the wrappings of the meal, but I said I'd take care of it. "Probably kids drinking beer." He got up from the table and then looked around before he smiled at me. "Looks like the coast is clear." He held out his arms and what started out as a mutual hug finished as a hot kiss that neither of us was in a hurry to end. It was just lucky we both'd had garlic. And then he was off into the night.

I knew that Dane wouldn't arrest the kids. He'd just give them a talking to and then get them to join his karate classes. His motto was keep them busy and keep them out of trouble.

I cleared up the table and reset it, making sure everything was perfectly aligned before going back to the kitchen. I made the crust and poured on the cherry filling. All the red brought to mind Tim's head again. Maybe Dane didn't want to poke the bear, but I had no problem doing it.

CHAPTER 13

As soon as Dane left, I looked at my watch. It was late by Cadbury time, but not by cop time, and I had Lieutenant Borgnine's cell number. Surely he wouldn't mind a call. After all, I was only trying to help.

I heard it begin to ring and was collecting my thoughts on how to tell him what I'd noticed without putting him on the defensive. I snapped to attention when a woman said hello. It wasn't just a greeting, there was an edge to it, and I considered hanging up. But there was no longer any anonymous hanging up, my number would show on the phone.

"Hello," I answered back with a tentative tone.

"Who is this?" she demanded.

"I was trying to reach Lieutenant Borgnine," I said. "It's official business."

"I just bet it is. Listen, I know all about you badge bunnies who see cops as these

159

romantic heroes. Teddy is taken." There was a finality to her tone and I was afraid she was going to hang up. It was hard for me to keep from laughing. Her husband had a bulldog face and a body shaped like a fireplug. His manner was gruff and impatient and certainly didn't inspire thoughts of romance in me.

"I'm calling about something that happened today. A man died on the rocks by Vista Del Mar. I was almost a witness."

I could tell by her breathing that she was evaluating what I'd said. "Then give me your name," she said finally.

"Casey Feldstein."

She took a moment to process. "The muffin girl," she said.

I wanted to correct her and say muffin woman, though I wasn't exactly sure at what age muffin girl changed to muffin woman. I was in my mid-thirties, but then my retreat bunch referred to themselves as the birthday girls.

"I want to thank you for getting Teddy off the doughnuts, but do you suppose you could cut the sugar out of your muffins? His sweet tooth needs taming."

"Actually, tonight I'm making what I call biscuit muffins. Barely any sugar. The sweetness comes from raisins."

160

She uttered a noise that sounded like approval before making a tsk sound. "I assume you aren't calling with an update on your baking. What is it then?"

"It's police business," I said.

She made a disapproving sound. "But aren't you the one he complains about interfering with his investigations?"

"I wouldn't say interfere. I am really about helping him."

"I don't know that he sees it that way. But if you hold on, I'll get him. He's just coming out of the shower."

"Borgnine," he barked in the phone a moment later. It was too soon for him to have had time to don more than a towel. Not an image I wanted stuck in my brain. "Who's this?" he demanded.

"C'mon, your wife and I just had a long conversation. She told you who's calling."

"Maybe she did. So what's so important?"

I considered how to phrase what I was going to say. I was calling to give him necessary information that he missed, not show off that I knew something he didn't. "I happened to run into Dr. Sammy Glickner," I began, but he cut me off.

"The magician? Don't tell me he got in trouble because of one of those magic shows of his. I'm telling you he should stick to straight illusions and lose that comedy stuff. I'm assuming it was planned, or did you just screw up and he did what he could to cover it up."

"How do you know about his magic act?" I asked, surprised.

"Number one, this is a small town, and number two, I'm a top cop, which means I know about everything. And I might have happened into a show he did for the group of doctors at one of the Pebble Beach resorts."

"I'll keep that under advisement," I said. "But my mentioning Dr. Glickner had nothing to do with his magic skills, more his doctor skills." I took a momentary pause to let it sink in before I continued. I explained telling Sammy about the incident on the beach and offered the detail that it appeared that the victim fell backward onto the rocks. "Somewhere in all of it, I brought up seeing blood on his forehead and how it had gotten on me. Dr. Glickner said that it seemed inconsistent with a backward fall." Rather than tell the lieutenant what I thought it meant, I left it hanging, hoping he'd come up with the same conclusion I did.

"Funny that Glickner would be commenting on the head of the victim since he's a urologist and his specialty is the other end."

I let out a sigh wishing he'd stop fixating on Sammy and pay attention to what I'd said. "This isn't about Dr. Glickner's specialty," I said.

"So then, what is the point of what you said?" Borgnine asked with a touch of impatience. I took a deep breath and hoped for the best. I was going to have to spell it out for him.

"I was just thinking that maybe the victim was hit on the head with something, like a rock. As in someone picked it up and did it," I said and waited for his response.

He surprised me by being silent for a few moments. "Maybe you're wrong about the way he was laying when you found him."

"About that," I said. "Someone else was there first. The person who called nine-one-one."

"But I thought that was you."

"There's no cell service at the beach," I said. "Someone had to go somewhere else to call."

"And you're sure that wasn't you," he said in his interrogation tone.

"Like I said, no. I barely had time to check for a pulse before the first responders arrived."

"Hmm," he muttered in an unhappy tone. "But back to the blood on his head. He might have hit his head and then rolled onto his back before you got there. Or maybe you're just wrong about how he was lying."

"I don't think so," I said.

"You saw him just for a few minutes. How can you be sure?" I could tell Lieutenant Borgnine was getting annoyed.

"I did only see him for a short time, but I know what I saw. He was flat on his back and I think he fell that way and that the blood on his head came from his being hit on his head."

"I'll talk to the first responders," he said. I knew he was trying to dismiss me.

"They just wanted to get Tim out of there before the tide washed him away. I don't think they focused on how he was arranged on the rocks," I offered.

"I'm sure the medical examiner will study his wounds."

"And when will that be?" I asked. There was silence on the other end. The doctor who served as medical examiner had a full practice since he wasn't often called on for medical examiner duties.

"I don't have to tell you that," he said.

"No problem," I said. "I'll check it out myself."

"What do you mean, you'll check it out yourself?" I was afraid my comment had made him snap to attention and I wondered if he'd lost the towel in the process.

"I'll check for blood residue."

"There's no way to tell where exactly he was lying and the tide came in and washed everything away."

"Even if the tide washed most everything away, I bet there's something left. And I have some luminol. Don't worry, I'll let you know what I find out," I said.

"Luminol? What are you doing with luminol?" the cop sputtered. Luminol was a substance that reacted with even the slightest trace of blood by making it glow in the dark. Sammy had gotten some thinking he could use it in an illusion. It had never panned out, but the bottle was in the storage area of my guesthouse along with the rest of his magic gear.

"Well, you can't spray all of those rocks."

"Don't need to. I can go exactly to the spot," I said in a confident tone.

"Don't do anything rash," he commanded. "You must have baking to finish. Those rocks are dangerous. You should leave it to the professionals. We should talk about this in person. Don't leave before I get there."

I barely had time to mix the biscuit muffins and put them in the oven before there was an insistent knock on the glass portion of the door.

"Good. You're still here," Lieutenant Borgnine said. The light reflected on his bristly salt-and-pepper hair and it was obviously still wet. There was no rumpled herringbone jacket this time. He was dressed for action in a navy blue tracksuit and white sneakers. He didn't wait to be invited before coming in and shutting the door behind him. "It's better if no one knows I'm here," he said, glancing out the window to the deserted street. I wasn't sure who he was worried about and I didn't bother asking. I'd riled him up enough already.

"You got the luminol?" he demanded.

"No. I don't carry it on me," I said, trying not to chuckle at the absurdity that I went around with luminol in my purse. "It's at my place." Just then the timer went off and I went toward the kitchen with him almost on my heels.

He sniffed the air and I had to admit it did smell wonderful. "The wife said you were making some sugar-free items."

I pulled the trays of biscuits out of the oven and he stepped closer to get a better view. "Are those them?" he asked. "So what are they, biscuits or muffins?"

"I'm not sure what the definition of either

166

of those is. They're kind of biscuits shaped like muffins."

"If this is a first-time thing, you really ought to let me taste-test them."

"You might want to wait until they cool a little," I said, setting them on racks. I finished with the pound cakes and rustic cherry pies and gave him the go-ahead to try one of the biscuit muffins. I'd changed from using fluted paper cups for the muffins to using squares of parchment paper that rose above the tops of the biscuits and made them look more dramatic. He took a tentative bite and I waited for his appraisal.

"I might need another to make sure," he said. I handed him a second and he bit into it. "I like it," he said finally. "And the wife can't hassle me about the sugar."

He waited while I packed them up and insisted on escorting me as I dropped them off around town. I think it was less about protection than worry that I was going to go to the rocks without him. I'd given him a bag of runts so he could let his wife taste them.

When we got back to the Blue Door he followed me to my place. When I say followed, it doesn't really cover it. The streets were deserted, but even so he rode the tail of the yellow Mini Cooper. Did he think I was going to make a run for it?

I pulled into my driveway and he parked on the street. Even so, he was next to the car door when I got out. "You want to wait here while I get it?" I asked. He thought about it for a moment and I guess he figured there was no way I could give him the slip and agreed. I probably should have told him that I wasn't trying to check it out without him, but I don't think he would have believed me anyway.

As it turned out he was trying to lose me.

"You can give that to me," he said when I returned with the spray bottle. "And then point me in the right direction."

"No way," I said. "First, I couldn't just point you in the right direction, and second, it's my luminol, so I get to be the one to spray it."

He looked gruffer than usual. "Okay, have it your way. I was just thinking of you walking on those rocks. I wouldn't want you to fall like the victim did." He didn't sound convincing. "But as long as you insist on going, I'd appreciate it if you kept this to yourself."

I nodded in agreement and we went across the street. Thanks to our sneakers our footsteps did not echo as we went down the driveway to Vista Del Mar. There was a deep silence on the grounds now. The only sound was the rhythm of the waves. The only lights on were in the Lodge and the lobbies of the guest room buildings.

We slipped across the grounds and took the boardwalk through the dunes. The white sand reflected the moon, illuminating the area well enough that I saw a deer family in silhouette making their way through the brush.

The breeze felt fresh and cold as it came off the water as we left the grounds and crossed the deserted street. We stopped when we got on the beach. The tide was out now and the sand seemed to go on forever. I led the way to the dark pierlike shape of the piles of rocks as they went out into the water. He offered one last time to do the heavy lifting and once again I refused.

I turned on the flashlight on my phone, glad it didn't need a signal to work. Here near the street the rocks were smaller and piled up, but as it went toward the water there were slabs of rock made smooth by the tide coming in and washing over them. I knew that was where Tim had been. I led the way past the area with the smaller boulders and stepped onto one of the slabs.

I kept my flashlight pointed on the stony surface. Even with the large mounds there were still plenty of crevices. Both the lieutenant and I were careful how we stepped. The crevices also had tide pools and more than once I saw a starfish clinging to the side of the rock in some water.

What I'd said earlier was kind of a bluff. I wasn't one hundred percent sure I could take him to the spot, more like I thought I could. I went to the approximate area I thought it was and began to look down. Maybe I was holding my breath a little thinking how bad it would be if I couldn't find the exact spot after all that I'd put the lieutenant through. And then I saw it and let my breath come out in a gush. My bluff had turned out not to be a bluff. I'd realized that I'd dropped my knitting and it made sense that it probably had been when I was kneeling next to Tim.

"Here we are," I said. "Pink marks the spot." The yarn and needles had gotten caught in one of the crevices. I left them for the moment and then oriented myself to the way I'd been facing when I knelt next to Tim.

I ran my flashlight over the area and noted that it was all smooth mounds of stone except for a jagged small rock.

I got down on my knees and took out the luminol. My heart rate had kicked up as I sprayed the smooth stone in front of me. I flipped off the flashlight quickly and we both looked at the dark surface as it came alive with bits of a blue glow that made an outline of where Tim's head had been. I clicked some photos.

"Good show, but it doesn't prove anything," the cop said.

I felt for the small rock and gave it the once-over with the luminol and spots of the blue glow lit up. "I beg to differ," I said, taking some photos before the blue glow disappeared. I flipped on my flashlight and shone it around the area, pointing out that the small rock was an abnormality. "As if someone brought it here," I said. "I bet if you take it to the M.E., the shape will match the wound on his head."

I heard him let out his breath in exasperation. "Okay, Ms. Feldstein, I see your point."

"You really should call me Casey after all we've been through," I said. "I'll send you the photos. I'm sure you understand what this means."

"Yes, Ms. — okay, I'll call you Casey, and I'll decide what this means." He paused a moment. "But don't think that means you can start calling me Theodore or Teddy. I will always be Lieutenant Borgnine to you."

"Okay, it's Lieutenant Borgnine all the

way," I said with a chuckle almost adding that what I really wanted to call him was Teddy Bear. "If I were you I'd start by finding out who called nine-one-one," I said, getting back to business.

"I can take it from here," he said. "Could you leave your knitting where it is, so I can get the area checked out in the morning?"

"Anything to help," I said in a bright voice as I heard him groan.

CHAPTER 14

"Hold on, Feldstein, I think you're getting ahead of yourself," Frank said. "I got that you took the local cop to the spot where something happened by way of your cockamamie knitting and you used some luminol to find blood residue — both of which must have driven him nuts — but am I to take that to mean someone died?"

I'd gotten back to my place so exhausted that I'd fallen asleep still dressed on top of the bed. I was amazed I'd managed to take off my jacket and give Julius a dab of goodnight stink fish. I'd awoken Friday morning with a start and a gritty tired feeling in my eyes — well, the tired feeling was pretty much everywhere. My first thought had been to call Frank and tell him about my triumph the night before. I'd forgotten that he had no idea what had led up to it.

I was holding the landline as I set the ceramic coffee thing on top of a mug. I put in the paper filter and spooned in the coffee grounds. Dane had gifted me with a filter setup so I could brew a single cup of coffee using real grounds. It was a definite step up from the instant I'd depended on and made more sense than brewing a whole pot. As soon as I poured in the hot water and it hit the grounds of the dark roast coffee, the pungent fragrance filled the air.

"Sorry, I forgot you didn't know." I heard Frank clucking his tongue.

"All this happened since I talked to you yesterday? You certainly lead a busy life."

"That was yesterday?" I said in surprise. "It seems like a month ago." The coffee had completed dripping into the mug and I took a big sip. The smell had knocked the door to my brain open and the liquid went right to my wakeup center. I let out a sigh as I felt more alert. "I better start at the beginning." I told him about the birthday group again since I figured he probably hadn't been listening that closely when I'd talked to him the preceding morning. There had to be some kind of drama in what I was telling him to get his attention. I heard him perk up when I mentioned interfering with the Silicon Valley group's retreat.

"Feldstein, you certainly know how to keep things stirred up. So the manager doesn't know that you're doing stuff for the retreat that he set up? The same person who you've told me doesn't like you and would love to trash-talk you to the owners so they don't give you a great deal on the rooms and your business falls apart." I heard the rattle of a paper sack on his end, and when Frank spoke again it sounded like he had a mouthful of something. "Is this leading up to whoever died?"

"Yes, you're right about Kevin St. John and I realize now it was probably a mistake to get involved with that group's retreat. And it was someone from Kevin's retreat who died," I said. I told him about the supposed accident, which led back to where I'd started telling him about my nighttime adventure with Lieutenant Borgnine.

"Whoever said small towns are boring hasn't hung out with you," Frank said. "So what happens now?" He didn't wait for me to answer. "I think I know. The cop is going to keep you out of the loop completely, but you're going to snoop around anyway. You know, Feldstein, most people wouldn't bother investigating if they weren't hired to do it, as in getting paid. It seems to me that with this one maybe you should stay out of it. Take your triumph with the luminol over the cop last night and walk away."

I took another sip of the coffee and mulled over what he'd said. "You could be right. Thanks for the advice," I said.

"That's what I'm here for," he joked. "Let me know what happens." And with a click he was gone.

I drained the coffee cup and went to get ready. I'd already planned to skip breakfast. I wasn't so sure having a lot of food in my stomach would go well with the morning's plans.

Even though I grew up in an apartment with a view of Lake Michigan my family weren't boat people. We were about looking at the water more than being on it. I'd taken the architectural river cruise on the Chicago River and gone to parties held on the excursion boats that left from Navy Pier to cruise along the coast to the north shore. In other words, I'd always been close to land.

So, when the birthday group requested a whale-watching outing, I'd arranged it and hoped my duties would be merely seeing them off from Vista Del Mar. But Aileen had made it clear I was to accompany them on the whole thing.

I threw Julius an envious look as he lay curled up on my bed for his morning nap. He didn't even awaken when I sat down on the bed to pull on my sneakers. I'd exchanged my usual turtlenecks for a V-neck taupe knit top and my favorite jeans that were pale blue from years of washing and wear. I slipped on a lavender cowl from my aunt's collection of her yarn craft creations. Figuring the wind would make a mess of my hair, I pulled it into a ponytail. There was another reason I wanted it out of the way. My lack of experience on the water left me worrying about getting seasick. I stuck on a baseball cap, grabbed a light-colored fleece jacket and headed to the door.

Julius never even looked up.

When I came outside, Deani was just closing the guesthouse door. She smiled when she saw me. "Just giving Fifi her morning walk and some attention," she said. I nodded as if in agreement, but I knew she was really dropping off the dog after sneaking her into her room overnight. *As long as she didn't get caught, why should I care?*

"Good idea not to take her on the boat," I said.

Deani and I walked across the street and down the driveway of Vista Del Mar. I kept expecting her to say something about the previous night, but she was acting like it never happened. I had a sudden thought, remembering how she'd said she had trouble sleeping. Maybe she had taken a sleep-

177

ing pill. I'd heard that people did weird things when they took certain sleep aids, like drive in their sleep and have no memory of doing it. Could that be what happened to her?

Madison, Iola and PJ were waiting outside Aileen's SUV in the parking area near the Lodge.

"Have you seen Aileen?" Madison said. "She didn't come to breakfast, and when I knocked on her door she wasn't in her room."

"You all know her better than I do," I said, "but she seems to have done the disappearing act a lot since you got here. It sounded to me like she wanted some alone time."

"I would have thought she had plenty of that since her divorce. But I guess it's different being away somewhere," PJ said.

"Here she comes," Deani said as Aileen rushed to join the group. Whatever Aileen was doing, it seemed to agree with her. Even with the utilitarian jeans and hoodie, her skin had a glow. Deani still had the car keys from the night before when she'd driven to the drugstore and stopped by the Blue Door. She went to give them to Aileen, but Aileen suggested she drive.

Deani beeped the doors open and said it was time to load up. I was hoping to ride shotgun, but Aileen opened up a single seat in the third row and gestured for me to get in. With the second row of seats back in place I felt a little claustrophobic but accepted that I was the hired hand and had to take the undesirable seat. The rest of them climbed in and Deani got in the driver's seat.

As soon as we were on the road, they all took out their phones, as I'd expected. It gave me some time for my own thoughts and I immediately went to thinking about Tim and his so-called accident. If I was right and someone killed him, the obvious suspects were the other people in his group. That meant there were four people who might have had a motive to get him out of the way. But which one and why?

Just as I was about to start racking my brain I thought about what Frank had said about letting this one go. I knew he was only thinking of my own good. I'd already stepped into the danger zone with Kevin St. John when I'd helped out his retreaters. Maybe it wasn't the danger zone yet, but if he found out, it would be the danger zone for sure. It would be even worse if he found out I thought one of his group was a killer. Maybe I should take Frank's advice and sit this one out, just let Lieutenant Borgnine do whatever he was going to do and stay out of the investigation. I let out a breath thinking I could just put it out of my mind and concentrate on everything else I had going on for the weekend. It sounded like a plan.

"I can't believe it," Madison said, looking up from her phone. "My daughter said my mother-in-law took them shopping and she's bought them the skimpy dresses I wouldn't let them buy." Madison held the phone up for them all to see. Well, except me. I couldn't see much of anything from the squished seat in the back row. She took the phone back and then let out a shriek. "She let them get tattoos. My eldest said it was funny that her grandmother was so much more with it than I am." She passed around the phone again and I assumed there was a photo of her daughters' new adornments. "I'm going to kill my husband when I get home. He's just asleep at the wheel while his mother wreaks havoc."

She touched her pink hair. "I was going to wash out the color before I went home. So I wouldn't embarrass them. But maybe I'll just keep it."

Aileen put her phone away. "It's better to talk to real people than to email or text." It seemed to have come out of nowhere. It served a purpose, though, by changing the subject.

"You never said where you went this morning," Madison said, leaning toward the front seat.

Aileen laughed. "Really? You're asking me to account for my time? I'm not one of your teenage daughters." We'd left Cadbury behind and were in Monterey, taking the route that ran close to the water. It was a big tourist area and the street was lined with motels and bed-and-breakfasts in interesting old houses. "If you have to know — instead of breakfast I went for a walk on the beach."

My ears perked up. Lieutenant Borgnine had said he was going to send a crew to check out the rocks first thing in the morning. "Where'd you walk? Were you near the rocky area?" I called out from the far backseat.

"Yeah, that's where I was," she said, nodding.

"Did you see anything interesting?" I asked.

"Just sand and water and of course rocks," she answered, and then looked out the window with a contented sigh.

Okay, something was off here. There would have been a police car and probably

181

a van. People would have been on the rocks. In other words, too much activity for a walker not to notice. So either he'd just been trying to pacify me with his supposed plans or Aileen wasn't telling the truth about where she'd been. I reminded myself that I was going to stay out of the lieutenant's investigation, so whatever he had or hadn't done was not my concern. Ditto for whether Aileen had been telling the truth. It was none of my business. Besides, I had other things to worry about — like the upcoming boat trip.

The boats left from the tip of Fisherman's Wharf and I directed Deani to a parking lot near there. The wharf was a tourist heaven with fudge shops, T-shirt shops and lots of places that sold raw and cooked fish, no doubt caught on one of the many fishing boats moored in the water nearby.

The sky was overcast and a chilly breeze blew off the water. I put on a brave face and led the group through the throngs of tourists. There was a brief stay in the boat lounge and the signing of waivers, which didn't make me feel any better. None of the boats I'd taken on Lake Michigan required the signing of anything. And then it was time to board.

You can do this, I told myself. With all the different things I'd done, spending a few hours on a small boat out in the middle of unbelievably deep water surrounded by huge animals couldn't be all that bad, could it?

I led the way onto the boat. There was a tiny snack bar and a little seating inside. There were two bathrooms on the outside and places to sit and stand. The motor made a grinding sound and we moved away from the dock. At first it went slow and we made our way around the other docks, and after we passed a buoy the boat picked up speed. I watched the panoramic view of the shore and the harbor get smaller and smaller as we went farther and farther into the open water. I did my best not to think about the map I'd seen of the mountains and deep canyon hidden under the water below us. The boat rocked and rolled over the rises and falls of the water. I was glad for the gunmetal sky, as even the thought of having the sun beat down on me made me feel queasy. The shore kept receding until it disappeared. Ahead there was just open water.

By now a couple of people had begun to look a little green and I noticed one of the boat people offering them paper towels and some advice. It was then that I noticed something about myself. The churning water and the rolling boat didn't seem to bother me at all. I began to make the rounds and check on my people in case their experience was different than mine.

Aileen seemed fine. She was at the front of the boat doing a *Titanic* move of holding her arms out and letting the wind make crazy salad of her brown hair. Madison had found a seat and wanted to know where the whales were. Iola had staked out a seat at the back of the boat. When I asked how she was she gave me a thumbs-up. Deani had gone inside and was checking out the snack bar.

And then I found PJ. She was slumped on a bench along the side of the cabin. "Are you okay?" I asked. She nodded half-heartedly. "I was going to tape something about being prepared for boat travel for the vlog." She pulled out a small makeup bag and showed me it was almost empty. "I didn't expect to have to use all the stuff on myself." She showed me she was wearing a wrist band that had a pressure point that was supposed to help with seasickness. There were only wrappers left from the ginger candy she'd brought. "Thank heavens I didn't have to use this," she said and pulled out the only thing left in the bag. It was a package of damp wipes with the lovely title of Vomit Patrol, which promised to leave the user fresh as a daisy.

"Maybe I should do the vlog entry. The point being that things don't always work out as you expected and you have to be able to step in and take care of yourself. The fact that it was me who had to do it might make it more compelling." She patted her hair, which like everyone else's was blowing across her face. "I'll just have to do the best I can to look presentable," she said as she pulled out a scarf and magically tied it perfectly around her head. She straightened her black jacket before she freshened her lipstick and pulled out her phone and used the camera to check her appearance. When she was satisfied, she began to tape.

I'd done my duty and went to find a seat near Iola just as the boat cut the motor and the voice over the loudspeaker announced we were there. Now that we weren't moving forward anymore, the boat really began to rock and I saw a couple of people head for the edge and hang their heads over. I thought of offering them PJ's Vomit Patrol wipes, but they weren't really mine to give.

I glanced at Iola. Not only was she quiet, but she was hopelessly nondescript as well. I was looking right at her and I had trouble noticing what she was wearing other than it seemed to be a beige jacket over slacks and those kinds of sandals that have a rubber layer along the front. They looked as if you could kick things and not hurt your toes. Her hair was literally a color without a name. It was somewhere between a honey blond and chestnut brown. It was cut short and seemed like it could use something to give it some life.

"Still okay?" I said to Iola, expecting a thumbs-up or -down. Instead she spoke.

"Boats don't bother me," she said. The sound of her voice startled me and surprised me, too. When she'd spoken before her voice had been so quiet I didn't hear the timbre. But thanks to the wind she had to speak louder and I heard the quality of her voice. I don't know what I'd expected she would sound like, but certainly not the husky sultry voice she had. She chuckled after that. "You looked surprised that I said something. I suppose the others told you I never say anything."

"Well, now that you mention it, somebody did say you were on the quiet side."

"Ha," she said in the low sexy voice. "They don't stop talking long enough for me to get a word in. Somebody has to listen to all their prattle. I think you should know that Madison is really upset with you."

"Really?" I said, looking in the direction of the woman with the pink hair. "What did I do?"

"She said you put on a workshop for those Reborn people." I remembered now that Madison had walked in during the workshop.

"I didn't think it would be a problem since your group wasn't using the room. I'm sorry," I added quickly. "We were just in your room for that time. Maybe I should go and tell her," I said, but Iola put her hand on my wrist.

"It's not that someone was using the room — it's who was using the room. She's not upset with you, it's them."

"Does she know them?" I asked, and Iola smiled.

"I guess you missed it when Madison was talking about what she does. She manages a shared work space place and they have an office there."

I was a little confused by the term *shared work space* and then I realized it was the new version of what used to be called an executive suite. There were private offices, but reception and a lounge with a kitchen were shared.

"Madison does more than manage the

place. She's the main receptionist who answers the phone and troubleshoots anything that goes wrong. That means those Reborn people go past her counter whenever they come in or go out or need something, which apparently is all the time. She wasn't thrilled when she saw they were here since she half expected them to dump some problem on her here." Iola let out a mirthless laugh and rolled her eyes. "But what they did was far worse. She went to greet a couple of them in the Lodge and they absolutely looked right through her. Those arrogant jerks are so into their own importance they obviously never really looked at a person they see every day."

"Wow, I had no idea. Well, maybe a little. I did get the feeling they think they're kind of entitled." I stopped as something occurred to me. "Didn't Madison say your knitting group meets where she works?"

Iola nodded.

"So then you all know them," I said.

Iola shrugged. "We have different degrees of familiarity with them, but believe me, they don't know us. They walked right past Deani without so much as a second look and she delivers their food."

"Did you know that one of them died?" I asked.

"The one that fell. He was the one who didn't play follow the leader and wear all black like the rest of them. Yes, Deani told us this morning. That's why Madison didn't say anything to you about being upset."

That made sense, but what didn't make sense was why Deani hadn't mentioned the Silicon Valley bunch were her customers when I'd told her Tim had died.

"Humpback on the starboard," a voice called out over the loudspeaker and everyone went to that side of the boat, making it list a little. Just then a large black creature breached the water as its blowhole made a whooshing sound. Its giant mouth was open and water poured in. After a few minutes its tail slapped the water as it dove back down. And then there were more. We were literally surrounded by whales having lunch.

I'd worry about Deani and the Silicon Valley bunch later. For now, I wanted to enjoy the show.

CHAPTER 15

The magic of the humpback whales was over and I was stuck in the tight seat in the third row of the SUV again, trying to tell myself I didn't feel cramped in. At least it was a shorter ride since the plan was that we'd stop for lunch at the Blue Door on the way back. I hoped I'd get a chance to talk to Lucinda about the information that Iola had dumped in my lap. It was a lot to process. It had never occurred to me that there was a connection between my retreaters and the Silicon Valley group and now I knew there was not only a connection but bad feeling toward the Reborn people from two of my people. I had to bring her up to speed on my nighttime adventure with Lieutenant Borgnine and how my opinion of what'd happened had changed.

I wasn't sure if Lieutenant Borgnine was sold on the idea that someone had hit Tim with the rock I'd found with blood residue, but I was. The jagged orb was too random when the whole area was made up of giant smooth slabs. The small rocks were piled in the area near the street where someone could have easily helped themselves.

Just then I remembered that I was going to let the whole Tim thing go. Oh, well, good plan while it lasted.

There was a lot more action on Grand Street than there had been when I'd gone to bake at the Blue Door the night before. The main drag of Cadbury was busy with tourists and townspeople. All the foot traffic gave the main street a lively air. I was concerned about giving Deani directions since my visual options were pretty limited in that third row, but she drove directly to the Blue Door with no help and parked right in front of the place. It knocked out my thought that she might have taken a sleeping pill the night before. My understanding was that people had no memory of what they'd done or where they'd gone. So I had to wonder all over again why she'd said nothing about her visit or that the Reborn crew were her customers.

The group waited until I squeezed out and then I led the way up onto the porch to the front door. Unlike when I'd arrived the night before, tables were set out on the far end of the porch. Though since it was past lunchtime only one of the outdoor tables in the corner was taken.

I held the door and ushered my group in. Lucinda was waiting by the door and gestured for them to follow her. Dressed in a bright yellow dress, it was as if Lucinda had brought the sun inside. I knew it was designed by some guy with a French-sounding name. All of her clothes were designer and she always looked completely put-together. She was wearing her hair short in what she called a carefree style. It was a warm brown now with golden highlights that seemed to act like a spotlight on her face.

I hung back as they went in. Iola held up the rear and I grabbed her as she was about to go inside.

"You told me about Madison and Deani, but what about you? Do you have any connection with the Reborn people?"

"If you're concerned that I'm angry you put on a workshop for them — I'm not upset. Madison and Deani are involved with servicing them." She shook her head. "I'm not." She looked ahead as her knit-together friends reached the other side of the main dining area. "I see the Reborn people in the hall and lounge. Frankly, I've never cared that they didn't acknowledge my existence here or in the office even though it goes against the 'friendly atmosphere' of the work space environment." She gave me a brief rundown of the business she and her husband had. They sold stuff online and made up little videos. No surprise, she did the voice-over. I bet they did well. With her husky voice I figured she could make straw sound exciting.

I'd held her up long enough and urged her to join the others. I stayed by the front, watching as Lucinda waited while they took their seats at the table on the sunporch and then handed them menus. She hung by the table and reacted with smiles and bows of her head as they read the back of the menu with the fairy-tale story of how Lucinda and Tag had been high school sweethearts and reconnected later in life. I noticed them looking around and I guessed it was for Tag. I couldn't hear Lucinda's explanation, but I knew she often shooed him out of the place toward the end of lunch so they could have some time off from each other before it was time to start serving dinner.

She took their orders and dropped them off in the kitchen before coming back to the front where I was. "Aren't you going to sit with them?" she asked.

"They're all friends and I'm like an outsider," I said and she nodded with understanding. She got me a stool and wanted to feed me, but all I would take was an iced tea.

The server took over dealing with my group and Lucinda stayed by the front in case there were any late arrivals for lunch.

"I feel so out of the loop," Lucinda said, leaning on the counter. "I'm used to being in the middle of things. This is the first retreat you've put on that I didn't attend. But I understand this isn't like your usual retreats. It's a private party."

"Exactly," I said. "And that's the same reason I'm not sitting with them." I leaned closer to my friend and boss. "But do I have some things to tell you."

"I'm all ears," she said. It was always hard to know where to start. I decided not to go chronologically and started with my adventure with Lieutenant Borgnine. She was laughing so hard by the end she had tears rolling down her cheeks.

"If only you had taken a video of the whole thing."

"Dealing with him was pretty funny, but finding the blood on the rock was serious and it explained why Tim had blood all over his face," I said. She wanted to know how the cop had taken it and all I could do was tell her the truth, that he'd seemed to go along with my assessment that someone had hit Tim with the rock, but that he might have just been humoring me.

"But there's more," I said. I told her about Madison being upset that I'd put on the workshop for the other group. "And Kevin St. John's group asked me to arrange another workshop. I have to do it," I said. "That group talked so much they barely had time to start their project. If I left things the way they are, I'm sure Elex would complain about it to Kevin St. John, forgetting that they'd come to me to put the workshop together."

"So, if it wasn't an accident and somebody killed Tim — do you think it was one of his people?"

"That would seem the most likely scenario, but now that I know some of my group knows some of that group, it adds to the possible suspects."

Lucinda and I sensed someone coming near and we both looked up as Deani approached. I hoped she hadn't overheard what we'd been talking about. "Have you seen Aileen?" she said, sounding worried.

It seemed she'd left the table right after the orders were taken and the food had arrived and she wasn't back. "I thought she'd gone to the restroom, but it's empty." She pointed at the open door in the back of the alcove between the dining room and sunporch.

"Didn't she say something about liking some time alone," I said, remembering her comments on the drive to Monterey. "Maybe she went out to check out downtown Cadbury."

The server who'd been waiting on them came by just then. "If you're looking for your friend, I saw her go out on the porch."

Lucinda, Deani and I went outside. Aileen was sitting at the far table alone. There was a dish with a crumpled napkin across from her and she was finishing her iced tea.

Aileen offered no explanation as she joined us and followed us inside.

CHAPTER 16

We walked outside to a blue sky and sunshine. It was so surprising that everyone on the street seemed a little dazed and was staring at the sky. It took awhile to get everyone back in the SUV. I was grateful that it was a short ride as I squeezed into the seat in the third row again. Of course, the rest of them spent the ride staring at their phone screens before they went back to unplugged land.

The blue sky and sun didn't last and by the time we pulled back onto the Vista Del Mar grounds the weather had changed completely and a thick fog was blowing in. When I finally left the tight seat and got out of the SUV, it seemed like I'd walked into a cloud. There was so much moisture in the air it almost felt like a light drizzle. They all scattered and literally disappeared in the thick whiteness to do whatever during the free time before it was time for the afternoon workshop. I went into the Lodge and right

197

into trouble.

I'd barely opened the door and taken a step inside when Madeleine Delacorte came toward me. Just as she snagged my arm I caught sight of Kevin St. John, Lieutenant Borgnine and a woman I'd never seen before huddled in front of the registration counter. Madeleine pulled me with her as she went outside. She seemed a little surprised at the fog, but it only lasted for a moment.

"Oh, dear," she said. "More trouble. Cora couldn't come, so I had to come alone. Kevin said that he'd handle everything, he was just notifying me what was going on." She shook her head with dismay. I knew she was upset because she didn't even mention the new jeans she was wearing. Thankfully, she'd gotten past wearing the pairs she'd gotten that came with tears and holes. She'd admitted to me that she kept getting her feet caught in the openings when she was putting them on, so it was really a safety factor that had led her to stop wearing them. Today's look was a more sedate darkwashed pair so dark they seemed almost black, which she'd paired with a black turtleneck. I wondered how the Silicon Valley group would view her. Would they think she was stealing their look?

198

She checked the area to make sure no one was nearby then muttered that with the fog it was hard to be sure. "I'll just talk softly," she whispered. "Cora is against it, but personally it might be nice to have some help dealing with Kevin. I'm tired of his condescending manner. Imagine telling me not to worry my pretty little head about whatever the latest problem is. If we had . . ." She looked around again to make sure no one was in earshot and dropped her voice even more. ". . . You-know-who on our side, I bet she'd come up with a sharp retort."

I brightened, thinking maybe there was hope after all that the Delacorte sisters would accept their newfound family. I really believed they would all benefit, but I'd meddled enough and now just had to let things take their course.

I played stupid and asked what was up. "You saw them, didn't you?" She pointed toward the door. "I suppose you know about the accident. It was just terrible that the man died. It wasn't actually on Vista Del Mar property, but he was a guest and I understand he was taking part in an activity that Kevin had arranged. The woman is his wife. I told her how sorry we were."

"So that's his wife," I said, wishing I'd

gotten more than a glance. All I'd noticed was a woman with long dark hair wearing a khaki trench coat.

"You're sure they said it was an accident?" I asked.

"The policeman in that awful-looking jacket said it wasn't official yet, but unofficially it was an accident." Madeleine let out a sigh. "She's going to stay until things get sorted out. I'm not sure what the sorting out is. When they got to that part Kevin dismissed me with that *pretty little head* comment." Madeleine's voice was back to a normal volume and she sounded annoyed. "Kevin doesn't seem to get that I've changed. Now that I've started this whole new chapter in my life, I'm ready to be in the middle of everything." She stopped to take a breath and let it out on a sigh. "I spent too many years being sheltered. I have a lot of catching up to do — even with dealing with events that aren't happy." She turned to me. "I hope the accident hasn't ruined your retreat. Such a fun idea having a yarn-filled birthday celebration."

I was still adjusting to all her talking. Madeleine was the older sister, but Cora had always been the one to take charge. Madeleine had been so quiet that for a while I wondered if she was able to talk. There was no doubt about that anymore.

"I'm sorry you aren't joining us this time," I said. It was really just a polite gesture. It would have been very awkward if she had joined the retreat as she usually did. "I think they're enjoying it, but I'm more or less an outsider on this one."

Something beeped on Madeleine's wrist. She looked at it in a sudden tizzy. "I have to go. I signed up for a golf lesson," she said. "Finally, my transportation seems appropriate," she added as she walked to her parked golf cart. I hoped she'd be all right driving in the fog.

This time I went all the way into the Lodge. As soon as Kevin saw me, his eyes tensed and he seemed to be turning Tim Moffat's wife to face away from me.

Lieutenant Borgnine was giving me the stink eye too. I took the cue and walked past them into the Cora and Madeleine Delacorte Café. Even with the stop at the Blue Door, I'd been too busy talking to Lucinda and worrying about my group to even drink the iced tea she'd given me. I needed a shot of something strong. Cloris was behind the counter wearing the gold jacket that was the café workers' uniform.

"You're everywhere," I said with a smile.

"I like getting as much experience as possible. The classes at the community college are fine, but nothing takes the place of learning how it all works by doing." She had a mixture of maturity and exuberance that made her a natural for a hospitality career. She picked up a stray sugar packet from the counter and put it back in the dispenser. "What can I get for you? How about one of the fancy drinks? Maybe a cappuccino. I'm working on making designs in the milk froth."

"You sold me. Make it a cappuccino with an extra shot."

"Tough morning?" Cloris asked as she started to fill the metal cup with finely ground coffee.

"How about not enough sleep and then taking my group whale watching and finding out that someone in my group was upset that I'd done the workshop for the Silicon Valley bunch."

"That's ridiculous. They don't own you." She sighed. "That group probably really needed the workshop, too. It must be tough on the Silicon Valley bunch to have one of their associates die." The strong coffee had begun to drip into a cup, filling the air with its strong scent. She steamed the milk and then poured it and the espresso into a cup. The final touch was a swirl on the top before she handed it to me. "I did it, a perfect heart shape," she said with pride. Then she waited while I took my first sip.

"Delicious," I said. I looked back toward the door. "About the Silicon Valley group — they seemed more confused than broken up. I saw Kevin St. John and Lieutenant Borgnine out there. I assume they've been talking about what happened. You seem to be in the middle of everything. Did you hear anything? You know, whether it was an accident or something else."

Cloris came around from the back and leaned on the counter next to me. "There was a lot of back-and-forth between Mr. St. John and the cop. I didn't mean to overhear, but they were talking in front of me like I was invisible. I got that it could be an accident or it could be murder." Her voice dropped to a whisper on the last word. "It seems like it's a matter of opinion about whether the man fell on the rock and it bashed his head or the rock bashed his head with some help. Mr. St. John was pushing for it to be called an accident and kept pointing out that the man used poor judgment to walk on the rocks when there was a *Danger* sign and he was wearing leather-soled shoes."

"I don't believe it. Kevin St. John is trying

to put the blame on the dead guy," I said, shaking my head. "What about the cop? What did he say?"

Cloris shrugged. "He agreed to call it an accident for now." It was great having someone on the inside like Cloris and I thought about something else. "Did Lieutenant Borgnine say anything about investigating the source of the nine-one-one call?"

"I forgot, they did talk about it. I think the cop checked the log of emergency calls and it came from one of the pay phones here." She automatically waved her arm in the direction of the Lodge's great room. "But there's no way of knowing who made it."

I was going to say something more, but I heard footsteps and when I turned I saw that Tim's wife had come into the café. I turned to Cloris and put my finger to my lips, signaling for her not to say anything more.

Cloris gave me a wink to show she understood and went back to her post behind the counter.

"Welcome, welcome. We feature espresso drinks of all kinds. Let me know what you fancy and I'll whip it right up for you."

The woman gazed at the menu with a blank look. No surprise that she was a little distracted.

By the way they'd acted, it was obvious that Kevin St. John and Lieutenant Borgnine didn't want me to talk to Mrs. Moffat. I assumed that was her name, but who knew — these days, so many women continued on with their maiden names. If I ever got married I was pretty sure I'd want to go by Feldstein. But the whole name thing was extraneous at the moment.

I checked the area to make sure her gatekeepers weren't going to swoop in and block me before I took a step toward her. "I saw you talking to Lieutenant Borgnine and Kevin St. John. You must be Tim Moffat's wife." I held out my hand. "Casey Feldstein."

Her expression came into focus and she looked at me. "Audrey Evans," she said, taking my hand. "Do you work here?"

"Not exactly, I arrange yarn retreats and hold them here." I was ready in case she asked what yarn retreats were since that was a common question when I told people what I did, but she let it go. "Did you arrange the retreat Timmy was here for?" I shook my head. "But you know what happened, right?" This time I nodded.

She turned to Cloris and said she'd have a coffee with lots of cream and sugar. "I usually drink it black, but I need a little boost. Please add it for me." I offered her the stool next to me at the counter, but she opted for one of the tables. "I don't have it in me to climb up on one of those." I thought that was going to be the end of it, but she invited me to join her.

Cloris did the honors with the cream and sugar and I carried the cup to the table. Audrey had already sunk into one of the chairs. The table was by the window, but there was literally no view. All that was visible was white from the thick fog. I didn't think it mattered as she didn't even seem aware there was a window.

Thanks to Lucinda and her taste in clothes, I knew all about designer duds. As soon as Audrey put her trench over the back of the chair, I knew it was a Burberry and probably cost almost as much as my entire wardrobe. Underneath she had on a black sweater over a pair of charcoal-colored jeans perfectly accessorized with a silk scarf that might have been a Hermès. She wore simple gold hoops in her ears and if the scarf was a Hermes, they were probably solid.

"I'm so sorry for your loss," I said in a somber tone. I was surprised when she rolled her eyes.

"This is very awkward," she said. "They

called me because I'm Tim's wife, but we're getting a divorce. I guess even though it's almost final, since we're still technically married, I'm his next of kin." She took a generous sip of the coffee that was almost beige. She swallowed and closed her eyes momentarily with satisfaction before turning toward Cloris. "This is perfect. Thank you."

She took a few more sips and it seemed to revive her. "I'd hoped to be able to take care of things right away. Tim always said he wanted to be cremated. They won't even let me pack up his stuff until everything is settled."

I was trying to think of something to say that would sound understanding, but it was certainly an odd situation. Finally I went with something simple and vague and just said, "I'm sorry."

She leaned back in the chair. "Thank you. It's good to have a little sympathy. The two I just talked to need some lessons in compassion. All the manager seemed to care about was putting the blame for what happened on Tim. And all the cop said was that I couldn't do anything until the medical examiner signed off on the manner of death." I looked back to Cloris, who was taking it all in, and we both shook our heads at how the two men had behaved.

Audrey started talking and it came out like a stream of consciousness. It didn't even seem like she was talking to me except that she occasionally looked in my direction. "It's not a contentious divorce. Our lives are just going in different directions. It was my idea. Not that he balked." She was still referring to him in the present and I could tell that everything hadn't sunk in. I doubt it had gotten through to her that there was now no need for a divorce and she wasn't a wife anymore, she was a widow. I was certainly not going to say any of it, though.

I did however ask her what they told her had happened. "I don't know. Something about him going for a walk on some wet rocks and falling. He hit his head. A stupid accident." She drank some more of the rich coffee. "Though the concept of Tim doing something like that on his own seems out of character. He wasn't interested in nature. I suppose it had something to do with the retreat."

I couldn't stay out of it anymore. "It was part of the retreat. They were supposed to go on an independent mindful walk." I hesitated and then continued. "I might as well tell you that Elex and Tim approached me about adding some activities to their

208

schedule." I reminded her that I put on yarn retreats and explained that knitting fit in with the mindfulness concept.

"Tim wanted to knit?" she said with surprise.

"Well, no. Actually, it was really Elex's idea. And as it turned out, the workshop came after his accident."

"I thought so. Tim wasn't into the whole mindful retreat thing. The only reason he came was that he thought it would be a good place to break some news to Elex." I was just thinking that she seemed to know an awful lot about someone she was divorcing when she must have read my thoughts. "He came by to drop off some papers and he told me about the weekend. We were still civil to each other."

She'd gotten my interest. I'd wondered what the whole dynamic was with the Silicon Valley group. "Were they partners?" I asked.

"I think that was how Tim looked at it. Tim was an angel investor. In the past he just invested in start-ups and stayed out of any real involvement. But I think he wanted to feel like he was doing something. He got involved in the day-to-day running of things with Reborn, but they have totally different styles. Tim was thoughtful and measured while Elex is passionate and impulsive. He'd tried to make suggestion to Elex about how to handle things, but Elex tuned him out. I think Tim was frustrated that Elex wouldn't take any advice and Tim was concerned that the concept Elex had come up with wouldn't work on a big scale. Tim wanted to do something that was a home run. He told me he'd already started working on something else totally on his own."

"So he wanted to tell Elex something like he was leaving their company?"

She nodded. "And that the second round of financing wasn't going to come through." She went for the coffee mug and I caught a glimpse of her hand. She was still wearing her wedding ring, which seemed strange since she'd made it sound like the marriage was over.

"Do you know if they had the conversation?" I asked.

"Knowing Tim, I'm sure he would have gotten it out of the way as soon as possible."

I was sure that the manager and the cop hadn't told her that I'd found Tim, but it seemed like something she should know. "I might have been the last person to see Tim alive," I said in a soft voice. She turned to me in surprise.

"Please tell me all the details. Was he

awake? Did he say anything," she asked, losing her cool façade for a moment and seeming almost frantic.

"No, he didn't say anything and he seemed unconscious to me. I really only had a short time with him and then the paramedics took him away. I'm sure they did everything possible to save him." I was reliving the moment as I told her about it. And then a vague image popped into my mind I'd forgotten about. Something that had happened when I first got to the sand. The thought only lingered a moment and then all my attention was back on Audrey.

She let out her breath, seeming uneasy. "I'm not sure what I'm supposed to do. I contacted my lawyer, but he's in Paris this weekend. He'll come here as soon as he gets back, and I can let him figure all of this out." She looked at the window and did a double take. "Is that fog?"

"It's pretty thick right now," I said.

"The manager offered me a room. Maybe I'll take him up on it instead of driving home to Palo Alto."

I thought back to the odd comments the Silicon Valley group had made when they were talking about Audrey. "Did the other Reborn people know about the divorce?" I asked.

"Only if there'd been a reason to tell them," she said. She drained the coffee cup. She had her back to the doorway and didn't notice Elex come in. He certainly noticed her and his reaction was to go a little pale. I looked away before he realized I'd seen him and he slipped back out the door.

"I just want you to know that I don't usually talk this much about personal stuff and particularly not to someone I don't know. It's just, well . . ." She let out a sigh. "A really strange time." She stopped for a moment and stared at the table as if she was thinking about something. She rocked her head and pursed her lips before muttering, "But Elex will get his money after all."

I couldn't let that pass without a comment. "What do you mean?"

"They had key man insurance policies for Elex and Tim for a million dollars each."

Wow, that put a whole new spin on things.

CHAPTER 17

I left shortly after Audrey did. Actually, I held down the fort for Cloris while she took Audrey to the front desk and made sure that she was given one of the rooms in a new building. I'd never seen the rooms but understood they were deluxe compared to the bare-bones rooms my people got. I thought that meant they had bathtubs and showers and were more spacious.

As soon as Cloris returned, I took off. My plan was to go home and bake cookies for the afternoon session. After hearing that Madison was upset with me for hosting the workshop for the Silicon Valley group — I always started to call them the Silicon Valley guys and then remembered they had a woman in their group — I felt guilty and hoped a batch of fresh butter cookies might smooth things over.

I was lost in the fog as I headed up the Vista Del Mar driveway. Both the thick white moisture outside and the swirl of thoughts going through my mind. Was Lieutenant Borgnine bowing to pressure from Kevin St. John? The mystery of the 911 call had been partly cleared up, but who made the call? What about what Audrey had said about an insurance policy? It sounded like Elex had a big payday coming. Then there was the issue that she was still Tim's wife. Was that a convenience or a coincidence? I didn't even know if all the stuff about how civil they were about the divorce was true. And to top it all off, I kept wondering about the vague memory that had surfaced and disappeared when I was talking to her.

The cloud on the ground made it hard to figure out my bearings as I went toward my place and I didn't realize I'd left the Vista Del Mar driveway and was on the street. It wasn't until I heard the screech of brakes that I looked up and saw the red truck inches from me. Dane glared at me from behind the windshield before he stuck his head out the window. "I'm giving you a jaywalking ticket." He kind of choked on the words as if he was trying to sound teasing, but was really stunned. "Wait over there by the curb while I get out my ticket book," he said. He'd added a grin to make his intent clear.

I finished crossing the street and walked up my driveway as he pulled to the curb and jumped out. "You do realize I could have hit you," he said, coming up behind me. "And then you'd have used that as the perfect excuse to break things off with me." I turned to check his expression. He was still grinning but there was some subtext of concern.

"Sorry," I said lamely. "You're absolutely right. I need to pay more attention to where I'm going."

"Apology accepted and there'll be no ticket," he joked before giving me a hug. He was wearing his off-duty uniform of jeans and a T-shirt and I was glad not to be smacked by all the stuff on his cop equipment belt. "What were you so busy thinking about?" he asked.

"Is it true that Lieutenant Borgnine is calling the death an accident even though he knows there's more to it?"

Dane's brow furrowed and he seemed perplexed.

"The man who died after falling on the rocks at Vista Del Mar yesterday," I said, trying to jog his memory.

"I know who you mean. It's not like there were any other deaths yesterday in Cadbury.

It was the last part about *more to it.*" He looked me in the eye. "How is that you know that Lieutenant Borgnine knows there is more to it?"

Dane had no problem with my investigating and had been a source of information on occasion, but he knew that Lieutenant Borgnine did have a problem with it. "Have you been up to something you haven't told me about?" he asked as a smile danced in his eyes.

"I don't want to talk out here," I said, taking his hand and leading him to the kitchen door.

"Okay by me," he said with a lift of his eyebrows.

"This isn't about romance," I said, trying to appear serious. "This is about murder."

"Whatever it takes for you to want to hold my hand," he said, giving mine a squeeze.

"You're hopeless. I should just jump in with both feet and then decide to leave and break your heart," I countered.

"Go ahead. Jump. I'll risk the broken heart. Besides, I know if you do finally give yourself over to me you'll never want to leave."

"Aren't you the cocky one," I said, shaking my head.

"Maybe I just see what you won't admit."

216

The grin was gone and I knew he was serious, which immediately made me nervous. Was it because I knew there might be truth in what he said?

Julius was waiting by the kitchen door. He welcomed both of us with some swirls around our legs followed by a plaintive meow before he went to the refrigerator.

"I'll do the honors," Dane said.

"Then you are my hero to brave the stench of stink fish." I did a flourish and a mock bow. He rolled his eyes as he took out the multi-wrapped can.

"I don't know why you make such a fuss about it." He pulled off the first layer and suddenly gagged. "Whoa, this stuff does stink. I *am* your hero," he said, looking at me and then at the cat. "How about a thank-you meow."

"I guess you don't know cats. They think we work for them," I said, watching as Dane held the can as far away as possible as he unwrapped the rest of the can.

Julius attacked his bowl with fervor when the precious pink blob had been put in it.

"Now, where were we?" Dane said. "Weren't you about to fall into my arms and vow your undying love?" His tone made it clear he was back to teasing, but underneath it there was a kernel of hope.

217

"I did agree to go to the movies in Cadbury," I said. "It's a small step, but still a step closer to your fantasy." I had wanted to keep our relationship on the down low, not wanting to be caught up in small-town gossip, but it was a waste of time. It seemed like everybody already knew anyway, so instead of having to go to Monterey on a date, I'd agreed to going local.

"I don't know why you put up with me," I said. "There have to be lots of single women in Cadbury who would love your attention."

"Really? You don't know why?" He rolled his eyes. "Is this a play for me to give you a list of what I lo, uh, like about you?"

"No," I said quickly, afraid of what he'd say and how I'd react. Okay, I was afraid I'd get all mushy and start crying. I wanted to keep things light.

When the stink fish had been rewrapped and put away, I went to the refrigerator and took out some rolls of cookie dough. I always kept the rich butter cookie dough ready to bake up for my retreaters. Dane pulled out a chair while I turned on the oven and sliced up the dough.

"There are fresh cookies in your future," I said, fluttering my eyes, which was my pathetic effort at being flirty. As usual it got me laughter in return. "And while you wait

I'll tell you about *the something more.*"

"I love it when you let me be the cop. Fire away."

While the air filled with the buttery sweetness of the baking cookies, I told him about my adventure with Lieutenant Borgnine the night before. Dane was shaking his head in disbelief by the end of the story. "I wish there was a video of that," he said. "Was he wearing his usual sport jacket?" Dane shook his head again. "You and the lieutenant climbing around rocks in the darkness with your luminol." He stopped for a moment. "Now it makes sense. He sent a detail to the beach this morning. I heard something about something pink and a rock you could fit in your hand. They were there a long time."

"Then there were cops on the beach," I said, half to myself. That meant Aileen had to have been lying about her morning walk. There was no way she could have missed a bunch of uniforms clamoring around the rocks.

"I thought Lieutenant B. agreed with me, that someone had brought the rock there and used it to bash Tim's head. Or at least that there was the possibility that happened. Would he look the other way because it's expedient to Kevin St. John to call what happened an accident?"

"Borgnine and I have our differences, but I've never doubted that he's a good cop. The manner of death isn't official yet anyway, so maybe he was just humoring the Vista Del Mar manager while he investigates with an open mind."

"Okay, I can buy that coming from you since you're on the inside."

Dane smiled and took on his cop stance. "Glad I could be of service, ma'am."

"Thank you, Officer," I said to counter his formal *ma'am.* I'd been slicing the logs of cookie dough during our back-and-forth and sliding the sheets into the oven.

"Uh, Officer, there's something else you might be able to help me with."

"At your service," Dane said, doing a grand bow.

"I heard that the nine-one-one call came from a pay phone at Vista Del Mar. But any idea who made the call? The dispatcher must have had something — a name, or at least an idea if it was a man or woman."

Dane broke a smile. "The cop gossip mill had a good time with that one when it came out that Mr. Top Cop had assumed you'd made the call and he didn't check. And then he did. What I heard was that the dispatcher just had J. Smith listed and had no memory if it was a male or female."

"Thanks, but it doesn't help." As I was saying it something stirred in my mind and I realized it was the vague thought that had flitted in and out when I was talking to Audrey. I tried to get it to flit into my mind and stay there. I must have had my eyes scrunched up and been gritting my teeth because Dane waved his hand in front of my face.

"What is going on in that head of yours?"

"When I tell you, you'll laugh," I said, letting my jaw relax. I explained trying to will a memory to come forward in my mind.

"Did it work?" he asked and I nodded.

"And the memory is," he prodded. "You're not making this easy."

"Sorry," I said. "As I was about to walk on the beach yesterday before I saw Tim or had any idea something had happened, I saw something go by out of the corners my eye. All I remember is a flash of something black. And then it disappeared. I went back on the street and looked but there was nothing there."

"Maybe it was J. Smith," Dane said. "The person who called nine-one-one."

I thought about it for a moment. "It seems like it could have been J., but if it was, where'd they go? And the timing seems off."

The oven timer pinged and I went to pull the cookie sheets out of the oven. I pushed the round discs out onto a rack to cool. Dane knew better than to try to snag one when they were just out of the oven. I had to admire his patience.

"It couldn't have been more than a minute or so later that I noticed Tim on the rocks. I barely had time to get to him and check for a pulse when the paramedics arrived."

Dane wasn't quite as patient as I thought and he took one of the not completely cooled cookies and popped it in his mouth. He pressed his fingers together and seemed to throw a kiss in the air. "My compliments to the chef." He went for a second cookie. "Most likely your memory of the timing is off. It might have taken longer than you think. Or maybe it was a crow — though to be honest, I haven't seen any around here lately."

"I was thinking maybe we could reenact the situation," I said. "You know, to see how the timing works." He grabbed another cookie and got up.

"Sure. Let's do it. I'm cooking for the karate kids, but I've got time."

The fog was almost gone when we went outside. There was just a subtle shroud of mist around the tops of the lanky Monterey pines that grew along the driveway to Vista Del Mar. I suggested we walk through the grounds separately in case Lieutenant Borgnine was hanging around. He frowned upon Dane getting involved with my investigations and punished him by giving him the worst shifts.

I passed by a group of the birders. It was easy to pick them out with their khaki vests and binoculars around their necks. They were just exiting the boardwalk that meandered through the dunes toward the beach.

I thought to ask them if they'd noticed any crows, but decided against it and simply nodded a greeting as I passed them before starting on the created pathway. The boardwalk looked like it was made of wood slats, but actually the "wood" didn't come from trees, but was fashioned out of recycled soda bottles.

I passed through the archway with a Vista Del Mar sign at the end of it. I was about to cross the street when Dane rejoined me. "Where did you come from?" I asked, surprised to see him.

"We cops have our ways," he said with a twinkle in his eyes.

He made sure we looked both ways before

we crossed the street after chiding me about my inattention before. The streets were all sleepy there, but I got his point.

I looked at the warning signs on the rocky pile thinking back to the previous day. I retraced my steps to the zigzagging pathway that led through the protected planted area to the beach. "This is where I was when I saw the flash of black."

From there we walked onto the sand along the side of the rocky surface. "I looked over there, and that's when I saw something that turned out to be Tim." We climbed on the rocks and I took him to the spot, which was easy to find because my yarn and needles were still stuck in the crevice. "Pink marks the spot," I said, pointing it out.

"I leaned down and felt for a pulse. The next moment I heard the paramedics pulling up." I looked across the rocky surface to the street and pointed. "Then they were coming toward me."

"So, your question is how'd they get here so fast?" Dane said. He'd crouched down but I'd stayed standing. "I'd like to say our services are that quick, but they would have had to be mind readers to have arrived that fast."

"So then it must have been somebody else," I said.

"Hey, what are you two doing up there?" a voice yelled. I saw Lieutenant Borgnine standing up to his ankles in sand. His bulldog face appeared angrier than usual. I stepped to block his view of Dane and waved my hand frantically, telling him to go. I didn't want it on my conscience that Dane would get another bad shift or duty. Dane hesitated. It was not his way to walk away from trouble, but he finally slipped over the rocks and went down on the other side before Lieutenant Borgnine realized I wasn't alone.

I leaned down and grabbed my knitting and held it up. "I just came back for this," I said. He shook his head with dismay and waited until I'd climbed down and then walked me back to the Vista Del Mar grounds.

225

CHAPTER 18

Lieutenant Borgnine rushed me through the boardwalk and abandoned me as soon as we were back on the grounds. I think his swift departure was deliberate because he was afraid I might start asking him questions. After what Dane had said about Borgnine being a good cop, I was giving him the benefit of the doubt and believed he had just been trying to pacify Kevin St. John.

Your loss, I said to myself as I watched the rumpled jacket disappear in the distance. Had he not been in such a rush, I might have offered him some information. I doubted that Audrey Moffat had told him half of what she told me. And wouldn't he have liked to know that it seemed there had been a mystery person on the beach. Someone dressed in black.

Dane was waiting by my kitchen door when I came back to pick up the cookies.

"I could have stayed," he said. "What

more could Borgnine do to me? I get the graveyard shift a lot, and dog cleanup duty."

"Sorry," I said, knowing it was my fault.

"I definitely don't like the dog-do duty, but the graveyard shift isn't all bad. I get to stop by the Blue Door when you're baking."

"You could come by the Blue Door even if you aren't working," I said.

He brightened and I expected some teasing remark about how I was finally succumbing to his charms, but his smile was just sweet. "Good to know," he said. He followed me inside my kitchen and I packed a tin with the cooled cookies and made up a bag for him. We walked back outside together.

"It's been fun," he said when we reached the end of my driveway. He glanced up and down the street, which was deserted. "I know you're not into public displays of affection, but who's here to see." He swept me into his arms and kissed me. He sensed that I was having a hard time pulling away.

Now he had the teasing smile. "I knew you'd come around. Just remember there's plenty more where that came from."

I'd never let on to him, but he was right. He was winning me over. I still felt a little giddy and weak-kneed when I got to the meeting room in the Cypress building. The door to the other room was open and I saw the Silicon Valley group was in there with Sky. It looked like they were working with coloring books.

I put the tin of cookies on the counter and was glad to see that Cloris had left the coffee and tea service. I was afraid she might have decided to use her own judgment about the birthday group's drinks as she had with the other bunch. She'd laid a fresh fire and lit it. It was already taking the chill off the room and adding a nice glow.

Now that I knew Madison was annoyed that I'd put on the mindful workshop, I wanted to make sure any hints of it were gone. I went over the table again to make sure there were no scraps of yarn from their knitting project. I was going to distribute the red tote bags when I realized a snag in my plan. I'd done enough retreats that I should have remembered that people tended to return to the same seats all weekend. Yes, the bags had names on them, but I didn't remember who had been sitting where.

Crystal walked in just as I was staring at the five tote bags and I told her my dilemma.

She shrugged it off and arbitrarily put a bag in front of each of the five chairs.

"They're not in kindergarten. They'll work it out."

"I was hoping to make it seem like everything was as they'd left it. It turns out at least some of our group knows the other group and I know for sure that Madison wasn't happy we put on the workshop for them."

"That's ridiculous. They didn't rent us for the entire weekend."

"I think it's more about Madison's relationship with Elex and his group than her being upset with us." I explained the shared office space and that she was the manager and Elex and his crew were tenants. "I guess they're a real pain to deal with."

"Well, there's one less of them now," Crystal said. Then she realized how cold that sounded. "Sorry. I'm sure everyone is upset about the loss of the guy with light blond hair."

"Tim. His name was Tim and I think one person might not be so sorry he's gone."

Crystal was all ears now, which I noted had an interesting mixture of hoops and dangle earrings that made her head seem a little lopsided. I didn't give her all the details of how I knew what I knew, but just that there was reason to believe, at least to me, that someone might have killed Tim.

"I knew you'd end up sleuthing. Anything I can do to help." She started to go over their group. I was about to tell her about Audrey. Crystal was divorced herself and probably knew a lot more about the emotions connected to it than I did. But this was not the time for it.

"We need to concentrate on what's in front of us. I don't want the birthday group to feel neglected. We can't do the other workshop for the Silicon Valley people in here. I was hoping we could do it at the yarn shop?"

"That would be great. It's easier for me and maybe we can sell them a boatload of yarn. Since it doesn't look like the Delacorte sisters are going to welcome us with open arms, we need to keep the yarn store bringing in the bucks."

"About the sisters," I began. "I ran into Madeleine. She'd just finished up a meeting with Kevin St. John and Lieutenant Borgnine about the so-called accident," I said. "I think she's softening. Kevin in his usual jerkdom said something to her about not worrying her pretty little head about the situation. Madeleine —"

Before I could finish, Crystal interrupted. "He didn't really say that. Let him say it to her when I'm there and I'll let him know that kind of comment doesn't fly."

"That's sort of what Madeleine said. She seemed to like the idea of having some help dealing with everything."

"All she has to do is say the word and I'll tell Kevin he can't talk to her that way. Imagine him saying such a demeaning thing."

Inside I was feeling a little more hopeful that the situation between the sisters and their new family members could be worked out. They all really needed each other. Maybe my meddling would turn out to have been a good thing.

I heard voices coming up the path and threw Crystal a shush. She nodded with understanding and we got ready to welcome back my retreaters.

I guess their noise bothered the mindful coloring going on next door because I heard their door shut with a sharp slap just as my group came in the room.

I counted four of them and was surprised to see that the missing person wasn't Aileen this time. "PJ will be along any minute. She left her jacket somewhere," Madison said. They went right for the drinks and cookies and brought them to the table. As I'd expected, they went back to the same seats they'd had for the first workshop. They didn't seem bothered that the bags were at the wrong seats and merely moved them around until they got to the right people.

When they'd settled in, Crystal started to stand up, but I moved to the head of the table before she could. I'd decided to deal with Madison head-on and clear the air.

I did a few minutes of greeting and said that I'd hoped they were enjoying themselves and then I got to it. "It's come to my attention that some of you were upset that Crystal and I held a workshop for the group next door in this room last night." I looked around the four of them as I spoke.

"I realize it was a mistake to have held it here and I want to apologize. I certainly didn't want to upset any of you. Just to let you know, the other workshop with them won't be here. It'll be off-site and won't interfere with any of your activities." I sounded so formal and businesslike I surprised myself. I looked to Madison and she nodded.

"I understand how Madison knows the Reborn group, but I don't know about the rest of you." I glanced around at the rest of them, as if to offer them the floor.

Aileen spoke first. "If you mean was I insulted that they didn't say hello when we passed each other in the Lodge yesterday?

No. I've seen them in the hall and the lounge at work, but we've never spoken."

"Then you have an office there, too?" I asked.

"Not an office really. I've made it into a classroom. I do home-schooling for people who want to homeschool, but have somebody else do it."

"I think that's called a tutor," Iola said.

"I don't think that's correct since I have five students." She turned to me. "I could have more if I could handle them. Home-schooling is quite popular now because kids have special needs or parents don't want to be forced into getting their kids vaccinated." She laughed at herself. "Listen to me on my soapbox. The point is I'm in the room with the kids or we're out in the world watching tadpoles hatch or something. By the way, PJ just comes for the knit group so I doubt she knows them. We meet in the lounge after hours."

Iola spoke next. She smiled at the surprised looks from the others. "Yes, I can talk when I have something to say.

"As I told you before," Iola said, directing her comment at me, "my husband and I have an online business and we have an office we use to shoot commercials and stuff. I've seen them in the lounge for Nachos

233

Night. Other than not seeming to know how to share, I don't have a beef with them."

PJ came in a little breathless. "Sorry for being late. I couldn't find my jacket and luckily brought a spare," she said, showing that she was wearing a sand-colored jacket. She found her place and sat down.

They all looked to Deani. I did, too, wondering what she was going to say. Deani had not mentioned any connection with Reborn when she'd stopped by the Blue Door. But Iola had told me Deani was their lunch service.

"Aren't you going to say something?" Madison said.

"All right," Deani said finally. "I had a connection with them, but not anymore." She seemed finished, but Madison prodded her.

"You can't leave it like that, what happened?"

"I wasn't supposed to say anything. Well, Tim Moffat kind of insisted that I not say anything, but I suppose it doesn't matter anymore. He's the money guy and I always had to get him to okay their monthly invoice. I met with him on Monday and he said to finish out the month, but then my service was canceled. He wouldn't say why, just that there were likely to be some changes. He said if I didn't keep it to myself, I wouldn't get paid for the last month of lunches. A while ago, he offered to help me get an app done for the service, but I didn't want him in the middle of my business."

I didn't say anything, but thanks to what Audrey Moffat had said I knew what Tim had been talking about. He was leaving and Reborn was going to be out of money.

"Is that why you didn't mention they were customers when you came to the Blue Door?" I asked.

"It was all too weird. You telling me that he'd died. I just wanted to stay out of it." She seemed tense as she looked down at the pink tote and made no pretense to hide Fifi as she reached in and stroked the little dog. I scanned the area outside the door and window and Kevin St. John didn't seem to be lurking in the bushes, so I let it go.

"Tim was the only adult in the group," Madison said. "He was a little older than the rest of them and certainly more businesslike. At least, I think he recognized me." She turned to me. "By the way, I was never really mad at you. It was just when I saw them sitting in our seats last night and they didn't even look up. It was worse than that. Those people walk by me almost every day and when I passed them in the Lodge and went to greet them, it didn't even register. I could have been invisible." She shook her head with dismay.

Crystal was getting fidgety and I noticed she'd looked at her watch a number of times. "Nothing personal, ladies, but we need to get started. You probably won't be able to finish the project this weekend, but you're all accomplished knitters, so once I show you what to do, I'm sure you'll have no problem." She was talking faster than usual. "Let's start by having you take one of the skeins of yarn and your hook." Madison was the only one to take a hook out of her pocket since she'd gotten it the previous night.

They did as requested and then Crystal brought out a sample of the finished shawl made in the same sparkly blue yarn they had. "I picked a project that showed off the benefits of crochet and included the basic stitches." She held up the shawl. "You'll note this is made the long way. It's easy to work the long way with crochet since you're working one stitch at a time, and not easy if you're knitting and you have to put all those stitches on a needle or cable." She waited until they'd all nodded in acknowledgment before continuing.

236

"I like to think that crochet is more playful than knitting. It's so much easier to try different stitches, and if you don't like them just rip them out with ease."

She had them start by making two hundred and forty chain stitches and told them to make a mark on a piece of paper for every twenty chains done so they wouldn't lose their place. The room was completely quiet as they concentrated on their work. When they were done, Crystal had them take out the paper with directions she'd included. It had instructions on how to do the different stitches and the rows of stitches that was repeated until the shawl reached the desired size. She demonstrated single crochet, extended single crochet, half double crochet, double crochet and finally treble crochet. The plan was that they'd finish at least one section with all the different stitches while they were at Vista Del Mar and could do the rest as a group when they went home. I was glad that Crystal had picked up that this group was anxious to do more than yarn craft during the weekend.

They stayed silent as they started the first row of single crochets, but it was a very long row, and once making the stitches became easy, the talking resumed.

"Did anybody notice the guy with the

gruff expression and the rumpled sport jacket?" Deani asked. "He looked kind of out of place, not like a guest."

"That Cadbury's beloved local top cop, Lieutenant Theodore Borgnine," Crystal said with a touch of sarcasm.

"What's a cop doing here?" PJ asked.

"He's probably investigating what happened to Tim," Madison said. "Isn't there always an investigation when there's a death, even if it's an accident?"

"If it really was an accident," Crystal said.

"Huh," Aileen said quickly. "If it wasn't an accident what was it?"

"Then somebody did it, as in killed him," Iola said in her sultry voice.

"Tell them what you told me," Crystal urged, and suddenly I had them all staring at me.

I didn't know what to do. Should I explain or not?

You could say I was saved by the bell. Before I could collect my thoughts, Crystal's watch began to ping. "Sorry, folks, but that means time's up. But the good thing about crochet is that it's easy to stop in the middle of the row, just make note of what stitch you were working on." She went on for a moment explaining about the benefits of taking notes to keep track of where you were in a pattern. "But as knitters, I'm sure you know all about that."

They packed up their things and filed out. As Madison passed me, she leaned in. "I'm sure you'll explain all at dinner."

At least I had some time to figure out what to say.

CHAPTER 19

With everyone gone, I did my usual little cleanup, gathering some scraps of yarn from the table and picking up a couple of paper cups. So much for it being an easy-peasy weekend. I was never going to say that to myself again. It seemed to be the kiss of death, literally. There had been some kind of trouble at every retreat I'd put on.

I regretted that I'd said anything to Crystal about what I thought had happened to Tim. But then who knew she would blab it to the group. Now they were expecting some kind of inside dope from me. Now that I realized so many of them had a connection with the Silicon Valley bunch, I really didn't want to discuss it. I mean, what if one of them was involved?

I straightened the last chair and flipped off the lights before I went outside. The door to the other meeting room was open and I heard the scrape of chairs as they got up. Sky was the first one out of the door. He looked over at me and gave me a friendly smile. "Be sure to tell your retreaters not to miss the Roast and Toast tonight. We're doing it mindful style."

His voice warbled a little when he said it and I picked up that he wasn't all that confident about it. It was another effort by Kevin St. John to take a regular Vista Del Mar activity and make it seem part of their retreat. Sky didn't have to ask me twice. There was no way I was going to miss seeing how he could make roasting marshmallows and toasting with cups of hot chocolate a mindful event.

The rest of the group came out through their door and headed up the path. Elex was in the rear. I noticed he had a softcover book under his arm. He picked up on me looking at it and rolled his eyes. "Mindful coloring," he said with distaste. He started to follow the others on the path and then he stopped.

"As long as we're stuck here, we really need another knitting lesson. I tried to work on mine this afternoon and, well, it's a mess."

"You were planning to leave?" I said.

"It's kind of hard to be mindful after what happened to Tim. But that cop in the rumpled jacket killed that plan." He looked at me intently. "What's with him? Some small-town cop who takes his job too seriously? It was a horrible accident pure and simple, so why keep hassling me with questions. And telling me the group has to stay here for now."

Hearing that Lieutenant Borgnine had put a hold on them and was asking a lot of questions made me believe that what Dane said was true. He was pacifying Kevin St. John by not making a point that it might be something other than an accident, but he was investigating it as though it might be.

"That's too bad. You'd think he'd have some empathy after what happened," I said. When I'd worked for Frank my main job had been making phone calls and getting information people didn't want to give. I figured out that the best way to get it was to be friendly and sympathetic. It was always good if they wanted to complain and were grateful for a willing ear, too.

Elex seemed surprised by my comment, but I noticed his expression relax. "That's what I thought. My business partner and good friend just died and he was grilling me about how Tim ended up walking on the rocks alone." Elex was looking off in the direction of the water. The days were so short at this time of year and the afternoon was fading into darkness. Without a visible sun to set, it was always very subtle. It always made me think of a dimmer switch going off in the sky.

Elex seemed lost in thought and I wondered how I could prod him to continue. I was curious about that walk too. "I never quite understood what the plan for the walk was," I said finally.

"Oh," he said, flinching, and I wondered if he'd forgotten that I was there. "The idea was that we'd walk somewhere on our own and focus on the moment, paying attention to the feeling of the ground, how the wind felt, stuff like that. We all went off in different directions. I had no idea where Tim was going to walk or I would have told him not to."

"And where did you walk?" I asked.

"I followed the roadway that winds through the grounds. And if you want to know what I noticed," he said, sounding like he'd been asked the question before. He offered a very detailed description of the cluster of newer buildings up the slope and a view of the ocean through an opening in the dunes.

"Sounds pretty," I said. "I suppose Lieutenant Borgnine asked you about your relationship with Tim," I said.

His eyes flared when he looked at me this time. "I just said he was my partner and good friend." He eyed me warily. "What's any of this to you?" Then he nodded his head in a knowing manner. "I get it. Didn't your partner in yarn say you played around with being a detective?" He seemed annoyed. "The only thing we need from you is another of those workshops. You said you'd let me know. Well, how about it?"

I was considering suggesting something else he might want to do with his needles when his face softened. "I'm sorry," he said. "This isn't the weekend I imagined for my group. I don't mean to take it out on you. But we really do need another workshop. I tried doing some on my own." He shook his head and smiled, thinking about it. "I somehow joined the two ends together and now it's a tube."

I was glad I hadn't made my comment about the knitting needles. Of course it made sense that he'd be stressed and upset after what happened and I knew more about it than he thought I did. I told him about the plan of having it at the yarn shop and he agreed. We agreed on a time for Saturday. "Don't worry, we'll undo the tube and show you what you did wrong so you won't do it again."

The dinner bell began to ring and he thanked me and went on up the path ahead of me.

I made a pit stop in the Lodge to use the phone to call Cadbury Yarn. Now that Elex had agreed, I wanted to make sure the time worked for them.

"Cadbury Yarn, we're closed," Gwen said when she answered. It was a real person and not a recording. I announced myself and she laughed. "For you we're still open. What's up? Please tell me it's not some problem with the Delacorte sisters." She stopped and continued in a fierce voice, "I didn't realize how difficult they are. They can't seem to understand that I don't want any of their fortune. I just want Cory to be connected to Vista Del Mar because he has such an instinctive love of the place."

I agreed they could be difficult but urged her to give it some time. "Just let it mellow for a while," I said. "At least through the weekend."

"You're right," she said. I heard her say good night to a customer. "Crystal already mentioned doing a workshop for that group. She said something about being mindful.

We'll set up some space for them and the two of you can do whatever you want. Tomorrow afternoon is fine." She suggested setting up a yarn tasting, as she called having the opportunity to play with different yarns, but I told her they weren't ready for that. However, I thought they might be interested in any kits she had for basic projects.

It was completely dark when I walked out of the Lodge. It didn't matter because the smell of hot food was like a magnet and led me right to the Sea Foam dining hall. The dinner bell had stopped ringing and I could see there was already a crowd inside.

Kevin St. John had done a good job of keeping it quiet about Tim's death. There was a din of lively conversation and everything seemed like a typical Friday night.

The food smelled delicious and I remembered I'd only eaten a few cookies all day. It would have been nice to sit down to a plate of comfort food, but I had a feeling that wasn't going to happen.

Deani, Madison, Aileen and PJ were at the same table they'd sat at before. I scanned the room and saw that Iola was sitting with the bird group again. She seemed quite animated and took a fork of her food and offered it to a man in a khaki vest. He smiled as he accepted it and then she went back to talking to the people around her. Talk about not judging a book by its cover — she was so plain as if to be almost colorless, but she was full of surprises. First the sultry voice and now she seemed to be playing up to some man. It was not my problem and I turned back to my group. I was hoping they'd forgotten that I promised to tell them what I knew about the investigation, but when I saw all four of them look at me with eager faces, I figured it was still on their minds.

I greeted them and saw that they'd already gotten their food. The meat loaf, mashed potatoes and peas looked delicious. My stomach rumbled, reminding me of how hungry I was.

"I'll just get a plate of food and join you," I said, leaving my jacket on one of the empty chairs. A reprieve for a few minutes so I could think over what to say.

I went through the entrance at the back of the room to the cafeteria line. Audrey Moffat was just ahead of me. She was looking over the food with the concern of someone who was used to having everything customized for her. I suspected she was super diligent about her diet and probably cringed at the butter pooling in the crater on top of

247

the mashed potatoes.

"It's all delicious," I said from behind her. She turned and smiled when she saw it was me.

"I never eat food like this. Fish or chicken and steamed vegetables with a dab of rice is my usual dinner. Every restaurant we went to would prepare what I wanted just the way I wanted it." She looked over the counter into the kitchen with the steam tables of food. "They don't work that way here, do they?"

She looked a little too thin and maybe a little peaked, too. But far be it from me to tell other people what to do. I saw that Cloris was working in the kitchen and I called her over. She remembered Audrey from the café and knew the situation. I explained Audrey's desire and Cloris shrugged.

"Don't say anything to the boss, but I can put something together for you." She nodded to Audrey, who turned to me.

"You have a lot of clout around here." Her shoulders dropped and her expression seemed tired. While we waited for Cloris to do her magic, I asked Audrey where she was going to sit. I couldn't really invite her to join the birthday girls, but I hated to see her sit alone. "I'll sit with the Reborn crew."

248

Cloris slid a plate over the counter with slices of chicken breast and a collection of steamed vegetables. There was just the tiniest dab of mashed potatoes, and she explained they didn't have any rice. "It's all about amounts. A little taste won't do you any harm."

Audrey thanked Cloris and me and took her tray and left. I thanked Cloris again.

"Mr. St. John has a hard time bending any rules. Sometimes you just have to. It's all about what our guests want."

"You're going to have a big career in the hospitality industry," I said.

"Probably not here," Cloris said, dropping her voice. "Mr. St. John isn't happy with the extras I do."

"Don't count it out," I said. "You never know what might happen."

Cloris made me a plate of food and I headed back to the table. Audrey had joined the Reborn crew, as she called them. I was curious about the dynamic. Elex seemed very cordial. He helped her with her tray and he pulled out the seat next to him. Julie was glaring at her from across the table. Josh and Jackson seemed more interested in their food.

The four occupants of my table watched me as I sat down and then Madison jumped in. "Tell us what you know about what happened to Tim. You implied it might not have been an accident."

Since Crystal wasn't there to contradict me, I kept it real simple. "Until the official ruling on the manner of death, everything is on the table," I said.

She looked disappointed. "Crystal made it sound like you were on the trail of something."

I saw Sammy walk into the dining hall. He kind of stood out since he had a tall teddy-bear build and he was the only one in a tuxedo. He came directly to our table and held up a bag. It actually said "bag of tricks" on the outside.

"Ready? It's showtime," he said to me before turning to the four women. He introduced himself and made a theatrical bow. "I'm afraid I have to steal Case away. I can't do the show without her."

I grabbed a bite of meat loaf and offered my apologies before leaving. He'd developed a corny show for the close-up magic he did as he circulated around the room. It was all in good fun and everybody loved it. I played the stooge, who in the middle of a card trick dropped the deck of cards and he'd joke, "And magically the cards are all on the floor." Of course, while everyone was watching me pick them up, he'd complete the trick he'd started.

"Kevin wanted me to start with his retreat group." He looked around the room and I subtly pointed them out.

When we got to the table, Sammy introduced himself and me. I saw a few eye rolls from Elex. Audrey appeared attentive. I'm sure she felt it was the least she could do after how much I'd listened to her in the café and the dinner I'd managed to get for her. Julie seemed bored. Jackson looked up from his meal with mild interest. Josh had an unhappy expression.

Sammy started things off by making the monarch butterfly appear from my hair. He'd made flowers and quarters appear from diners' hair and ears in the past, but Kevin St. John had gotten worried about people being upset about being touched and potential lawsuits. So all the stuff appearing from body parts was done to me.

Sammy did some card tricks. The comedy stuff caught them off guard and Sammy seemed to have won over the table, except for Josh. I don't think it was Sammy's act. Josh seemed lost in his own upset. He barely looked at Sammy and when he did, he glared at him.

Sammy did all the standard tricks with

magic wands turning into bunches of flowers and a rabbit (a toy one) appeared from a hat. I knew he was going to finish with pulling out the silks. I noticed that Josh was eyeing Sammy's pocket.

"Aren't you finished yet?" Josh said in a petulant tone. "Maybe you need some help." Sammy was lost in his patter and didn't seem to hear Josh. Then I understood that he was going to pull the silks out of Sammy's pocket to try to mess up Sammy's performance. I'm sure everyone knew that Sammy had stuff up his sleeves and in his pockets, but having someone point it out ruined the show.

I was trying to think of a way to stop Josh, but before I could do anything, Sammy turned to him. "There's something that I've never tried before, but I believe I can turn you into a magician." He waved his wand over Josh's head. "Now reach in my pocket and I bet you can make silks appear," Sammy said.

"Hey, man, I'm not in the mood," Josh said. He pushed back his chair and stormed past Kevin St. John, who'd just come in. The manager glanced from Josh to me with an accusatory grimace.

I knew how much doing the magic at Vista

Del Mar meant to Sammy. I had to make it right and rushed out after Josh.

CHAPTER 20

The small lights along the side of the pathway were meant to show the boundaries but did little to illuminate the space in between. There was no sign of Josh at first. I kept going in the direction I thought he'd taken and caught sight of him as he walked up the stairs to the deck outside the Lodge.

I was intent on reaching him and hadn't even considered what I'd say when I did. I was sure his reaction hadn't really been aimed at Sammy, but more likely was caused by some internal upset. But that didn't mean he wouldn't blame it on Sammy.

What did I know about Josh other than he had a really bad zit on his forehead? I'd have to use the skills I'd developed working for Frank. Make friends and be a sympathetic ear.

The interior of the Lodge was quiet because most everyone was still at dinner. I noticed the guy I'd met the first day — the one whose name made me think of peanut butter — was sitting with someone in the area by the fireplace. They had papers spread out around them.

I surveyed the whole room for Josh, and when I didn't see him, checked the café. He was just paying for a bottle of beer. I waited until he took it to a table before I approached.

"Hey, Josh," I said, standing next to him.

"What are you doing here?" he said. He took a gulp of the beer and let out a sigh.

"Bad night, huh?" I hoped my face had a sympathetic expression. "I just wanted to apologize. It seemed like the entertainment made it worse."

My words worked like magic, real magic. His eyes widened and his mouth softened as he gazed up at me.

"I guess I acted like a jerk. Sorry." His face might have lost the angry expression, but his shoulders were still stooped and he had the look of defeat about him. He looked like the stereotype of a techie type with no vanity when it came to his appearance. The black turtleneck was baggy, as were his pants. He probably just kept his dark hair cut short enough so he didn't have to comb it.

"Is there anything I can do to help?" I

said. I pointed to the chair and asked if I could sit. He seemed a little awkward as he answered with a nod.

He drank some more of the beer and let out a few sighs, which made me believe he was thinking before he spoke. "No one knows this," he said finally. He paused again. It seemed like he was having some kind of internal battle. Of course, what he'd said had fired up my imagination and I really wanted to know now. I couldn't let it show, though. Then he definitely wouldn't say any more. I decided to see if I could prime the pump.

"Does it have anything to do with what happened to Tim?" I asked in a calm voice. There was a light in his dark eyes and I knew I'd hit something.

"I suppose I could tell you. You're not involved with our business." He looked around the area, which was deserted. "It's just so unfair. I was about to get a really big opportunity and then just like that it's gone. And no matter what Elex says, without Tim, Reborn is on life support."

"Was the opportunity connected to Tim?" I asked.

"He's was going to leave and take me with him," he said with a gush of breath.

I already knew that Tim was leaving and

taking his financial backing with him, but I didn't know he had been taking anyone with him. Audrey hadn't had any details of what Tim was going to do.

"Was it going to be something similar to Reborn?" I asked.

"Tim kept it close to the vest and never told me what it was, just that it was going to be really big. A lot of stealing of ideas goes on so I wasn't surprised he kept me in the dark. Tim was money and idea. I was going to be the tech guy."

I thought back to seeing Tim's room when I'd dropped off the goodie bag. His computer had come on and I'd gotten a glimpse of something. Now I realized it was probably what he was working on.

I considered if I should tell Josh about the key man insurance policy, thinking it might reassure him, but it also might seem odd that I knew about it. I decided to leave it be. What I did say was that Elex seemed optimistic about the company's future, hoping that would make him feel more positive.

"Elex thought this retreat would make us more of a team. But so far everybody is still sniping at each other. Julie thinks we're all against her and Jackson thinks he's superior to me. I was so looking forward to seeing Jackson's face when I announced I was leav-

ing. But that's not going to happen now."
He pushed the empty glass away. "Hey,
thanks for talking to me. I feel better now."

It was mission accomplished. I was confident he wouldn't be complaining about
Sammy, and if I'd lifted his spirits, all the
better. I pushed back my chair to get up.
"One more thing," he said. "You know
anything I can do about this?" He pointed
to the prominent red spot in the middle of
his forehead.

Sammy had finished working the room by
the time I got back and was ready to leave.
The dining room had cleared out and a
cleaning crew were going through the tables.
My plate of food was long gone and the
kitchen was closed. Cloris would have gotten me something to eat, but she'd been
doing so many extra things for me, I didn't
want to bother her. I'd fill up on marshmallows and hot chocolate at the Roast and
Toast Mindful Style.

I apologized to Sammy for leaving him in
the lurch before explaining what I'd done,
including the pit stop to get some cover-up
for the zit. "Thanks for looking out for me.
Case, you're the best," he said as we walked
to the door together.

I decided to hang around until the Roast

and Toast. When Sammy and I reached the steps to the deck outside the Lodge, I said I was going in. There was an awkward moment when we stood facing each other. Sammy thanked me again for all my help. There might not be a sizzle in his kiss, but there was a soft spot in my heart for Sammy. I reached out and gave him a hug, but I pulled away quickly. The truth was I felt comfortable and safe in his arms.

I climbed the wide stairs to the wooden deck knowing he was still standing there. The dark wood of the building almost melted into the darkness with just rectangles of light coming out of the windows.

It was a completely different scene than I'd walked into when I'd been running after Josh. It was filled with people, and instead of silence there was a loud din of conversation. The rustic chandeliers offered bright light and the amber-colored glass shades on the table lamps tempered the harshness with a warm glow. Someone had added wood to the fireplace and the fire burned brightly. There seemed to be people everywhere. Card games were going on at some of the small tables spread around the room. I heard the thwack of Ping-Pong balls and some cheers as someone made a particularly good shot.

I noticed Lieutenant Borgnine coming out of the door that led to the business area. He wasn't alone. The lone woman member of the Silicon Valley group was with him. I tried to read their expressions to figure what had been going on. Lieutenant Borgnine had his usual gruff expression and she glanced around, seeming uncomfortable. They parted company and she slipped out the door on the driveway side of the building.

The cop in the rumpled jacket saw me and looked away. I thought he was going to slip back into the business office, but I caught up with him first.

"Aren't you supposed to be at the Blue Door baking?" he said.

"It's too early. I go in when the restaurant closes," I said. "What brings you to Vista Del Mar? Investigating Tim Moffat's fall, perhaps?"

"That's for me to know and you to not find out," he said. "Just because I let you go with me the other night doesn't mean you have access to any information."

"It was more like you came with me," I began. "If you recall, I had the luminol and my knitting took us to the exact spot where he'd fallen." I glanced around the room. "But I don't need your information. I have

260

a lot of my own."

"Oh, no, Ms. Feldstein, we agreed you weren't going to get involved in this," he said, dropping his voice.

I probably should have just walked away, but I couldn't resist dangling that I had information he might not know. He jumped for the bait.

"You have to tell me," he said in a stern voice. "Withholding information is interfering with an investigation. I'm sure you wouldn't want to spend your night in a jail cell."

"You wouldn't," I said, regretting that I'd let on I might know something he didn't. And he nodded with a smile. He was probably bluffing, but I couldn't afford the chance that he wasn't.

He gestured for me to follow him and led me to an empty spot next to the row of phone booths, which seemed to offer a little privacy. "Okay, spill," he commanded.

"Did you know that Tim Moffat's wife is in the process of getting a divorce? Pretty convenient for her that he died while they're still married. And she seems in a rush to get him cremated." That wasn't everything, but hopefully enough to keep me a free woman.

"Hmm, I didn't know the rush to get him cremated part. But it's not going to happen until the investigation is closed." He looked at me intently. "Anything else you want to share?"

I debated telling him that my retreaters came from the same area and their paths had crossed Tim's. It seemed disloyal somehow. He noted me hesitating and of course figured out that I was holding something back. "Ms. Feldstein," he said in a warning tone, "don't make me use them." He'd opened his jacket to show the handcuffs hanging from his belt. I didn't even know that he traveled equipped. I had to throw him something else, preferably something he already knew.

"I found out that Tim was the money guy for the company." I watched the lieutenant get a smug smile. I knew he was thinking that he had so much more information than me. I decided it was best to leave it that way.

"Are you staying for the Roast and Toast?" I asked and he almost growled.

"I have important business to attend to. There's no time for roasting marshmallows." He uttered a terse good night and turned on his heel.

Kevin St. John walked up to the massive wood counter that separated the registration area from the large room. He surveyed the crowd and made one vain attempt to get everyone's attention before banging on the counter. The noise cut through the din of conversation and everyone turned in his direction. Sky had just come in and the manager waved for him to join him. "The Roast and Toast will be starting in a few minutes. Tonight in honor of our retreat group from Silicon Valley, we're having a Roast and Toast Mindful Style." Sky had reached his side. They certainly made an odd pair. Kevin St. John in his formal-looking black suit and Sky in yoga pants, a T-shirt and bare feet.

"And don't forget, tomorrow night our Saturday special event is a Sound Bath," Sky said. Someone yelled out asking what a sound bath was and Sky smiled. "It has to be experienced to be understood."

Sky crossed the room toward the door that led out on the deck and waved for everyone to follow him.

I joined the throng going out the door. The fire circle was located just before the dunes began. It wasn't really a circle and was more like a half-oval-shaped enclosure. A layer of glass kept the wind out and rows of benches made a square shape around a firepit. I stood back as the crowd moved in and found seats. The area was lit by a few spotlights when something was going on and I watched the crowd for familiar faces.

It was easy to pick out Madison. She was the only guest with pink hair. Deani followed her and had her pink tote. I wondered if Fifi was inside. More people moved along the benches. I thought I might have seen Iola, but she didn't have any outstanding feature that made her stand out. Though the activity had been touted as being in honor of Kevin St. John's retreat people, I didn't see any of them at first. Though with their black clothes they did blend in with the darkness. Finally, I spotted Julie. She hardly appeared enthused and I wondered what Lieutenant Borgnine had gotten out of her.

Kevin St. John directed someone from the kitchen staff to roll in a cart and park it near the firepit. He seemed ready to start. I took one last survey of the crowd and what I saw totally surprised me and made me wonder. Elex and Audrey had come into the fire circle. They were walking close together and it seemed like they might have been holding hands. I couldn't tell for sure because of all the shadows.

The manager started recapping what he'd said in the Lodge about the specialness of this Roast and Toast. Then he waved for Sky

264

to join him. Even in the semi darkness I could make out Sky's hesitation before he walked to join the manager. He began with an explanation for the people not part of Elex's group who might have no idea what mindfulness was.

"Being mindful means focusing on the moment and using all your senses." As he offered some examples, I kept watching the pair trying to determine what was going on between them.

"What are you looking at?" a male voice asked. I turned just as Jackson climbed over the bench and sat next to me.

I pointed to Elex and Audrey. "Do you know anything about that?" He was staring now too.

"You mean like are they together?" he asked, still staring. "I don't know. He's single and I guess she is now." He shook his head. "I don't know."

"Am I right that Elex and Tim were partners?" I figured why waste the opportunity to see what I could find out since Jackson was sitting there.

He shrugged noncommittally. "Elex had the ideas, but Tim brought in the bucks. Yeah, I guess you could call them partners. But Elex was the one who made the decisions. Honestly, I didn't know Tim that well.

I could never figure why he seemed to favor Josh. I'm so much better at everything than he is." Jackson sounded angry and I suddenly had a feeling that he knew Tim had offered a job to Josh. "Let's see what this doofus does with marshmallows."

We both turned our attention to Sky, who was holding up a marshmallow. "In mindfulness we get lost in the moment. Tonight we have a moment of marshmallow." He got a couple of volunteers to pass out the marshmallows.

"Now that you all have them, feel how spongy they are. You can smell the sweetness." He held his marshmallow to his nose and urged the audience to do the same. "But when you add fire, the marshmallow transforms." He stabbed his marshmallow with a long fork and put it in the fire. He must have missed the lesson that it was roasting marshmallows, not burning them. Instead of turning a soft brown with an oozing inside, his caught on fire and in moments turned into black ash with maybe a dab of sweet fluff on the inside.

"The final mindful moment comes with the tasting." He blew on it until it was cool and prepared to put it in his mouth. "You savor the flavor." He took a bite of it and was speechless for a moment. I don't think he was savoring the flavor. It was more like choking on the ash.

He lost control of the crowd as they moved toward the firepit, grabbing long forks and cooking their marshmallows.

When the hot chocolate was passed out, he wanted everyone to take some in their mouth and swirl it around, letting their senses take in the flavor and the fragrance of the now lukewarm drink.

"Hey, it's not wine," someone called out. Sky seemed dumbfounded by the heckler. If I were him, I would have turned it into a mindful moment that focused on the heckler's bad manners.

Kevin St. John finally stepped in and reminded the crowd of the movie afterward.

Movies were a Friday night ritual as well. Hummingbird Hall was transformed into a movie theater complete with bags of popcorn. I wondered what the movie choice was. Had Kevin St. John found something that went along with the mindful theme? I laughed when he said, "In honor of the mindful retreat, tonight's feature is *A Beautiful Mind.*"

I heard Jackson laugh next to me. "Really? He's a doofus, too. Does he think everything with mind in it is about mindfulness?"

Everyone started to file out. I tried to see

what Audrey and Elex's hands were doing as they left, but I still couldn't tell. When they'd all gone I approached Sky. He looked desolate "That was a bust," he said. I couldn't argue with him.

"I was really trying to get the yoga business from Vista Del Mar. When people put on retreats and needed a local yoga instructor, I hoped Mr. St. John would recommend me. He talked me into being a facilitator for this mindful thing as an audition. He makes up a ridiculous program and then expects me to make it a success. Mindful marshmallows, really?" He shook his head with hopelessness. "My only hope is pulling off the Sound Bath." I had the same question someone had shouted out before and asked him what it was. "Words can't describe it. You have to experience it to understand."

I left him to gather up the roasting forks. I still had miles to go before I slept.

I cut through the Lodge, which was quiet again. Apparently, the crowd had gone with the movie offer. The café was just closing and Jackson walked out holding a bottle of beer.

"That was underwhelming," he said, gesturing toward the firepit. After what Sky had told me, I wanted to somehow defend him. While I was considering what to say,

Jackson continued. "His name isn't really Sky, you know. I think it's Bob or Robert. He told me he'd developed an app. Something weird like setting up dog playdates. Turns out he got angel funding from our own dead Tim. But it all crashed and burned. Hence his new name and new profession." He smiled to himself. "*Hence* is such a great word. Don't you think people should use it more often?"

I was too busy thinking about Sky's connection to Tim to answer.

CHAPTER 21

I was free to go, but my night was far from over. I was looking forward to the peace of baking at the Blue Door. Just me with flour, sugar, eggs and more. Who was I kidding? Ever since it'd become public knowledge that I was going to be there working on desserts and muffins, it had become a guessing game of who would show up. Last night's visit from Deani wasn't one that I would have even considered.

Downtown Cadbury was a little livelier since it was Friday night and the restaurants stayed open a little later. The lights on the movie theater marquee went off just as I was parking my Mini Cooper.

The first thing I always did as I walked into the restaurant was to check the front counter for the status of the desserts I'd made the night before. I was always relieved when there were just crumbs left on the pedestal-stand plates. It was silly, but I always worried something would happen, like the whole town would decide to go on a diet and give up dessert. I guess part of my fear was that nobody would even tell me and I'd walk in to find the whole cakes and pies I'd made the night before. I laughed inside at my own ridiculous thoughts.

The main dining room was empty except for a pair of diners at the end of their meal. Tag was standing in a corner staring at the table with a tense expression. Lucinda was next to him and her arm was on his, restraining him. I glanced back at the occupied table and found the subject of his distress. The man had set his coffee cup on the table instead of back on the saucer. It was just the sort of gaffe that drove Tag crazy.

Lucinda gave in to his obsessive behavior most of the time, letting him follow behind the servers as they set up the tables and he straightened any knife or fork at a tilt. But when it came to his rearranging customers' settings, she drew the line.

I heard her sigh of relief as the pair left their table and passed me on their way to the door. Tag was on it before the door even closed. My boss and friend came across the small room to join me. She looked down at their story on the back of the menu sitting on the counter and shook her head. "If they only knew . . ."

Even though it was the end of the evening, she still had fresh lipstick and every hair in place. Without actual knowledge, I assumed the same couldn't be said for me. I didn't even remember if I'd smoothed my hair after the boat trip in the morning.

She added the menu to the stack and grabbed one of the recycled grocery bags that had my supplies for the muffins, and we went across the dining area. "I really could have used a yarn retreat this weekend."

"Sorry I couldn't include you. I certainly miss your presence." In the past Lucinda had been my partner in crime, or really partner in solving a crime. She was my sounding board, and on occasion my lookout when I went somewhere I wasn't really allowed. That didn't even cover all the times she acted as host at meals because I was otherwise occupied.

"Did something happen?" she asked in a whisper, stopping on the sunporch.

"So much," I said. I was trying to figure out how to begin when Tag called to her from the door. He was suddenly frantic that he'd left the coffeepot on at home. She rolled her eyes at me.

"The pot shuts itself off after an hour, but once he gets a thought that he's left something on there's no reasoning with him. I really want to hear about everything." He had the door open and was beginning to hyperventilate. "Got to go. The kitchen's all yours."

It was always a bonus when I didn't have to deal with the chef. I continued on into the kitchen and put down the bags. I went back into the dining area to turn on the soft jazz I liked as an accompaniment.

I glanced toward the glass portion of the front door after I'd adjusted the radio. Dane was standing with his face inches from the glass. I opened the door with anticipation, hoping he'd brought food.

He was in uniform, so it was break time. I looked down at his hands but they were empty. My expression must have told it all.

"What's wrong?" he said, glancing around the interior for the source of a problem.

"You came empty-handed," I said.

He smiled and rocked his head. "I knew it. It's all about the food I bring."

I put up my hand to stop him. "You know I always love to see you, but remember when you came over and I gave you some cookies? Well, the couple that I ate were it for me today." I told him how I only got a bite of dinner and the disappointment of the Roast and Toast.

"What do you want?" he asked.

"Anything but something sweet. Making all this sweet stuff has kind of turned me off to it."

"You do realize we're standing in a restaurant."

"I'd feel funny about using any of their food."

"Do you really think your friend Lucinda would begrudge you some eggs and toast?" he said, taking the lead back to the kitchen.

"You're probably right. It's just that —"

"Oh, no, you, the dessert and muffin queen, don't know how to scramble eggs?" he said, incredulous.

"I know *how* to scramble eggs in principle, but they never turn out." He laughed and waved me out of his way.

"Carry on with what you were doing and I'll make the eggs."

Lucinda had requested my cherry cheesecake, which was fine with me. I went to the refrigerator just as Dane came away from it holding eggs and butter. We played the game of trying to stay out of each other's way, but we kept ending up facing each other.

"Is this where I ask you to dance?" he said with a merry expression. "If it is, you have to change the music. You can't dance to jazz."

I put the cream cheese on the counter. "This needs to get soft anyway. The kitchen is yours."

He made delicious pasta and sauce for the kids who came for karate and for me, but his skills went way back. Due to her problem, his mother had been undependable, to say the least, and he'd taken over making sure they were fed. He'd made sure to tell me that no one guessed how he carried the responsibility of his family and that he had the image of a bad boy.

"It's kind of fun cooking in a restaurant," he said as he swirled the butter in the pan to melt. Since I couldn't get on with my duties, I set up a table for us in the sun-porch.

He brought out plates of eggs and toast with artistically sliced strawberries as a garnish. "This is what happens when you let me loose in a place with gourmet tools."

I ate my eggs and most of his. Like everything else he cooked, they were amazing. I let out a contented sigh. Then I turned to him. "As long as we're sitting here," I began. "You have your ear to the ground. You must hear things."

"Sure. When I'm not giving someone a

ticket for littering."

"Do you have any updates on the lieutenant's investigation? Like if it turns out to be a homicide, who he thinks of as suspects?"

"I'm just food and information to you," he said. His grin let me know he was joking. "Actually, I don't know much of anything. When I saw the lieutenant earlier, he clammed up as soon as he saw me."

"I was considering if I should share some information with him that he might not know."

Dane suddenly looked serious. "Don't do it. He won't take it well." He reached across the table and touched my hand. "How about we talk about something else, like why don't you come by when the karate kids are there. We could use a feminine touch."

"Are you kidding? Do you remember how they teased us?"

"Maybe they did. I didn't care, but if it bothers you, how about this then. We work it out so we have a day off together. I know this place up near Santa Cruz with a forest of redwoods. So tall you can't see the tops and they're thousands of years old. It kind of puts things in perspective. There's a river, too. And no one to tease us if we hold hands."

His mention of holding hands made me

think of Audrey and Elex. "I wonder if they're a couple," I mumbled to myself. "And if so, for how long."

"What?" Dane said, leaning closer to hear. Then he blew out his breath. "You weren't commenting on my offer, were you?" I shook my head with an apologetic smile. "It had something to do with what you said earlier, right?" I nodded. "You just can't keep your mind off of crime."

"Guilty," I said. "But the redwood forest sounds wonderful. Let's work it out."

Dane's radio crackled and there was something about an altercation at a fast-food restaurant over undercooked fries. "That's the life of a small-town cop." He threw up his hands as he got up.

"Don't you owe me a hug?" he said.

"Probably," I said with a chuckle. "I suppose you want to collect it now." He nodded and opened his arms.

I stepped into his embrace and one thing led to another. The hug turned into a kiss and then a hotter one. There was some touchy feeling stuff going on, too. I'm not sure what would have happened if there hadn't been a knock on the glass. It brought me back to the present and I pulled away with a jump.

He insisted on acting as my protector as

we went back into the main dining area. The light on the porch illuminated two figures. Crystal and Madeleine.

Dane opened the door and I invited them in.

"Cora doesn't even know I left the house," Madeleine said with a giggle. Her eyes were bright with excitement. "Crystal said she'd show me the other side of Cadbury. What goes on when the town is asleep." She looked at Dane with puzzlement. "Why is there a policeman here? Is something wrong?"

Was Madeleine the only one in town who didn't know that Dane and I were sort of an item? Crystal held in a laugh and rolled her eyes.

"No, nothing wrong here," Dane said in an upbeat voice. "I just stopped by for a muffin report." He turned to me. "I hope you can drop some by my place on your way home. There's nothing like a hot blueberry muffin."

Madeleine seemed perplexed by his comment and I reminded her that in addition to the desserts for the restaurant, I baked muffins for the coffee spots around town.

"I'll leave you to it," Dane said, giving me a cheeky salute. "Got to keep the streets of Cadbury safe for you ladies."

Madeleine watched him go. "He's kind of cute. I think he likes you."

Crystal and I traded glances and I shook my head, hoping she wouldn't tell Madeleine the real situation. I quickly tried to change the subject. "How did the two of you end up going out together?" They certainly made an interesting pair. Crystal had a shocking pink shawl over her outfit. She was still wearing the mismatched earrings that made her look lopsided. I assumed her socks didn't match, but she had sheepskin boots on so it was impossible to tell.

Madeleine wore faded jeans, a white shirt tucked in the front only with a jean jacket. She noticed me looking at the colorful shawl wrapped over the jacket. "It's Crystal's. She thought I might be cold." Madeleine looked at the younger woman with a warm expression.

"Cora is being a real pill about finding out that Crystal's mother is our brother's child." She reached over and patted Crystal's arm. "She can do what she wants, but it doesn't mean I have to. I saw Crystal leaving the yarn store and told her that I'd like to spend some time with her. She suggested this adventure." She glanced around the closed restaurant. "This is only part of it.

We already went to the all-night grocery store in Carmel."

I was already behind schedule, but since the cheesecakes didn't require baking, it was okay. "I'll give you the grand tour," I said, leading them back to the kitchen.

Madeleine seemed mesmerized as I began to mix the cream cheese and whipped cream for the cheesecake and then she began to talk about Vista Del Mar. "The accident with that poor man dying was just terrible. I hope Kevin is handling it properly." Madeleine made a tsk sound. "He insisted that he could handle putting together that retreat and didn't need anyone in your position," she said, looking at me. "I didn't think it was a good idea, but Cora gave him the okay. She's old school and thinks that men are supposed to run the world." She smiled at her newfound grand-niece. "Crystal told me those people in the black clothes weren't happy with what Kevin planned and that the two of you had to add some activities and provide them with some extras." She made another tsk sound. "Wait until I tell Cora about that. Maybe that'll give her something to think about."

I froze. Was I going to end up in the middle of a battle between all of them? I was sure to be the one who came out badly.

I rushed to try to smooth things over and urged her to let things be for the weekend. "There's no reason to stir things up now."

"You're probably right," Madeleine said.

Crystal's eyes were flaring. "You mean Cora lets Kevin St. John run things because he's a man?"

"Not totally. But he keeps saying that he understands how to run Vista Del Mar better than we do and she believes him," Madeleine said.

"Somebody needs to bring Cora into the modern age," Crystal said.

Crystal and Madeleine stayed until I'd made the graham cracker crusts and poured in the filling for the cheesecakes before moving on. Crystal was going to take Madeleine to the McDonald's drive-through in Seaside for a soft-serve ice cream cone to cap their evening. Thankfully that was the end of my company and I was able to hustle through making the cheesecakes. Despite what Dane had said about blueberry muffins, I made more of the biscuit muffins. I hadn't heard any feedback on them yet and hoped they were a hit.

I rushed through distributing them to the coffee spots along Grand Street and then drove home. All seemed peaceful and quiet as I got out of my Mini Cooper. But before

I could go to my back door I heard a rustling in the bushes that surrounded my house.

My heartbeat kicked up, but then I figured it was probably Dane coming to collect his muffins. "I know you're in there. Come out," I commanded.

A moment later Deani revealed herself. "Sorry if I scared you," she said. "It was an automatic reaction when I heard someone drive up." She looked toward the guesthouse. "I was just coming to check on Fifi."

I looked down at the tote bag she was carrying. In the dark I couldn't tell if the dog was in the bag or the guesthouse as she implied, but I gave her the benefit of the doubt. She wished me good night and then hustled down the driveway and across the street.

I finally went to my back door. When I opened it a slip of paper fell out. I waited until I was in the light to check it out. The smell of the marker lingered on the page. Sprawled in big letters it said: KEEP YOUR NOSE OUT OF WHERE IT DOESN'T BELONG. BAD CONSEQUENCES IF YOU DON'T.

CHAPTER 22

"Hold on a second, Feldstein, you lost me. Who's Jackson? And I thought the plan was to sit this one out."

I took a sip of coffee and tried to center myself. Frank was right, I was throwing too many things at him at once because that's the way they were in my mind. As soon as I'd awakened that Saturday morning I'd called him. I didn't have Lucinda to talk things over with and I couldn't trust Crystal not to blab.

I'd started with the threatening note, but before Frank could react I'd gone on talking about the previous night. I'd left out the whole Roast and Toast since there was a good chance my former boss would have fixated on the marshmallows and hot chocolate.

I took a deep breath and tried again.

"I was thinking about staying out of it, but information keeps falling into my lap.

That's where Jackson comes in. He's one of the people in the mindfulness retreat. Last night I found out that he felt slighted by the dead guy. And then there's Sky."

"Sky?" Frank said, sputtering. I had a feeling some liquid had just sprayed out around the area where Frank was sitting. "Who's he and what does he have to do with any of this?"

"He's the facilitator the manager hired to handle the mindfulness activities. Turns out he has a connection to the dead guy, too. And his wife showed up — the dead guy's wife, not Sky's." I explained her almost-divorced status. "Tim, that's the dead guy, was the money guy for the business. I'm pretty sure he was personally loaded. She seemed anxious to make arrangements for him to be cremated."

"Sounds like she wants to get rid of some evidence. It's certainly convenient for her that she's still his wife. She probably gets everything and she could be the beneficiary of an insurance policy," he said.

The mention of the insurance policy made me think of Elex and what Audrey had said about the policy where Elex got a bunch of cash. Frank knew all about key man policies. "I heard that Tim, the —"

"I got it, Feldstein," Frank said, cutting

me off, "the dead guy's name is Tim. You can just refer to him by his name for the rest of our call. As you were about to say . . ."

"Well, I heard that he was going to tell Elex during the weekend that he was leaving the business and some funding they were expecting would go with him."

"Do you know if he told him?" Frank asked.

"His wife — Tim's wife — thought that he would have wanted to tell Elex right away, so I'm guessing that he did." I took a moment to breathe. "And it turns out my retreat people, at least most of them, had some connection to Tim, too." I was about to give him the lowdown on Tim canceling Deani's food delivery service, but Frank stopped me.

"Here we go again with you throwing too much info at me. Here's what I think. You're probably right that it wasn't an accident, and if someone bothered to leave a threatening note, you must be stepping on some toes. Though a threat in a note seems like something out of Nancy Drew's playbook. If I wanted to scare somebody off, I'd throw in a dead something. Even better, one of those life-size rat gummies. Better shock value than the real thing. Or from the way you make that hotel sound, you could probably just pick up something dead out of the bushes."

"I'm glad whoever it is doesn't have the same mind-set you do," I said. The note was jarring enough. A dead anything would have given me pause, but he was right that a life-size gummie candy in the shape of a rat was the worst. The idea of candy and rat would have made me throw up.

"So, you didn't go running to your cop friend for protection?" Frank asked with a chortle.

"I can take care of myself," I said, leaving out that showing up at Dane's house in the middle of the night would put me in jeopardy for another kind of trouble.

"You said the information keeps falling into your lap. Does anyone know you're investigating?" Paper rattled on his end and I assumed it was food-related. It was a little early for lunch in Chicago, but Frank was known to have a midmorning hoagie sandwich. I knew I was right when I heard him grumble they'd been stingy with the mayo.

I took another deep breath. "I'm afraid everybody knows. My yarn helper told the mindfulness bunch and my friend who owns the restaurant where I make desserts told my group." That's when I realized that

Frank didn't know that I was helping with the other group's retreat. I started to explain and he stopped me.

"You've outdone yourself this time. All these names and groups with no faces to go along with them have me totally mixed up. I don't know why you're pursuing this anyway. It sounds like a bunch of mixed-up knots. Why not leave it to the cop? Nobody hired you to find out what really happened to the guy, did they?"

"Well, no. At first I was just worried Lieutenant Borgnine might try to sweep things under the rug so it would be ruled an accident, but then all this information started falling into my lap and it's become a challenge."

"Fine, if you want to be the white knight and figure it out for the good of all, here are a few tips. Remember that people lie, particularly killers. Go with the basics of motive, means and opportunity."

"You're right. That's the way to go," I said, launching right into it. "When it comes to motive, there seems to be a lot of people who might have one. Means — well, anyone could have picked up the rock. There was literally a pile of them nearby. Opportunity," I said, shaking my head. "It was supposed to be a solo walk." I suddenly remembered something. "Someone was there before me and went to call for help. And somebody else rushed by me just before I found Tim." I was going to explain how I'd figured they couldn't have been the same person, but Frank spoke first.

"I didn't mean for you to start going over the motive, means and opportunity with me now. I was trying to give you a push in the right direction. I know you can do it. You were trained by the best." He paused then, either to let the comment sink in or to swallow a bite of the sandwich.

I had to withhold a laugh at that comment. Frank's training had been to hand me a phone and list of people to call with the information he wanted me to get out of them. I'd figured out how to do it on my own. Still, it had been my favorite of all the temp jobs I'd had and he did still give me advice.

He continued on. "You'll weed out all the innocent people and give that cop the guilty one. Anything else?"

"You've been very patient on this call. Usually you'd have cut me off before now."

"I could tell you I was just being a nice guy, but I'm stuck on a surveillance. I've got the van parked in an alley waiting to see if a guy who I watched roll around in a wheel chair all day yesterday is faking it. I think the insurance company is going to lose on this one."

"Glad I could be the entertainment," I said. It was going to be a first with me being the one to say I had to go. I opened my mouth, but of course he beat me to it.

"Gotta go, Feldstein, the mark just came out the back door with a skateboard tucked under his arm." Then the phone clicked off.

I wasn't sure if I was any more focused than I'd been before the call, but it still felt good to talk to somebody about what happened to Tim. I dressed quickly and was out the door as the breakfast bell made its first gong. Breakfast was my favorite meal at Vista Del Mar and I didn't intend to miss it. I sniffed the air as I approached the Sea Foam dining hall and my stomach gurgled at the prospect of a plate full of breakfast treats.

People were straggling in as I entered. I put my bag down on one of the chairs at what had become my group's table. I wasn't waiting for anyone this time and went toward the food line. I grabbed a tray and looked over the counter into the kitchen.

"Is Cloris working?" I asked. She always made up a special plate for me and it was like having my own mini buffet. The older woman glanced around and then pointed to the open doorway between the kitchen and the dining area. Cloris was talking to Kevin St. John. I made a quick decision to delay getting my food and went back to the table.

Not only did I want Cloris's assistance in getting my food, I wasn't ready to deal with Kevin St. John without at least a cup of coffee first.

Iola was sitting at the table when I came back to it. Her knitting needles were going at a quick speed and she wasn't even looking as the metal spear moved into a stitch and created another. I couldn't tell what it was, only that it was purple.

I was tempted to say something about her finally deciding to sit with us since she'd eaten with the bird-watchers for the other meals, but I just greeted her with a good morning and sat down. She saw me looking across the room at the empty tables where the bird-watchers had sat.

"They're off on an early morning adventure," she said, but offered nothing else and asked me to pass her the coffeepot. I turned the lazy Susan until it was in front of me and grabbed the pot. Taking a lesson from Lucinda, I got up and walked over to serve her. Steam rose from the dark liquid as it streamed into her cup. She glanced around at the empty chairs. "It looks like they're all sleeping in."

I asked her how the movie had gone for everyone.

"Okay, I guess. We didn't sit together. I tried to sit with Aileen, but she wanted to sit with some man."

"Really? Which one?" I asked. "Was it someone from the mindfulness group?" I asked.

"It could have been. It was too dark to see. She's been acting weird all weekend. She said this weekend was about Madison but I think she's the one who needed to get away."

I looked up from my coffee and saw Kevin St. John crossing to the door. The coast was now clear. I offered to get food for Iola and went back to the cafeteria-style line.

"Good, you're here," I said to Cloris.

"The usual?" she asked, grabbing an empty plate.

I nodded and asked her to make something up for Iola as well. "I saw you talking to Kevin St. John. What's up? I hope it wasn't trouble."

She loaded tastes of all the breakfast items onto the plate. "Just the opposite. He's upped my job title and guaranteed me more hours. I'm now an assistant-at-large." She laughed and explained that it really just meant she got stuck with odd jobs that didn't fit in anywhere else. "I already got my first assignment. One of the housekeepers found some clothes in an outdoor trash can. Mr. St. John thinks it was a mistake and the owners will come looking for them. My task is to see that they're cleaned and at the desk."

"Congratulations, I guess," I said. "I hope you got a raise too."

"Barely enough to make a difference, but I like working all over the place." She handed me my plate and began working on one for Iola. "There's something more." She dropped her voice and leaned closer. "He wanted me to be the eyes and ears around here and let him know of any weird stuff going on, like people breaking the rules." She loaded some eggs onto Iola's plate. "I refused that part of the job." She chuckled. "If I'd have taken it, the first thing I would have had to report is myself taking all the bottles of kombucha to the Silicon Valley people's workshop."

"Good for you for not taking that part of the job. You'd have to report me, too," I said with a smile. "You don't have to worry about getting any more drinks for that group. We're putting on another workshop for them, but it's going to be at Cadbury Yarn during their mindful free time."

"Good," she said. "Mr. St. John is extra keyed up. He didn't give any details other than he's expecting someone important to come by today."

I brought the plates of food back to the table and by then Madison and PJ were there. They eyed the plates of food with tastes of everything and I took another thing from Lucinda's playbook and offered to get them plates made up the same way.

I acted as host with the coffeepot and got plates of food for Deani and Aileen when they finally showed up. By the time I sat down to eat everyone else had finished and the dining hall was emptying out.

"Isn't our workshop starting in a few minutes?" Aileen asked, looking at my plate just before they all headed to the door.

CHAPTER 23

Cloris was wheeling in the coffee and tea service as I went into our meeting room. She quickly unloaded the cart and lit the fire before heading back to the door. "Got to get these clothes taken care of." She pointed to something dark on the lower shelf and I remembered what she'd said about her new assignment. All I could think was thank heavens she hadn't agreed to the other one — spying on everyone.

Cloris had just left when Crystal arrived, followed by my group. Crystal did her setup at the end of the table while the rest of them dropped off their things and headed to the counter for refreshments. I was glad there were cookies left from the previous day.

I made sure the door was shut since there was a sign on the next door saying *Quiet Please, Meditation Session in Progress.*

Crystal stood and began to talk to the group and asked them to take out the crochet project they'd begun the day before. They'd all finished making the chain stitches and were working on the first row. As expected they'd all picked up the single crochet stitch with ease. They worked in silence for a few minutes and then Aileen picked up Crystal's finished sample and compared it to what she'd completed so far.

"Once you get the sequence of the rows down all you have to do is repeat it," Crystal said.

"I like the texture," Aileen said, running her fingers over the hills and valleys.

"That's all from working in the back loop of the stitches," Crystal explained.

Just then the door to the room opened and Kevin St. John took a look around before walking in as though he had every right to interrupt. The manager had made sure he closed the door behind him before he went to the head of the table, waving his hand to signal that Crystal should move aside. What was he up to now?

He plastered on a concerned look and looked around the table at my group. "We're all so sorry about what happened to one of our guests, and we're doing everything possible to keep it from impacting your weekend here. I just wanted to check that everything is going well and to remind you that we have something very special planned for tonight. I urge you all to attend the Sound Bath in Hummingbird Hall. It will be a one-of-a-kind experience.

"My hope is that if anyone were to ask you about your stay here that you will have good things to say." His gaze moved around the group and he waited until each of them had nodded in agreement.

"There is a normal investigation going on regarding what happened to our guest. Lieutenant Theodore Borgnine is overseeing that investigation and he's been having a conversation with all of our guests to try to gather as much information as possible."

Kevin St. John was certainly an expert on verbiage and I waited for him to get to the point. "I hope you don't mind but I agreed to let the lieutenant talk to you all." He said it as if they had a choice. None of us had a choice, including Kevin St. John. If he had, there was no way he would have given the okay to have the guests questioned.

The manager went to the door and opened it for Lieutenant Borgnine. I watched the reaction of my crew as he came in. They didn't look particularly happy.

Lieutenant Borgnine was dressed as always in his rumpled jacket and it seemed like he'd tried to soften his gruff expression.

Kevin St. John seemed only too happy to turn over the floor to him and made a hasty exit.

"Thanks for agreeing to talk to me," he began. I noticed that no one nodded and they all had wary expressions. Even though Kevin St. John had introduced him, he introduced himself again and seemed to be trying to keep things on a friendly basis.

"I've been talking to all the guests to see if they might have seen anything that will help us understand what happened. We know that someone made a nine-one-one call from one of the phone booths. They're not in any trouble. We'd just like to talk to them. The call was made around four o'clock on Thursday. The day you all arrived. I believe you had a workshop that afternoon," he said, clearly trying to jog their memories. His gaze made the rounds of the group and then he asked, "So, did any of you happen to see anything?"

Madison looked panicked. "Someone could have seen me in one of the phone booths around then. I was calling home to check on things. That was before I found out that my mother-in-law was trying to make points with my daughters by letting them get tattoos and dresses the size of tank tops," she said. She looked the gruff cop in

297

the eye. "Do you have kids? I bet no one undermines you when you are gone for a while."

He smiled uncomfortably. "That's really irrelevant," he said.

"So, you're saying you want to find the person who called about the man who fell on the rocks?" Madison asked. Her breath seemed choppy.

"That's correct," Lieutenant Borgnine said.

"It definitely wasn't me. But if there was any way those people could have gotten me to do it, they would have dropped it in my lap," she said.

The cop seemed perplexed with her comment. "Could you elaborate on that?" he asked. "Are you saying you knew the victim?"

"Yes, I knew Tim and the rest of them. I manage the shared work space where they have an office." She looked around at the rest of her group. "We all knew him."

Lieutenant Borgnine looked like his head would fall off. "You all knew Tim Moffat?" he said. "Why don't I know that?" He glared at me. I wasn't sure if it was a real question or a rhetorical one, but I decided to treat it as the latter and kept silent.

He pulled out his notebook and was looking at Aileen, who was in the seat next to Madison. "You want to tell me what your relationship with Moffat was?" Though it was said like a question, it was clearly a demand. Aileen looked uncomfortable suddenly being in the cop's crosshairs.

"I only knew him in passing, as in passing him in the hallway and sometimes the lounge. I use one of the offices as a classroom," she said. "I wouldn't expect them to recognize me."

"What about you?" he said, pointing at PJ.

"I didn't really know him. I have a vlog that offers hacks," she said, holding up her phone as if it was somehow proof. "My only connection is that I help make the food she delivers to them." She pointed to Deani. He turned to stare at her.

I glanced down at her tote bag, hoping she didn't have the dog with her. She seemed nervous as she answered. "I have a service that brings in lunch to offices and Reborn are customers."

"Don't you mean *were* customers?" Iola said. "Didn't I hear that they canceled you and Tim was the one to do it?" Deani gave her a sour look and the cop did a double take at Iola's sultry voice.

Lieutenant Borgnine was looking more

upset by the minute, probably realizing what I had — that there were a lot more potential suspects than he'd thought. "What about you?" he said to Iola.

"I knew Tim like Aileen did. We have an office there, too, and I passed him in the hall."

"But when you all saw Tim here, you must have said hello and commented on the fact you had some connection," Borgnine said.

Iola spoke first. "Hardly. He and the rest of them had to see Madison every day when they went past the reception counter and yet they looked right through her when they saw her here." She turned to Madison. "Isn't that right?"

Madison looked uncomfortable. "Yes, I was upset about that, but I didn't realize one of them was going to die. It seems kind of unimportant now."

They had given up enough of their work-shop time and I wanted to end his interview. I moved next to him. "They only have a short time to learn how to crochet. It looks like you got the answer to your question," I said. "No one saw who made the call." I walked him to the door and he pulled me outside with him.

"Why didn't you tell me your people knew the victim?" he demanded.

"You didn't ask, so I didn't tell." He didn't seem happy with my answer.

When I came back into the room, Madison was beside herself. "Why did I say I was in one of the phone booths? It's like I was making an excuse for being there. Now he probably thinks I'm the person they're looking for." She looked at all of us. "It wasn't me. I didn't make the nine-one-one call."

"But maybe you saw who did," Iola said.

"You've sure become the Chatty Cathy," Deani said, glaring at her. "What happened to the wall of silence you always were in our group? I wish you hadn't mentioned that Tim had canceled my service."

"Sorry," Iola said. "I didn't know it was a problem."

"The cop could think I had a beef with Tim," Deani said.

"I don't think I saw anyone else in the phone booths, but I wasn't really paying attention," Madison said. "Maybe I should find the cop and tell him that."

"Relax, everybody," Aileen said. "He said he was just looking to fill in some information. Isn't that right?" They all looked at me.

I wasn't that worried about the threatening note, but I did find it just after seeing

Deani hanging around my house. It didn't seem like a good time to give them inside information, so I stuck with the company line and just repeated what Lieutenant Borgnine had said and reassured them what they'd said was fine.

It took a while to get them back to crocheting, but when they did, they seemed to calm down. When the workshop ended, they decided to continue on and moved to the lobby of the Sand and Sea building.

I was released from duty, and after reminding Crystal of the mindful group's workshop at the yarn shop in the afternoon, I headed for home. But I only got as far as the Lodge. I was surprised to see a black limousine parked in the driveway. It was a no parking zone and strictly enforced, apparently except for now.

Curious what was going on, I went inside. At this time of day the cavernous room was always quiet as the guests were off doing activities. A tall man in a white linen tunic over matching pants was standing by the registration counter with Kevin St. John. I could tell by his body language that the manager was tense. He was doing a lot of gesturing with his arms, as though indicating the grounds.

Sky was half hidden in the shadows near

the entrance of the café. He was watching the interchange with a reverent expression. I slipped across the room unnoticed and joined the facilitator.

"Do you know who that is?" he said in a whisper when I reached him. It seemed to be a day for rhetorical questions so I didn't even try to answer. "Wind Markham," he said in an awed tone, as if it was supposed to make me swoon.

I answered with a shrug. "I don't believe you don't know who he is," Sky said, incredulous. "How about he is like the guru to the gurus. He's the author of *You Are the One, A Glorious Life Is Your Birthright, The Magic of Silence* and a bunch of others." He gazed at the man again. "I can't believe he's here."

"Speaking of that, what is the super guru doing here?"

Sky's topknot bobbed with excitement. "He wants to do a retreat in the area and he's considering Vista Del Mar. I think he's going to spend some time here, seeing what the facilities are like." Sky almost swooned. "Mr. St. John could hire me to be a facilitator again. It would be a much bigger retreat. Do you have any idea how many followers Wind has?"

I laughed to myself. Now I understood Kevin St. John's comment to my group about saying good things about the place. He was thinking about Wind Markham. I rolled my eyes, wondering what his real name was.

Just then I got in Kevin St. John's line of sight. His expression froze and he tried to surreptitiously wave me away.

I slipped out the side door. Kevin St. John had his work cut out for him trying to impress a big-shot guru when Vista Del Mar was in the middle of a murder investigation.

CHAPTER 24

"Too bad you weren't here for lunch," Cloris said. She was behind the registration counter wearing her blazer uniform. I noticed she had a tag now that said Assistant to the Manager. "Mr. St. John really put on a show for the man in the white outfit. Mr. Markham has a lot of, uh, needs," she said. "We had to cordon off a table so that he wouldn't be bothered by the other guests. The lunch menu had to be scrapped at the last minute and we had to make sure it was all plant-based. If he does the retreat here, that's how it would have to be for the whole place for the weekend. He insists there be no fumes of cooking hamburgers."

"It sounds like quite a show. I'm sorry I missed it, but the lure of a nap won out." I yawned. "Burning the candle at both ends yesterday." She nodded with understanding. "Now it's back to work. Once I see my re-

305

treaters off for their afternoon adventure, I'll gather up the Silicon Valley bunch for their workshop." I glanced around the Lodge for any signs of the manager and the guru. "What's Kevin St. John up to with him now?" I asked.

"He's escorting him on a tour of the area," she said. She dropped her voice, which was really unnecessary since there was no one else around. "I think he wanted to get him off the grounds before Lieutenant Borgnine came back to investigate some more." She leaned a little closer. "Mr. St. John really, really wants the retreat. Just a heads-up, he's acting a little crazy about looking for anybody not following the rules."

What was new about that? All I cared about was that Kevin St. John was off the grounds and I didn't have to worry that he'd see me dealing with his retreat group.

I was waiting in the driveway next to the Lodge when my group showed up. At their request I'd arranged a winery tour for them. I wasn't going along, but knew that they'd be leaving all the cloudy skies behind. It was like going from a black-and-white movie to color when you traveled into the Carmel Valley. The sunshine, blue skies and green grass-covered mountains were a feast for the eyes. There would be treats for their taste buds as well. The tour ended with a wine and cheese tasting.

So that there would be no issue with drinking and driving, I'd arranged for a van to drive them to and from. Deani had the pink tote with her and I asked about Fifi after Cloris had said that Kevin St. John was on the hunt for anyone breaking the rules. She opened the tote bag and Fifi popped her head out and let out a few yips.

"I hope I get some hacks about wine," PJ said. "The winery must have Wi-Fi. I'll put it up while I'm there." I almost didn't notice Iola standing next to her. She'd gone back to being quiet and her plain looks made it easy for her to blend into the background.

"I don't care about hacks," Madison said. "Just bring on the wine, lots of it. I'm not even going to call home," she said. "I don't want to know what else my mother-in-law has done while I'm gone."

"Where's Aileen?" I asked as the van arrived.

"Maybe she's in her room," Deani said. "She said something about taking a nap."

I told them to get in the van and tell the driver there was one more and then I sprinted up the slope to the Sand and Sea building. I had to squeeze around the housekeeping cart and went up to Aileen's door and gave it a quick knock. There was no answer and I tried again. When I saw one of the housekeepers come out of a room down the hall, I explained my plight. "I'm afraid she might still be asleep and I've got a van of people anxious for wine."

"I can let you in, I guess," she said and unlocked the door. The room was empty and the bed still made. Then I saw the laptop open on the table and realized it was Tim's room. I was careful to avoid bumping the laptop this time, remembering how it had come on.

"Wrong room," I said, rushing back in the hall and pointing at the one next door. I didn't bother trying to knock and had the housekeeper open the door. The room was empty, but when I saw Aileen's knitting at least I knew I was in the right place.

I rushed out of the building and back to the van. I was relieved to see Aileen was just about to get in. "Good, you're here," I said. I stuck my head in to wish them a nice afternoon and told the driver they were good to go.

I watched the van drive away and let out a breath of relief. They were all accounted for, and if Deani had the dog in the bag, at least it meant Fifi wasn't on the Vista Del Mar grounds.

I'd arranged the same meeting spot for the other group, and as the van pulled away, they began to show up. I was surprised when Audrey Moffat was with them. She smiled at me. "I hope it's okay. I could use a little mindfulness. I'll drive on my own. Just tell me where to go."

I assured her it was fine with me. I was sure that Crystal still had the tote bag we'd made up for Tim. One of us could show her the ropes and bring her up to where they were. I gave her directions and she went to the small parking area adjacent to the Lodge and beeped open a white Mercedes. The rest of the group went to a black SUV parked nearby. Elex climbed into the driver's seat. Jackson rode shotgun and Josh got in the back, leaving the doors open for Julie.

She was standing near me, looking at the ajar door. "Screw that," she said. "I've had more than enough of all of them. Can I ride with you?"

"Of course," I said. She started to walk away with me, but then saw that the door was still open and Elex was backing up the vehicle. She walked up to the moving car and pushed the door shut.

"Did you see that? He probably would have driven all the way there with the door open. Tim was the only one who paid attention to anything."

We waited until the SUV passed the stone posts that marked the entrance to Vista Del Mar, and then I took her across the street and pointed to my yellow Mini Cooper.

"Cute ride," she said, getting into the small car. As soon as I started the engine, she closed her eyes and leaned back in her seat and sighed with pleasure. "It's a bitch being the token female. It's like I'm Wendy and they're the lost boys." She chuckled half to herself. "But I think the lost boys listened to Wendy and she didn't have to wear these depressing clothes."

"So I take it they don't listen to you," I said as I turned onto the street.

"It's beyond not listening to me. They ignore me. I tried to make some suggestions for the produce truck and Elex wouldn't even let me talk." She pulled her long wavy hair into a low ponytail.

"Then the obvious question is why did they hire you?"

"I found out that Tim said they needed to have a woman in the group. I gather he thought it looked bad to have all guys. Tim's the one who interviewed me and told me I got the job." She looked down at the baggy black outfit. "I went to him about this nonsense of wearing black turtlenecks and black pants. I thought he'd understand, since he didn't go along with it himself, but he refused to do anything. He said I had to be part of the team."

I wanted to hear what else she'd have to say and was sorry it was such a short ride into the heart of town, but I milked every minute of it.

"Since it seems like Tim was your benefactor, I guess it'll be tough now that he's gone."

"He might have started out as my benefactor, he wasn't anymore." She pressed her lips together as if to keep herself from talking and I thought that was going to be the end of it, but she let out a sigh and continued. "Not when he told me he was leaving and taking that moron Josh with him instead of me. I could have helped him with his new venture, whatever it was." She sounded angry and hurt.

I asked her how she felt about Audrey coming to the workshop. Julie shrugged. "She's stuck here until they release Tim's body so she figured why not join in on some of our activities."

"Then you know her from before?" I asked.

"Not really. Tim didn't talk about his

311

personal life. The rest of them . . ." She rolled her eyes. "They don't have a personal life to talk about."

It was a little awkward but I asked her if there was something between Elex and Audrey, remembering that they might have been holding hands the night before. She laughed in response. "If there is, it's all on her. Elex has no game."

I turned off of the main thoroughfare onto a side street and pulled the car to the curb in front of Cadbury Yarn. Like the Blue Door, Cadbury Yarn was in a building that had once been a residence. It was bungalow-style and had a porch in the front with a rainbow-colored windsock that blew in the constant breeze. The Mercedes and SUV were both parked nearby, and once Julie and I got out of my car, the rest of the crew got out, too.

We gathered at the base of the stair, and when I looked over the group they all seemed a little intimidated.

"You're not going in there to get a tooth pulled," I said, trying to loosen them up. "It's going to be mindful and relaxing." Elex separated himself from the bunch and took the lead and waved for them to follow.

Crystal was waiting by the door as we came in. She took the group back to what I surmised was the dining room when someone had lived there. For now the room was used for social knitting. There was a nice oval-shaped wood table and enough chairs for everybody. She directed them to find a spot and was relieved to see that they'd all brought their tote bags with them.

She handed the leftover tote bag to Audrey. "Why don't the rest of you have a look around while I give Audrey a quick lesson." Crystal pointed out a table that had been set up with the easiest of kits.

I followed along with them as they walked around the yarn shop letting them know I was available to help them. I liked working with this group because I knew how to knit well enough to actually be able to help them.

It was a typical Saturday afternoon at the shop. Gwen was handling sales and a number of customers were browsing the extensive supply of yarn. I noticed a couple of women had pulled two of the easy chairs together and were knitting and talking.

Crystal's son Cory made an appearance, bringing a supply of bags from the back. He was tall and lanky, at the age where his body was still working out its proportions. The front door opened and the Delacorte sisters came in just as Cory gave the bags to his grandmother. Cora was in the lead and seemed agitated. She went right up to Gwen and it was obvious some kind of confrontation was about to happen. I moved closer to hear what was happening.

"I thought as long as you people are making a play for our family business, we should claim part of yours," Cora said in a snippy tone. She was overdressed as usual in a Kelly green knit suit with a boxy jacket. She wore heels and a lot of green eye shadow.

"What are you doing?" Madeleine said. "You told me you wanted some yarn to make a pair of fingerless gloves."

"I had to give you some excuse," Cora said in a haughty voice. "It doesn't matter what I said anyway." She turned back to Gwen. "I bet you don't like having someone come in and say they're entitled to part of your business."

"Have you lost your mind? Shush, be quiet. Don't say anything else," Madeleine said, trying to control her sister. In her boyfriend jeans and white tunic, Madeleine appeared years younger and much cuter than her sister. Instead of the oversprayed helmet hairstyle Cora had, Madeleine wore hers in a swingy bob.

"You be quiet," Cora said. "All that denim has gone to your head. If they're going to claim a piece of Vista Del Mar, I want part of their yarn shop."

Gwen seemed stunned. I was too. It sure seemed like Cora had lost her mind. She was the one who was always so concerned about proper behavior and what people thought and here she was coming unglued in a yarn shop.

As soon as Gwen got her bearings, she saw how confused her grandson looked and sent him to the back, telling him to stay there. Gwen had kept him in the dark about his newfound family even though she was only acknowledging it because of his affection for Vista Del Mar.

Madeleine seemed wistful as she watched the teen boy leave the scene. She had taken a liking to Cory before she knew he was actually related and now she understood that he reminded her of her brother. She tried to grab her sister's arm. "We're leaving," she said, trying to sound forceful.

Cora viewed her sister with disdain. "You might be the older sister, but I'm the one who Mother left in charge. I'm the one who has always taken care of everything. And I'm going to take care of this." She glared at the yarn shop proprietor.

Gwen was a no-nonsense sort of person. She wore earth tones and sensible styles. Her earrings and socks matched, or I think her socks matched, I'd never actually seen them. In other words, Crystal and her mother had totally different styles.

The one thing they had in common was that they could be fierce, particularly when it came to Crystal's children. As soon as Crystal heard the ruckus she made a beeline to the cashier table and joined her mother.

Gwen put her hand up to stop everyone and stepped close to the sisters, dropping her voice to a whisper. I was close enough to hear what she was saying.

She looked Cora square in the eye. "The only reason I decided to make our familial relationship known to you was that my grandson has such an affinity for Vista Del Mar. But as much as he loves the place some things just aren't worth it. I would have thought you would be happy to find that you had some family." I could tell Gwen was restraining herself. Crystal stayed next to her mother for moral support, but let the older woman handle the show.

"Cory knows nothing about his relation to your brother. And now he never will. So, I've decided to drop the whole thing. You can keep Vista Del Mar and everything else. Hopefully you'll still let Cory work there summers. We'll just forget that we're related and life will go on for you as it was."

316

This was not how things went in Cora's playbook. She was used to being the one who said how things were going to be and she was speechless. Madeleine appeared distraught and she glared at Cora before locking her fingers around her sister's arm. "We'll talk about this at home."

Gwen, Crystal and I stood together watching the sisters leave. The amazing thing was that no one in the store had realized what had just occurred. With them gone, Crystal took a deep breath, pulled herself together and handled the workshop as if nothing had happened.

CHAPTER 25

The afternoon was winding down when I got back to Vista Del Mar. The cloud cover was thin enough to let the sun through and for once the orange disk could be seen slipping toward the horizon. Despite the dustup with the Delacorte sisters, Crystal had done a great job with the mindfulness workshop. The actual mindful portion had been rather short, as she'd had to refresh their memories on how to knit and undo some of their mistakes. But it ended with them asking for one more session.

Julie and Audrey had made friends at the workshop and driven back together, which was fine with me since it meant there was no chance Kevin St. John would see me with anyone from his retreat.

I made a stop in the Lodge to look for the birthday group. The workshops were over and people were back from afternoon excursions and had started to congregate in the large room to enjoy a glass of wine before dinner or to play a few hands of cards. Kevin St. John was standing by the registration desk watching as Lieutenant Borgnine moved around the room.

"I don't know why he is insisting on talking to every guest who was here Thursday afternoon when the incident happened."

"It was more than an incident. Someone died," I said.

"Yes, and it was terrible, but we must remember the other guests and do our best to see that they have the best weekend possible. Particularly now." His usually placid face lit up. "I think it's going to happen," he said in an excited voice. "You must have seen Wind Markham here earlier. He's interested in holding a retreat here. He wanted to look at the other resorts in the area, but we're the frontrunners. He loves how rustic Vista Del Mar is and how it feels like it's away from it all. The fact that we're unplugged is a plus too." He looked around the large room, seeming almost cocky. "It will forever change Vista Del Mar. If someone as important in the spiritual world as Wind has a retreat here, others will follow. I'll be doing it turnkey for him and then all those other groups." He had a malevolent smile. "Too bad, but we won't be able to accommodate your little retreats anymore. I know you think you have a special relationship with the Delacorte sisters, but I'm sure they'll turn everything about Vista Del Mar over to me once they understand the importance of what I've done."

I half expected him to let loose with a creepy laugh like a Disney villain, but he just dismissed me with a quick wave of his hand. At the moment, I didn't think he'd have a hard time convincing the Delacorte sisters to cancel my special deal. After the past afternoon, they'd probably want to run me out of town.

As the dinner bell began to ring, I suddenly realized this might be my last retreat. I was determined not to let anything on to my group. They deserved to get every minute of enjoyment out of their weekend.

The dinner menu was always special on Saturday night. Normally I would have been excited at the prospect of roast beef and Yorkshire pudding, but it barely crossed my mind as I headed to my group's table.

"Nice that you're all together," I said, noting that Iola and Aileen were sitting at the table with PJ, Deani and Madison.

"That's right," Madison said. "I guess I shouldn't take it personally, but the two of you did seem to be MIA a lot." She turned to Aileen. "You almost missed the winery trip. We had to send Casey looking for you."

"Really?" Aileen said, looking at me. "Sorry for being a bother."

"It was no big deal, other than I ended up in the wrong room. At least this time I didn't knock into the dead guy's computer."

"Do you mean his stuff is still in his room and it's near ours?" Madison asked.

"Relax. It's not like his ghost is hanging out there," Iola said.

"His wife will clear it out as soon as everything is settled," I said.

"Settled?" Aileen asked. "You mean like when they say it was accidental?"

"If that's what it was," Madison said.

"Of course that's what it was," Deani said in a decided tone. "Let's talk about something more pleasant." She turned to me. "Too bad you missed the winery trip. It was fun." I nodded and suggested they all get their food.

I was too keyed up to eat and just drank some iced tea while they dug in. As the meal was winding down, Kevin St. John came in. He seemed more self-important than usual as he worked the room. He ignored me when he got to our table and urged my group to go directly to Hummingbird Hall for the Sound Bath.

"I read the sign in the Lodge," Madison said. "But it really didn't explain what a Sound Bath was. It seemed like a lot of hype." She looked to me.

"It'll probably be a unique experience," I said and suggested that we walk there together.

Hummingbird Hall was similar in design to the Lodge with a few changes. It was built into a hillside and had a small lower floor. The upper floor had a large open interior with a stage and alcoves on either side of the main area and at the back. When it was used for movies or entertainment rows of chairs were brought in, but tonight it was all open with rows of floor mats and rolled-up blankets. A staff member stood by the door and instructed everyone to leave their belongings on the long table set up in the alcoves and then to wrap themselves in a blanket and lie on one of the mats. I glanced up at the stage, which was set up with gongs and chimes and metal bowls of different sizes.

Deani looked at the pink tote. Nothing had been said, but I was certain the dog was still in there. She seemed at a loss of what to do until I agreed to take it. The rest of them left their bags and things on the tables and did as they'd been told. I stayed in the alcove with the pink tote and watched as the open area filled up. I looked to see if the Silicon Valley group was there, but wrapped in the blankets they looked like a bunch of identical burritos.

When everyone was in position, Kevin walked out on the stage holding a microphone. He did a few minutes of welcoming and reminded everyone there was a reception after the event. Then he introduced Sky. A musical note swelled as the barefoot facilitator came out. He gestured with his arms and the lights dimmed. As it grew darker, he suddenly lit up and I realized he was wrapped in a string of tiny lights.

"Close your eyes and let the sounds carry you wherever your mind wishes."

I watched as he hit the gong. The sound reverberated through the room and I could actually feel the vibrations in my body. A hum started from something and it grew louder and sounded almost like a plaintive cry. Sky began to chant and suddenly I felt the pink bag began to move. Fifi stuck her head out and began to howl. I rushed out the door.

The grounds were dead and it seemed that everyone had followed Kevin's order to go to the Sound Bath.

It was a cappuccino moment if there ever was one. I needed the boost of caffeine tempered with a fluff of milk. The Lodge was deserted, but the door to the café was open. I was glad that Cloris was behind the counter. She was busy doing cleanup from the crowd earlier and looked up when I came in. She noticed the pink bag with Fifi's head sticking out.

"You better not let Mr. St. John see you. He's dying to catch that dog in a guest room so he can tell the Delacorte sisters that someone in your retreat broke the rules."

"I'll take her across the street to my place," I said, starting to get up. Cloris waved me to sit.

"You should be good for now. He's tied up with the Sound Bath." She reached across the counter to grab a paper cup, but it tipped and coffee poured out onto the counter. Before she could stop the stream it dripped over the side. "I'm filling in. The new hire got scared of the steam from the espresso machine and quit on the spot and left this mess." She looked down at her clothes. "I guess I should be glad that the coffee is cold."

I leaned over the counter to assess the damage. "Lucky you," I said, gesturing toward her black pants. "It doesn't show."

"But it's still there. My pants smell like coffee now." She wrinkled her nose and then smiled at me. "I assume you came in here for a drink. What can I get you?"

I ordered my cappuccino and she went to measure the espresso. A moment later I smelled the smoky scent of the dark coffee as it trickled into the cup. She steamed the milk and finished making the drink.

She did a little more cleanup while I downed the drink.

"You're my last customer," she said, turning everything off. "Now it's back to the registration desk." She went under the counter and grabbed something black. "I think Mr. St. John is wrong. I don't think anybody is going to claim these even though I put up a note. But they're all clean in case they do."

I tossed my cup in the trash and grabbed the pink tote and gave the tiny dog a snuggle.

"What happened with the workshop at the yarn shop?" she asked.

"It went okay, but they still want another session tomorrow morning."

"Same place and same drinks?" she asked as she got ready to shut off the lights.

"I'm thinking of keeping it less complicated," I said. "But they did like your selection. I kept meaning to ask you how you chose what to bring."

She smiled. "It's simple. I asked them what they wanted."

"You did?" I said, surprised. Then I was curious about the who and the when. After I heard her answer all I could think of was something Frank had said: *Remember that people lie, particularly killers.*

CHAPTER 26

I was still processing what Cloris had said when I went outside. I could hear gongs and chimes. The Sound Bath was still going on but for how long? I wanted Fifi safely away from being discovered. I rushed across the street with the small dog. I gave her a little outside time and then brought her into the guesthouse. She seemed happy to be out of the bag and scampered into the crate before rutting around and making a comfortable spot for herself. I made sure she had some treats and water before I left her. My mind was clicking as I went back to Vista Del Mar.

The closer to Hummingbird Hall I got, the better I could hear the sounds and feel the vibrations of the Sound Bath. Over the gongs and tones, Sky was urging everyone to join in with a final chant of *Om.* The sound swelled and then gradually diminished into nothing. I was standing in the doorway by then. The lights came on and the human burritos unwrapped themselves.

I looked over the crowd trying to pick out individuals. I knew I could just tell Lieutenant Borgnine what I'd just figured out, but I wanted to be sure before I spoke to him. I watched as everyone moved toward the back of the hall.

A curtain had been pulled opened that had closed off the back alcove. A long table was covered with refreshments that seemed at odds with the ethereal quality of the Sound Bath. There was a bowl of punch made of ginger ale, frozen strawberries and floating islands of orange sherbet. Potato chips and dip were next to a chocolate fountain with cookies to dip into it.

"And now for a different kind of Sound Bath," Kevin St. John said from the stage. Dance music started to play. "Feel the beat and move to it," Sky said as he jumped off the stage and began to dance and urged anyone who wanted to to join him.

I noticed a few people going out the exit, including the person I wanted to talk to. I followed along, not sure what I was going to do. Then people began walking in different directions. I started to follow the one I wanted to talk to, who seemed to sense it and picked up speed. I saw a figure slip in

328

the doorway on the lower area and followed. Inside I saw a doorway open and I rushed to follow just as someone went into the unisex handicapped restroom. I pushed myself inside before the door could close.

"What do you want?" Elex said. He was trying to edge around me but I flicked the lock and blocked it so he couldn't get out.

"I know that you were with Tim," I said. There was a flicker of distress on Elex's face and then it disappeared.

"It was a solitary mindful walk," he said. "Like I told you, I walked through the grounds of Vista Del Mar."

I told him about my conversation with Cloris. "She said that you and Tim were walking together when she asked you about your drink choice. She heard you say you knew just the place to go."

Elex froze, realizing he was cornered. "I tried to tell Tim the point was for us to walk alone, but he insisted we go together."

"It was because he wanted to tell you something and get it off his chest," I said.

"How did you know?" he said, looking worried.

"It was about him leaving and pulling his financing," I said. I explained what Audrey had told me and that she'd said she thought Tim would have wanted to talk about it right away.

"I knew Tim wasn't happy with the way things were going, but I didn't think it was that serious. I tried to tell him he hadn't given it enough time. But he wouldn't listen. He said he was tired of watching me burn through money on weekends like this and expensive food delivery. He wanted to be in control and call all the shots." Elex looked down. "He said he was already working on something. He said we were all loser nerds." His mouth settled into a grimace. "I was so mad. I wanted to do something."

"So you led him to the rocks, knowing he was clumsy and wearing slippery shoes. What did you do, push him and then when he fell you smashed his head?" I glared at him. "You'd figured out another way to get the money you needed." He looked blankly at me. "The key man insurance policy."

Elex seemed to be melting before my eyes. "You know about that." He put his face in his hands. "I'm screwed." He looked up at me. "I didn't smash his head. I swear when I went to get help, he was alive." His shoulders drooped. "I admit I led him to the rocks just like you said. All it took was a push and he fell backward. He knocked himself out. I was so angry I wanted him to die and I thought about hitting him with a rock, but I couldn't do it. So I went for help. I was so panicked I didn't realize the tide was coming in."

He leaned against the wall for support, seeming stunned and relieved at the same time. "I'm not good at intrigue. I don't know what happened. Maybe he came to when I went for help and tried to get up and then fell and hit his head."

"You didn't come back after you went to call?" I asked, thinking back to what I'd seen.

"No. I didn't want be involved. I know that sounds stupid now, but I thought maybe Tim wouldn't remember that I'd pushed him."

"Did Tim tell you what his project was?"

Elex shook his head with a sigh. "Unlike me, Tim was good at intrigue. He didn't give a hint other than I got the feeling it was a product and not a service." He swallowed and looked at me. "I guess I have to tell that cop all this."

While he'd been talking some pieces had been coming together in my mind. The first was that I believed him and the second was I thought I understood what had happened. "Hold that thought for now."

I was on my way out the door before I'd finished what I was saying. The path was empty since everyone was still at the reception. Time was of the essence. I had to check this before everyone came back to the Sand and Sea building.

I rushed into the Lodge, grateful that Cloris was working the registration counter. Between heavy breaths, I asked for the master key. It was more like I demanded it with no explanation. She sized up that I was in the middle of something and gave it to me without question. "The clothes," I said, trying to catch my breath. "Don't let anybody take them."

I was back running through the grounds before I was sure she understood what I meant.

This time I went to the right place and opened the door to Tim's room. All was as it had been the last time I'd seen it. The computer was still sitting open and all I had to do was touch a key and the screen came on. I caught a glimpse of what was on it and was going to scroll down and see what else there was when someone grabbed me from behind.

"I'll take that," a voice said, pushing the laptop away from me. I started to react, but my arms were wrenched behind me and I felt something going around my wrists, and when I tried to move them I felt a plastic cable pull tight. "Zip ties are the best. You never know when they'll come in handy."

I looked over my shoulder, startled. "I'm surprised you're not videoing this for your vlog," I said to PJ.

"No time for that now." She bent down, and before I could move my feet, she'd used a zip tie to hold them together.

"Now, let me look at that laptop," she said, grabbing it. As she looked at the screen she began to shake her head and make angry sounds. "He absolutely ripped me off. That louse." She turned the screen where I could see it. A clear cellophane bag held small toasted squares with a small strip of orange. The sticker on the front of the bag called them "The Perfect Bite, melts in your mouth and your soup too."

"When I tell you what he did, you're going to understand. He said we'd be partners. I had the product and he had the know-how and means to make it into something big. He was sure we'd end up selling it to a major food company and have a big payday. I should have never listened to him or trusted him. He said he had to know the recipe and process for making them. I'd taken months working it out and it seemed like I had no choice but to share the information with him. He was one of Deani's customers so I trusted him." She looked at the screen. "This belongs to me."

"It's the pop-in-your-mouth mini grilled cheese sandwich snack that we had that first afternoon, right?" I wanted to keep her talking so I could figure out how to wiggle out of the hand restraints.

"Yes, weren't they the most delicious thing you ever had," she said. I agreed they were tasty, but I wasn't sure they were the most delicious thing I'd ever had, but under the circumstances I didn't want to argue with her so I agreed.

"I hadn't heard from him in a couple of months, and when I saw he was here, I cornered him and asked him what was going on." She let out an angry grunt. "First he pretended not to know who I was. Then he insisted his product was nothing like mine. Right. He used margarine and I used butter. I was beside myself. This was my shot. I've let people walk over me before, but not this time."

"You saw him after he fell," I said.

"I saw them walking to the beach and I followed them. I was just so angry. I saw Tim fall. As soon as the guy with him left, I went up to him. And I just lost it and started hitting him with a rock. I could see the tide was coming in and thought it would carry him away. Then I saw you coming and I took off.

"Finding this computer is a bonus. I heard you talking about it before and then when I saw you going in this room, I realized this was my chance. Maybe I can use whatever he's already set up." She seemed to be thinking to herself. "I just have to get rid of you."

They were hardly comforting words and I made another play to loosen the zip ties. I knew there was a way to get out of them, but I was a little too panicky to think it through. She was taking something out of her bag and talking to herself. "I always carry a trash bag. Useful for so many things. It can be a raincoat with a few snips, a laundry bag, a blanket in an emergency, and a means to take out a pest." I heard the rattle of the clear bag as she unfolded it. "It says right here that it's a suffocation hazard. One person's hazard, another's solution," she said in her vlog voice. I couldn't do anything to stop her as she opened it up and put the clear bag over my head. I felt something go around my neck. Another zip tie, perhaps? She must carry a supply of different sizes.

I ordered myself not to panic, which didn't completely work. Even though I still had some air, I felt like I couldn't breathe. She was packing up the computer and going toward the open window. I could hear noise coming from the hall. I thought I recognized Kevin St. John's voice. I considered yelling, but because the doors were so thin, everyone was conditioned to ignore any sounds coming from inside a room because, well, it could be embarrassing.

There had to be something I could do. She was ready to climb out the window and take the computer with her. And then it hit me. There was one thing I could do that would get Kevin's attention. That would make him barge in the room. I took in a deep breath of what air I had and I began to bark and make yipping sounds. It might not have been the most authentic impression, but I hoped that Kevin was so coiled and ready to react that he wouldn't notice. I was barely on the second round of barks when the door burst open and Kevin barged in.

"Aha, caught you," the manager yelled. "That's it. You're in trouble now."

CHAPTER 27

"Where's the dog?" Kevin said, looking around the room.

I moved my arms around to get his attention. "Get this off me," I said from inside the bag. He looked up from his search and finally noticed my situation. He shook his head with reproach and then ripped it open. I took in a gush of air and ordered him to undo the restraints on my hands. I took care of the ones around my feet. Once I was free I ran to the window, but PJ had disappeared in the dark. I knew where she was headed and climbed out the window.

"Casey, I demand to know what's going on. And where did you hide that dog?" the manager yelled after me.

Really?

I didn't bother with the path, but ran through the tall dry grass on the slope that led down to the Lodge. I was so intent on what I was doing I barely heard the sound of sirens growing louder. I burst through the door and saw that PJ was at the counter dealing with Cloris. Despite what I said, it seemed like Cloris was going to hand over the discarded clothes. In a last-ditch effort, I boosted myself up on the huge wooden counter and slid across it, grabbing the black clothes out of PJ's hands.

The sirens were loud now and I saw the reflection of flashing lights coming in the windows. PJ tried to make a run for it, but the door on the driveway side opened and cops and paramedics flooded inside.

The commotion had gotten Lieutenant Borgnine's attention and he came in the door on the other side still holding his cup of punch.

"Grab her," I said. "She killed Tim Moffat." I held up the black outfit. "She was wearing these clothes. They've been washed, but I'm sure there's still blood residue." I offered to get my luminol to show them.

"You can't prove they're mine. Lots of people wear black leggings and tops," PJ said.

"Except those people don't put them on their vlog as a travel hint. How a black outfit hides spills. Or have a little red heart on the shoulder."

"Arrest her," Lieutenant Borgnine said,

338

looking for a place to put down his punch cup.

The lights from the police cars and ambulance were still flashing. All the noise and lights had attracted the attention of the guests at the reception and people began to crowd in the side door that opened on the deck.

Kevin realized he had to take control and told them to go back outside. The door on the driveway side opened and Wind Markham walked in followed by Dane.

The spiritual guru did a sweep of the room with the cop handcuffing PJ, the flashing lights reflecting off the walls, the grumbling crowd being pushed out into the darkness and me with the remnants of a plastic bag still hanging around my neck. He made eye contact with Kevin St. John.

"I think not," he said and then turned and went back outside. Dane shook his head as he looked around the room and his eyes stopped on me.

"Who said nothing happens around here," he said.

CHAPTER 28

Deani, Aileen, Madison and Iola were already at the table when I came in for breakfast on Sunday morning. They had been part of the crowd that came into the Lodge the night before as PJ was being taken away. They'd also been part of the crowd that Kevin St. John and Lieutenant Borgnine had teamed up on and told to go back to their rooms. I'd barely been able to give the birthday group the barest of details before Lieutenant Borgnine took me into the closed café and wanted a statement.

Dane was waiting when the cop finally released me and walked me home. He wanted to stay but he was still on duty.

"What's going to happen to her?" Madison asked.

I grabbed a chair and poured myself some coffee. "They might charge her with voluntary manslaughter since it seems like she didn't plan it out. There will be some charge for what she did to me. Maybe attempted murder." I took a deep breath with new appreciation for air after the bag incident. "I don't think they're going to give her bail."

"I feel terrible," Deani said. "It's kind of my fault. PJ worked for me making the food I delivered. She took advantage of the kitchen I used and worked on the grilled cheese snacks. She wanted to get feedback, so I let her make up sample bags and I left them with my customers. I guess Tim must have contacted her from the business card she stuck in the bags. She never told us any details, just that she was working on building them into something bigger. I wish I'd known."

"It's not your fault she did what she did," Madison said. "It's not any of ours fault. I'm appalled what she did to that man and to Casey." She looked at me with a sympathetic expression. "We'll do what we can to support her, like help her get a lawyer and talk to her daughter. But life has to go on."

The mood in the room was subdued after the events of the previous night. Kevin St. John came in, looking dejected now that his dream of having a superstar guru let him arrange a retreat at Vista Del Mar was dead. He threw me an angry glare, as if it was my fault that Wind Markham had shown up in the midst of an invasion by first responders.

It wasn't me at all. Audrey Moffat thought PJ had fallen out the window and had used her satellite phone to call in the emergency.

I was sure Kevin St. John would put in a bad word for me with the Delacorte sisters. Not that he really had to. Cora might have already talked to him.

It was no surprise that nobody felt like eating. I reminded them that the last workshop started shortly after the meal.

Crystal and I were waiting in our meeting room when they showed up. Cloris had left coffee and tea. There were cookies still in the tin. "I hope this works," Crystal said, looking out the open door to the path.

"It's the perfect solution," I said, hearing voices. The birthday group came in and went to take their regular seats. A moment later the Silicon Valley group came in. Their number was back up to five since Audrey was with them. The two groups looked at each other and then turned to Crystal and me.

"What's going on?" Elex said

"I thought you people would probably need help with your mindful knitting after you leave. And these ladies are experts," I said, gesturing to the birthday group. I saw Madison's back go up and knew she was about to object.

"There is a catch," I said. "I want you to look at my retreaters carefully." Elex and his crew followed my orders and I saw them beginning to shrug.

"Really?" I said, glaring at them. "You don't recognize these people?" I pointed to Madison. "How about you see her every day when you go through the reception area to your office." They all stared at Madison and a look of recognition lit their faces.

"Right, the woman who runs the place. I don't remember that hair, though," Julie said. Madison took a moment to explain the hair color had just been a weekend thing.

"This is Deani. She's the one who provides you with meals."

"Provided," Deani corrected. "Tim canceled my service."

"We can't have that," Elex said, sounding panicked. "We'll starve." He nodded to Deani. "Consider yourself reinstated."

"And you should recognize these two people, too. Aileen and Iola both have offices in the same shared work space suite."

Aileen and Iola both struck poses. I wanted to mention how rude and arrogant the Silicon Valley group had seemed, but I wanted to mend fences, not scold. In that

343

moment, Elex gave them all a hard look and then his eyes lit with understanding.

"It must have been seeing you all out of context," he said. "I guess we've all gotten a little too into ourselves. I'm sorry. I'm really sorry." He sounded like he genuinely meant it.

It was amazing how powerful those few words were. The words *I'm sorry* were like magic, and my group easily forgave them. Now that the ice was broken they began to talk to each other. The Silicon Valley group showed off their mindful projects and my group said they would be glad to help them and mentioned how they met in the office lounge.

All Crystal and I had to do was stand there while they all began to work on their projects and talk at the same time. As expected, the conversation went to what had happened the night before. Elex admitted what had happened between him and Tim, making sure they understood he'd gone to get help for him. He'd told Lieutenant Borgnine the same thing and the cop had said it seemed they'd just had a scuffle, and since Elex had gone for help there was nothing criminal. "It's a relief, but I'll still always have regrets about what happened."

Madison said something similar to what

she'd said at breakfast. "No matter what, life has to go on." She looked at Audrey with a question.

"I'm afraid we've never officially met. I'm Audrey Moffat. Tim's widow."

"She's going to be working with us," Elex said.

"I always thought the produce truck was a great idea and am excited to be involved. I hope we can do something with the grilled cheese snacks too and give a share of the money to the woman's family. I had no idea that Tim stole her idea. Julie and I were talking and we have an idea that can help the produce truck and bring quality food to so-called food deserts. I don't want to be the person who just writes the checks. I want to be in the middle of things."

Elex looked surprised. "You mean because you'll inherit Tim's money?"

"Oh, no. I have my own."

When the hour ended, I was pleased that everything had worked out for the two groups, which seemed like one now. I heard they were all going to sit together at lunch.

And then it was time for the goodbyes. I was waiting when the birthday group came into the Lodge to check out.

"I hope you have a happy birthday, whenever it is," I said to Madison. She still had the pink hair and seemed sorry for the retreat to end because of having to face her daughters and her mother-in-law. Aileen was late as usual, and when she came in she wasn't alone.

"Everybody, I'd like you to meet Reese." They were arm in arm and clearly a couple. Now I understood why she'd been doing the disappearing act and who she'd been doing it with. Everything made more sense when she explained. She and Reese had met a year ago at Vista Del Mar. She was there for a homeschooling retreat and he was there to see a client, as he did every year on the same weekend. "That's why I insisted we come this weekend," she said to the others. "I was hoping to meet up with Reese again now that I'm divorced."

He looked at her with love in his eyes. "And now all we have to do is figure out how to have a happy ending."

Iola was standing with one of the bird group. "This is my brother," she said. "I had no idea he was going to be here. I had some meals with him. It gave me a chance to meet his girlfriend."

Deani had the pink tote and was not trying to hide Fifi anymore. I blew the dog a kiss, realizing she'd helped save my life.

I was going to walk them out to the SUV, when the door on the driveway side opened and two teenage girls made a noisy entrance.

"Mother," they cried in unison and rushed up to Madison. She turned her head, trying to avert her eyes, but it was useless and she looked at the two young women.

"Okay, let's see the tattoos," she said with a groan. The girls started giggling and took off their jackets to display elaborate artwork on their arms. Madison almost choked. Then one of them licked her finger and began to rub her arm. The color faded and started to disappear. "Faked you out. We did them with a special pen."

"What about those dresses?" Madison said.

"It's so easy to make you crazy," the other one said. "Grandma buy us hot dresses, ha!"

"What are you doing here?" Madison asked.

"We missed you so we thought we'd come to get you. Boy, do we have a lot to tell you about Grandma. What a pill. She made us count the dust balls under our beds, only she called them dust bunnies." The older one looked at her mother and shook her head. "Pink hair, really? It looks like you're trying too hard."

"It looks like I'll be riding home with my

girls," Madison said, beaming a big smile. And then we all went outside. The Silicon Valley group came outside a moment later with Kevin St. John. Sky was trailing behind.

"I hope you'll spread the word about the mindful retreat to all your start-up buddies." He tried to give Elex a high five. "Should we put you down for a repeat?"

Elex rolled his eyes and shook his head. The manager seemed totally confused when his group and my group offered goodbyes, handshakes and hugs to each other. The manager gave me a dirty look before he went back inside shaking his head. Then everybody got into their vehicles and we watched them all drive away.

I gave Sky a high five. "We're done."

I went to the meeting room to pack my things in the wheeled tote. I stopped in the Lodge to thank Cloris for all her help. She was behind the registration counter on her own.

"Something's happening," she said. "I'm not sure what it is, but I think it's big, really big." She pointed toward the café. I walked over and peeked in. Cora and Madeleine were sitting with Crystal and Gwen. I checked their expressions and they were all friendly. Crystal saw me and waved me in.

"Thank you," Cora said, giving me a

round of applause.

"Huh?" I said, confused.

"If it weren't for you, we all wouldn't have found each other."

"But I thought —"

"We all said some things we shouldn't have. We worked things out," Gwen said with a bright expression.

"We're ready to go public with it, too," Cora said. "We know that our brother would want his great-grandson to have a stake in Vista Del Mar."

"We're all going to work together," Madeleine said. "And take a more active role in running Vista Del Mar. In other words, we are going to worry our pretty little heads about things," she said with a twinkle in her eye. "We'll be wanting input from you, too." I nodded enthusiastically, already thinking I wanted to help Sky do more with Vista Del Mar. He'd only faltered on the activities that Kevin St. John had planned. Everyone was raving about the Sound Bath and how he'd mixed the meditative aspects of the gongs and singing bowls with the fun of rock and roll and dancing. I certainly wanted to put in a lot of good words about Cloris. She was an employee to be treasured.

"We'll talk later," Cora said. "But right now we're all going to meet with Kevin St.

John and let him know there are going to be some changes."

Oh, to be a fly on the wall for that meeting.

Everything closed early on Sunday night and the streets were practically rolled up by the time I headed for the Blue Door. There were loose ends still hanging. I had to call Frank and tell him what happened. He'd be surprised to hear who'd left me the threatening note. Though looking back on it, it made sense that it was Kevin St. John. He didn't want me investigating since he was trying to sweep the whole thing under the rug. Cloris had been the one who tipped me off. She'd found an earlier attempt in the trash and figured out what it was.

I owed my mother a call, too. Sammy wanted to break in some new illusions, and Julius was out of stink fish.

Lucinda and Tag had already gone home and the restaurant was dark when I unlocked the door. I dropped off the bags of muffin ingredients in the kitchen and then went to turn on the soft jazz I liked to bake to. I glanced out the window at the quiet street. It felt like the whole world was taking a break before the new week began.

I had just taken out the ingredients for carrot cakes when I heard a knock at the door. Dane was holding up a paper bag and a holder with two cups of coffee when I went to the door.

"You know the way to my heart," I said, looking at the bag.

"Always," he said with a smile. "Now tell me everything."

MINDFULNESS TIE

Finished dimensions approximately 2 inches by 60 inches

SUPPLIES
Size 10.5 (6.5mm) knitting needles
1 skein Fair Isle Sutton yarn, 119 yards,
  3.5 oz, 109m, 100g, 100 polyester
Tapestry needle

DIRECTIONS
Cast on 6 stitches
Row 1: Knit across
Repeat Row 1 until approximately 60 in/
  152 cm
Cast off and weave in ends with tapestry
  needle

RAISIN TO BE,
AKA BISCUIT MUFFINS

(Makes 12)

2 cups unbleached flour
4 teaspoons baking powder
1 teaspoon salt
1 tablespoon sugar
4 tablespoons butter cut in small pieces
3/4 cup raisins
1 teaspoon vanilla
1 cup milk

Preheat oven to 450 degrees. Line a 12-muffin pan with paper muffin cups.

Sift flour, baking powder, and salt into a large bowl. Add sugar and stir. Work butter into flour mixture using pastry blender. Mix raisins into flour mixture. Add vanilla to milk. Make a well in the flour mixture and add milk all at once. Mix for about 20 seconds. Spoon into muffin cups.

Bake for 12–15 minutes until golden.

ACKNOWLEDGMENTS

It's a crisp, sunny October day as I sit here in Chicago writing these acknowledgments. Outside the window I can see the leaves are just beginning to turn on the tree across the street. It seems like a long way from all the white skies and fog of Cadbury by the Sea, California. But it is time to say goodbye to this manuscript before it goes out in the world to readers. It's time for me to move on to my next project, which happens to take place in Chicago in October.

I always have a hard time writing the acknowledgments because I know it is my last touch with a book.

I want to thank Bill Harris for his editorial advice. He has a great eye for making suggestions to improve the manuscript. Dar Dixon once again has come up with a fabulous book cover. I have been with my agent, Jessica Faust, for a long time and I give her credit for making my dream come true. I appreciate her persistence and how I always have her ear to run ideas by.

Back in the San Fernando Valley my knit and crochet group are probably sweating in the October heat wave. We have moved locations a number of times and people have come and gone. But our core group of Rene Biederman, Diane Carver, Terry Cohen, Sonia Flaum, Winnie Hinson, Elayne Moschin, Vicki Stotsman, Paula Tesler and Anne Thomeson have stuck together to stitch and talk. We all miss Linda Hopkins and Lily Gillis.

This is the first time I haven't been able to include Roberta Martia as my cheerleader, but I'm sure she's here in spirit. She would be so excited about my next project.

My family is probably sweating from the hot day in the Valley, too. Burl, Max, Samantha and Jakey have been great about giving me the space I need to come up with my books even if it gives them pause to think that I spend so much time figuring out weird ways to kill people.

ABOUT THE AUTHOR

Betty Hechtman is the national bestselling author of the Crochet Mysteries and the Yarn Retreat Mysteries. Handicrafts and writing are her passions and she is thrilled to be able to combine them in both of her series.

Betty grew up on the South Side of Chicago and has a degree in Fine Art. Since College, she has studied everything from improv comedy to magic. She has had an assortment of professions, including volunteer farm worker picking fruit on a kibbutz tucked between Lebanon and Syria, nanny at a summer resort, waitress at a coffee house, telephone operator, office worker at the Writer's Guild, public relations assistant at a firm with celebrity clients, and newsletter editor at a Waldorf school. She has written newspaper and magazine pieces, short stories, screenplays, and a middle-grade mystery, *Stolen Treasure.* She lives with her family and stash of yarn in Southern California.

See BettyHechtman.com for more information, excerpts from all her books, and photos of all the projects of the patterns included in her books. She blogs on Fridays at Killerhobbies.blogspot.com, and you can join her on Facebook at BettyHechtman Author and Twitter at @BettyHechtman.

The employees of Thorndike Press hope you have enjoyed this Large Print book. All our Thorndike, Wheeler, and Kennebec Large Print titles are designed for easy reading, and all our books are made to last. Other Thorndike Press Large Print books are available at your library, through selected bookstores, or directly from us.

For information about titles, please call:

(800) 223-1244

or visit our website at:

gale.com/thorndike

To share your comments, please write:

Publisher
Thorndike Press
10 Water St., Suite 310
Waterville, ME 04901